The Secret of the Lost Soul

A Ben Street Mystery

Book One

by

Tobias Cooke

To Adeebk

best wishes

Tobias Cooke

First published in Great Britain by Pen Press

All paper used in the printing of this book has been made from
wood grown in managed, sustainable forests.

ISBN13: 978-1-907499-80-7

Printed and bound in the UK
Pen Press is an imprint of Indepenpress Publishing Limited
25 Eastern Place
Brighton
BN2 1GJ

A catalogue record of this book is available from
the British Library

Cover design by Jacqueline Abromeit

Dedication

For Pauline, Millie, Yasmin, Danielle, Lauren & Matthew, with thanks for all your inspiration.

Tobias Cooke lives with his wife and children in Sussex. They have been the inspiration for his first novel. Their encouragement continues to feed his passion for writing. Apart from his writing he works helping some of the less fortunate in society.

CONTENTS

ir weapons, nonetheless. Dr Bird strode quickly
strument case toward the meteorite's resting
ather coat flapping against his legs, as Jeffrey
ind, clumsily struggling to carry a large glass
:.

up slowly descended into the crater made by
, a large black insect the size of a full-grown
sprang from behind an oblong stone. The
around wildly, then peered at the men with a
uoise glare. It waved its huge, wiry legs
ed momentarily in front of them, and then
small rocket. In less than a second, it was
of sight. All four men stood rooted in shock.
e logged how many of these things have
at?" Dr Bird said sharply.
ird one, sir," replied a sergeant. "The other
somewhere nearby."
you to stay here," Dr Bird commanded.
ordered by General—"
what you were ordered," snapped the
This is a job for me and me alone. Jeffrey,
You carry my bag and follow ten paces
f without waiting and walked out of sight
ong rocks. Jeffrey picked up the bag, and
s mentor as instructed.
inutes, there was sudden clamour, and
Bird shouting for him. "The antidote,
te, over here, quick!" Jeffrey ran in the
ice, and found Dr Bird lying on the
is left forearm, which was dribbling
vas the cage, now containing one of the
clawed and scratched viciously at the

an antidote kit from the doctor's case
ed to indicate one of the substances.
m above the elbow," ordered Dr Bird.
noment, the needle poised above the

CHAPTER 1

The darkest day

Wiltshire, England – 1946

The sound of excited laughter could be heard coming from
the children of the William Ingram School of Performing
Arts on their annual school trip. They poured from the bus
without hesitation, and then stood marvelling at the stone
structure before them. An ancient civilisation had placed
these great, tall stones, called Stonehenge, in a circle.

The day had started out bright and sunny. As eleven
o'clock approached, the kids were all grouped in the centre
of the monument, listening to the gentle rise and fall of their
teacher's voice, as Mr Streeter held forth on the history of
Stonehenge. Suddenly, a shadow began to gather right over
them, and then gradually spread out and moved sideways
over a nearby field. It was not a cloud. It formed a perfect
square of absolute darkness. The children gasped and stood
motionless, their eyes transfixed skywards.

The black mass grew by the second. Suddenly, Mr
Streeter called out in panic, "Run for the bus! It's a
meteorite!"

The galloping herd of terrified kids and teachers were all
back in the bus and driving away in seconds. Within
minutes, the bus was several miles away. The meteorite
struck earth, causing an enormous tremor and a terrifying
bang, which reverberated around them. The bus wobbled
and kids collided with each other. Shaken up, they looked

out of the windows to see a massive mushroom cloud of dust rising into the sky.

The following morning, Dr Edward Bird was working diligently in his laboratory at the Department of Entomology. A slimly built man, his frame bore out his name. With his tufted hair going grey where he wasn't losing it, his bushy eyebrows, and his wide eyes behind round spectacles, he looked very much like some rare bird as he perched over his laboratory desk, pecking away at his latest theories. Suddenly, the telephone rang, jarring his concentration. Despite being the foremost living expert on insects, calls to his lab were very rare.

"Edward Bird speaking," he said into the phone.

"Dr Bird, this is Tony Chatterton, the Minister of Defence," said the voice on the line. "Please listen carefully."

The doctor went pale as he listened over the next several minutes and then replaced the receiver with a shaking hand. As he turned, he spoke sharply to his assistant, who had been watching the scene with growing interest. "Jeffrey, gather up a set of sample bottles, the largest cage we've got, and all the antidotes," he ordered. He began racing about the lab, placing surgical instruments into his case. "Don't stand there gawking, man. Move!"

"Yes, Doctor," said Jeffrey. "But what's it all about?"

The doctor paused, looking deep into Jeffrey's eyes.

"That thing that landed in Wiltshire. You must have heard it on the news. The Minister of Defence, by order of the Prime Minister, has asked us to go and urgently investigate—" The doctor hesitated to finish the sentence. He started to whisper. "Look, this is top secret. Not a word. Our lives may depend on it. That square meteorite which landed yesterday split into four perfectly shaped pieces. It's been seen crawling with unknown giant insects. The army has cordoned off the area."

The doctor's lips quivered with nervous tension. He snapped closed his briefcase and picked up the phone ready

to call his wife. "You'll
know if I can manage i
things I need, and th
worried, Jeffrey went
orders.

Dr Bird rang his
"Heather, my love," h
sorry, dearest, but
government busines
unfortunately."

"Oh, Edward," e
know how Sonia h

"Why? What's

"Today is t
competition. Yo
practising for w
"She'll be crush

"I am so so
can't be helpe
promise."

He said hi
alarmed as hi
returned fro
crushed by
Heather wo
that very
suspected

It was
Austin v
the mete
the sol
them.
all bef
soldie
their

cle

fingered the
with his in
place, his le
followed bel
and wire cag

As the gr
the fallen roc
cat suddenly
insect looked
menacing tur
around, bounc
flew off like a
completely out

"Has anyon
flown off like th

"That's the t
two came down

"I want all of

"But we were

"I don't care
irritated doctor. "
I'll have the cage
behind." He set of
in between the obl
meekly followed h

After a few m
Jeffrey heard Dr
Jeffrey! The antido
direction of the vo
ground, clutching
blood. Next to him
giant insects, which
walls of its prison.

Jeffrey withdrew
and the doctor nodd
"Inject it in my left a
Jeffrey hesitated for

target. "Do it now, man! I may only have thirty seconds before the venom kills me," shouted the exasperated doctor. Jeffrey took a deep breath and plunged in the needle.

Despite their orders, the soldiers gathered around where Dr Bird lay. Jeffrey pointed at the closest man. "You! Radio for an ambulance!" He turned to examine the doctor's arm. "He'll need to get to a hospital at once."

"No! Absolutely no ambulance," ordered Dr Bird. "No information is to leave this area." Though pale and sweating profusely, the doctor seemed to be recovering quickly. He sat up and wrapped a tourniquet around his wound. "Only a slight nip. Feeling better already." He stood up, wobbled slightly, but shook off the steadying hand that Jeffrey offered.

"There are no more of these creatures here that I can see. Jeffrey, let's have the containers. I want samples of that jelly over there." The doctor moved to examine the rock's surface and ran his hand over it, dislodging a handful of goo. "It's like treacly frogspawn. See the little black critters in it, just waiting to grow." The doctor placed the sample into a large jar and wiped his hands on a rag. He looked at the alarmed soldiers.

"Contact General Howe and arrange to burn all this sort of goo substance, wherever it can be seen. It's dangerous. Oh, and send a piece of this rock to geology for analysis," he added. "You must never tell anyone what you saw today; it's all an official secret. Just remember that."

Dr Bird pulled a cloth from his case and put it over the cage. Jeffrey took it and the rest of the equipment back to the van and waited while Dr Bird settled himself gingerly into the passenger seat. Jeffrey drove them both back leaving the doctor to nurse his small puncture wound.

"What happened?" asked Jeffrey.

"It got the better of me for a moment, and stung me," muttered Dr Bird. "I suspect it's a form of parasitic fly. It may even need a host to complete its birth. I'm relieved that universal antidote I developed worked." Dr Bird chuckled.

5

"I developed it for the war effort, to combat insect venom anywhere in the world. I guess it truly is universal, since this one came from outer space."

Jeffrey thought for a moment. "If it came from outer space, how did it enter the atmosphere without burning up?"

"I am sure the rock acted like a protective eggshell, containing possibly hundreds of eggs," replied Dr Bird. "That thing in the cage is more like a foetus than a fully formed young insect. It's probably blind, which is why I was not attacked until I touched it. It may not be able to see for weeks." Dr Bird relaxed back into his seat and closed his eyes. "I'll report it to the Minister in the morning. Ah, Jeffrey, I'll be able to do some extraordinary research on this one. I'll be published in every journal in the scientific world. The world won't know what's hit it." The doctor seemed to have all the answers.

The news reported that a piece of rock from outer space had simply fallen to earth. The weeks and months passed, and the falling meteorite became a distant, unimportant memory to the public. The government kept the truth about it a complete secret. Dr Bird carried out numerous experiments on the giant insect, piling up data and filing periodic reports with the Minister of Defence. Until the day he came to work to find a broken window and the iron bars over it bent wide. The creature had vanished.

Wiltshire, England – 1947

Mrs Quigley began to scream in pain as her trolley was raced down a hospital corridor, accompanied by a concerned nurse, Dr Cameron, and her husband. She was expecting, but this baby was kicking and pushing like no other the doctor had ever seen. They wheeled the patient straight into the maternity room as her screams became even more piercing. Two more doctors arrived and rushed to join the team. A very worried Mr Quigley was marched back out and sent to the waiting area; over the sound of her screams, Dr Cameron took command.

"I'll have to operate. I can't risk you or the baby. It's a caesarean." But as the doctor turned to prepare himself, Mrs Quigley had the worst contraction yet. Her body convulsed, and her stomach began to undulate visibly, as if the baby was wiggling violently inside her womb.

"Doctor, I can see the head," Nurse Biggins cried out. Dr Cameron moved around to examine the progress. As he did so, Nurse Biggins recoiled in horror. The doctor stumbled backwards, raised his eyebrows and took a sharp breath as he caught sight of an abomination, something he had been warned about, but never expected to see. He knew the procedure. He lifted the telephone on the wall.

"Put me straight through to the Health Minister. Quote code Z417 – emergency." A female voice came on the line almost immediately.

"Hello, can you please confirm your name and location?" questioned the female voice.

"It's Dr Cameron, Cragerton Hospital delivery unit," he replied nervously.

"Confirm the code for me, Doctor," requested the woman.

"Code Z417 emergency," replied the doctor.

"That's 'insect syndrome', Doctor. Can you confirm that is your request?"

"Unfortunately, yes."

"The Minister is coming to speak with you now. Please hold," stated the female flatly.

The others in the delivery suite had all now seen what Mrs Quigley was delivering. It was about the size of a baby, but there was nothing human about it; six long, black hairy legs waved about, and its piercing turquoise eyes did not seem to focus on any one point. The creature began to hum and buzz, as it lay on the bed, now free of its host. The staff all stood back waiting for Dr Cameron to give orders.

Mrs. Quigley called out to them. "Well, what's the matter? Have none of you seen a baby before? For God's sake, is it a boy or girl? Well? Well?" she hectored, expecting a proper answer. Mrs Quigley could not see what was sitting at the end of her bed. The staff all looked on with pained expressions, hoping Dr Cameron would end his call and take charge.

Dr Cameron hung up the phone and reached for a nearby blanket, throwing it over the insect and wrapping it as if it were a baby. "I'm sorry, Mrs Quigley, but I'll need to take your baby to intensive care. The staff will stay with you here, and I'll come back as soon as possible." With that he rushed from the room, and ran outside towards the hospital incinerator. A brick on the walkway caught his shoe and he tripped and fell, holding the blanket tightly. But, his grip was not enough. The beast slipped out of his grasp and scuttled away out of sight.

Shocked and frightened, the doctor jumped to his feet and ran straight to reception, muttering the whole way, "Dr Bird, Dr Bird." Grabbing the nearest telephone he furiously entered the number.

Dr Bird listened as the frightened physician explained how the newly born fly had escaped before it could be destroyed, and reassured him as best he could.

"It's unfortunate, Dr Cameron," said Dr Bird, "but I promise you, the creature is too young to survive on its own. Wherever it got to, it will likely be dead within the next hour or two. I suggest you turn you attention to consoling your patient."

None of them were to see or hear of these creatures ever again. But the rumours continued for decades to come of sightings of a giant fly in London that day. It was all routinely denied by the government and never mentioned on the news. Dr Bird's family were deeply affected by all of these events. A dark shadow fell on his family. It was even called a curse by some.

Two years later in 1949 Dr Bird came to work looking very pale. Jeffrey came straight over to him.

"Jeffrey, I had to tell you this personally. I'm still in shock." He sighed and a small tear formed in the corner of his eye as he spoke. "The school called yesterday when I got home. My beautiful, lovely Sonia—" The doctor's face screwed up momentarily with the pain. "She fell and broke her neck in an accident at the school theatre."

"Oh my goodness. I'm so sorry. Has the hospital said if she will—" Jeffrey stopped as he saw Dr Bird's head drop.

"She died, Jeffrey." There was a pause while the news sank in.

"I am so, so sorry," Jeffrey replied as he put his arm around Dr Bird's shoulder. Dr Bird left for home shortly afterwards.

The real reason for the death of Sonia at the William Ingram School would remain secret for over sixty years.

CHAPTER 2

Ben Street and the audition

Berkshire, England – 2010

For Ben Street, it was just another ordinary day after school. Ben was an unusual twelve-year-old boy, with scruffy dark brown hair and sparkly grey-blue eyes. He was tall for twelve, had strong arms and was good at sports. He was a little shy in some ways, but wonderful at acting, singing and even dancing; hip hop, street dancing and tap. His parents hadn't noticed how good he was. They never did. They could only see his faults. He sometimes answered back, often left his room in a mess and spent hours phoning his friends. He hated doing chores.

As usual, the first thing he did when he came home from school was to ask his mother to move her bags, clothes and magazines. He was tired of finding them blocking his way to the computer in their small living room. He would soon be networking with his friends if he had his way. Homework came second. Instead, he had to settle for reading the daily newspaper, which he began to unfurl.

"All I get from you is grief!" screeched Mrs Street from another room. "I get your packed lunch, wash your clothes, make the tea. I suppose you'll have us ferrying you here, there, and everywhere when you're a teenager," she continued, in a slightly more tempered tone of voice.

Mrs Street was a petite lady who did not bother over her appearance, and looked every one of her thirty-seven years.

Her dark blonde hair was shot through with grey strands and she wore little make-up. She was the kind of person who would say what she thought, loudly and without hesitation.

"Mum," sighed Ben, "I just need to practise my routine and do my homework. I can't do it if you've covered the table and filled the room with junk.

"Stop bothering your mum," snapped his father, entering the front door and putting his coat on the peg next to it. "Anyone would think we were your slaves."

Jim Street was tall and dark, with thick sideburns and a full head of dark brown hair. He had few interests apart from his work as a storeman: television, football, darts and growing his beloved marrows in the greenhouse out the back. He looked ordinary, and really quite like lots of dads. Ben could not imagine for a moment being anything like him when he grew up.

"Kate, how long 'til tea?" his father inquired of Mrs Street. As usual his mother didn't bother to answer her husband's question.

I love my mum and dad, thought Ben, but they're not interested in my aspirations at all. Ben started scanning the newspaper, when he noticed a prominently placed advertisement. He read it through to himself more than once with excitement and butterflies building inside his stomach.

> **The William Ingram School of Performing Arts (WISPA) Scholarship Auditions, to be held on Saturday 19th July. All details on the school website where applications can be downloaded, for submission no later than 15th July. Aspiring stage school students will be informed if they are to attend auditions by 17th July.**

It was the 10th July; Ben had no time to lose. He had read the website several times in the past, and had held a little dream that some day he might attend WISPA. Should he apply? His parents would not like it, would they?

Ben was so caught up in his musings that he never noticed his mother standing beside him. She glanced over his shoulder at the paper, and ripped it right out of Ben's hands. "Oh, don't be daft," she barked. "Stage school is not for the likes of us. Your Uncle Tim will tell you. He never got anywhere," she chortled condescendingly. "All that time at school, and what happened? Still works in a shop and earns peanuts. Now, you don't want that!" she said with a scoff.

Ben sat silently, not responding, but promised himself that he would apply and let nothing stop him! Parents never stop moaning, he thought. Why couldn't they just be chilled and cheerful like he was?

He took himself up the garden, passing Dad's marrow producing greenhouse. There he was, madly planting and watering as if his life depended on it. "Don't tread on my petunias," his father bawled gruffly. Ben kept walking, quickly moving out of sight of his father's little oasis of pleasure.

There was a square of concrete right at the end of his long thin garden strip, surrounded by trees and almost overgrown bushes where no one could see him. Ben often practised his dance routines there. The only trouble was that his garden backed onto a park and sometimes the football players would jeer and tease him as they saw his movements through the greenery. He didn't care. He was going to show them one day. That evening he went into the front room and downloaded the application form for WISPA and began the task of filling it in. Then he crept into his father's study in an upstairs bedroom, and removed last term's school report from the file.

"Come outta there. If your dad finds you rummaging in his office he'll go mad. Use your own pens and paper," his mother trumpeted. She had seen him leave, but not what he was holding.

"Is supper ready yet, Mum?" Ben enquired politely, trying to take her off the scent.

"Well, you could help for a start," retorted his mother.

Ben went straight to his room and clipped the school report to his application. He would post it tomorrow, and then there would be the wait of a week before he would hear his fate. The excitement and anticipation was unbearable. How would he get through waiting a whole week? What if they turned him down? He had made up his mind to be positive. That's how he wanted to stay.

"Come down, Ben. Supper's on the table getting cold." Knowing his mum's cooking it was probably almost cold already and would be something vile like a rissole, or otherwise covered in an indeterminately flavoured sauce bought from the supermarket. It would be accompanied by home grown marrow without fail. Yuk!

The phone went and his father, who had come in, picked it up before Ben could reach it. Ben sat down and started with the first awful mouthful. He really didn't know if he could survive to the end of this meal. It had confirmed his worst fears. It was a stew with dumplings. Stew was a loose description for his mother's made-up recipe. She would throw in any leftovers whatsoever, whether or not they had any likelihood of tasting good together. He could see pieces of chicken, beans, old mushy broccoli and even some cucumber and lettuce under the dribbly thick brown glue she called gravy.

"It's a Laura for you. Says you know her from school."

Ben rushed off his seat virtually falling to get away. He had shared the idea of going to WISPA with Laura for some time and wanted to tell her about the advertisement. "Don't be long now coz it's supper and your mum—" He didn't hear the rest as he closed the door to the dining room and grabbed the phone.

"Hey, Laura, how's it going?" Ben half whispered excitedly.

"Have you seen the advert?" she questioned pointedly, in her very well-spoken voice, quite unlike the Street family. She was a step ahead of Ben who thought he'd seen it first. They didn't need to say anymore. They both knew.

"Yes and I've downloaded an application. I'm posting it tomorrow. How about you?" Ben replied.

"I'm doing mine tonight. Only thing is I can't find my last school report. So I'm getting another one at school tomorrow to send in with the application. My dad says he can collect it all at school because he's going that way anyway. Then he'll go to WISPA tomorrow afternoon and drop mine in. So if you give me yours tomorrow morning—"

"Oh, that's cool. You're so lucky your folks are up for it. My mum thinks I'm crazy wanting to go to WISPA," Ben pined in a shaky voice full of emotion.

"Off that phone, Ben. Why does your mum bother to make supper if you let it get cold?"

Ben didn't want to hear his embarrassing father's voice and hoped Laura didn't hear it either. He hurriedly said goodbye and returned to the dining room. The word 'dining' did not fit the activity he was forced to endure there. It was more like tortured taste testing for animal feed. Still, Ben knew he must keep his strength up and practise his showpiece to the last moment. He just had a mum who couldn't cook.

Laura Munday was from the other side of town and a rather posh family. Her father was 'something in the city' and he clearly had lots of money. Her mother was a socialite who played tennis and had coffee mornings to raise money for 'the needy'. They lived behind large imposing iron gates in a Georgian style mansion that was worth a packet. Luckily Ben never felt jealous and was friends with Laura on account of being in a school play together. His parents didn't even know he was in it, as they rarely spoke to Ben except to issue boring instructions like, "You can brush your hair better than that", or, "Work hard and we'll help you through that plumber's college".

The countless number of times Ben had to explain he did not want to be a plumber, carpenter, electrician or anything else his father regarded as a 'proper job' really upset both he and his parents. He knew they were worrying about his future, but he had it mapped out and they would not listen to it. Bad luck he thought. In fact he didn't want that life or the life led by the Mundays in their posh house. None of that would make him happy. It was something else he was after.

"Laura, darling, be a dear and find my gold necklace; the one with the sapphire pendant." The Mundays were going to a function tonight with some of Mr Munday's business associates and they were dressing up. Not that Laura's mum ever dressed down. She was called Patricia and wouldn't countenance anyone calling her 'Pat'. It would be a surprise if you saw her wearing anything remotely casual.

"And who were you phoning, Laura?" her mother asked smiling falsely to extract the answer. Laura arrived with her large jewellery box.

"Oh, it was Ben from school. He's applying for WISPA too and Dad's taking our applications in there tomorrow." Laura was a sweet-natured girl but could be very feisty if pushed. She would stand up for herself and give any adult all the reasons under the sun why she was right and they were wrong. She was growing up to be a pretty young lady but did not share her mother's interest in trinkets. She had slightly darker than blonde hair of a natural tone and was tall for her age.

Her mum started rifling through her enormous store of sparkly jewels, no doubt worth hundreds of thousands. She was a tall, imposing lady of formidable character and very well mannered. She had a long slim face with a figure that could have been modelling a few years ago. Her hair was a natural golden blond. She was always dripping with jewellery and trying to know just the 'right' people. Laura loved her but had no truck with her snobby attitude.

15

"That's marvellous, darling", she continued, too effusively for most people to bear.

"Is Ben your age?" she enquired hoping for an answer she liked.

"Yes, he's twelve I think and in my year. We were in the musical production show together last term, remember?"

"Goodness, I do and it was just delightful. And what does his father do?" Somehow it always mattered to the Mundays and their type what someone's parents did. Laura did not understand the point of the question and resented it on Ben's behalf.

"Well, I think he works for that pharmaceutical company." Laura was cut off by her mother squeaking with delight at the sound of the word 'pharmaceutical'.

"Darling that's wonderful. Is he one of the managers?" Laura knew her mother well enough to know where this pointed question was leading. She was determined to stick to the truth without couching anything in 'acceptable terms' for her mum's benefit.

"He works in the stores I think," Laura stated bluntly.

"Ooooh, well," sighed Patricia, as if let down like the world's largest balloon. Laura felt let down too, at her mother's crazy way of thinking. Ben was a good friend and that's all that mattered.

Her father entered half dressed in his dinner suit and searching for his bow tie and cufflinks. He was still only in his late thirties and amazingly successful. He thought nothing of spending thousands for a weekend away. He was very tall indeed and of a good stature with a commanding voice everyone would listen to. His complexion disclosed a little of the Mediterranean in him. His full head of hair was fairly dark and he had deep hazel eyes.

"Have you put them somewhere, Patricia?" he blasted, far too rudely for the situation at hand. "Nothing's ever where I left it," he complained. He had a kindly loving nature, but little patience for the bits and pieces of life such as getting ready or having to find something. He just expected everything to be there and all that mattered on the surface was being successful in business and being on time.

"I think they're on the shelf with your belts, Rupert dear." He made for the area purposefully. The Mundays had a walk-in wardrobe the size of most people's bedrooms with a clean, leathery, expensive sort of aroma. There were rows of shoes and suits on one side and an endless stream of cocktail dresses and swish outfits on the other. It looked more akin to a small boutique than the storage of someone's own clothes.

"I can't see them so you must have put them somewhere else," he retorted, even more irritated than ever. Patricia glided into the wardrobe elegantly and found the bow tie and cufflinks just as she had explained. Handing them to him, she pulled a smug frown as she announced,

"Your apology is awaited, Rupert." He forced a reply from his reluctant lips.

"Well, I thought you meant the other shelf. Sorry anyway," he muttered, not feeling the control he exercised at work. Laura butted into the all too usual incident.

"Daddy, if I don't see you before I leave for school tomorrow morning, remember you are picking up the WISPA applications for Ben and me.."

"You don't think I'd forget that do you? Your mother and I would love to see you at stage school if that's what you really want."

Laura's mother would have adored stage school, but she was never offered the opportunity. She just imagined immediate success and meeting the stars without any thought that it may take years of hard graft and there was no certainty much would happen at all. She was determined to live her dream through her daughter, but there was no pressure on Laura to perform, just encouragement. At least her parents got that right.

"I really, really, really want to go there," Laura exclaimed in a squeal of excitement. "I know I can do it."

"So do we, dear, but there's always finishing school if —" her mother calmly enthused, not actually wishing to finish her own sentence. Finishing school for posh girls. Well, that's where she'd been sent. "I suppose we'll have to buy you loads of clothes and attend all your shows! I can hardly wait," she giggled clapping her hands with delight.

"Oh, Mum," Laura shrieked. She could not imagine anything worse than her parents turning up at her stage school, trying to impress everyone by arriving in their Bentley, but somehow she knew they would. They would treat it like a premier show to which royalty were invited and expect to find a white-gloved footman with a red carpet rolled out to invite them to their specially saved seats. No way! Laura ran off to her bedroom.

Quite unlike Ben's home she had a magnificent view across a lake from her room. She was so used to it she hardly noticed these days.

She was almost too young to remember the ordinary house she once lived in with her parents. This was before her father's career took off into the stratosphere. She had a very large bed and a study annexe with fitted furniture and her own bathroom. She didn't care for girly pink and had a strong sky blue colour on the walls. She still had toys and looked lovingly at her doll collection and set of books on the shelf.

"Are you in bed yet? Your babysitter's here." She heard her mother's screeching voice wandering up the stairway. 'Babysitter' did not feel like the right word. She was capable of looking after herself at twelve and did not need this mollycoddling.

"No," she called back defiantly. "I'll go when I'm ready." Laura peered out of her room through the landing and balustrade to see the enormous double wooden front door, half cocked and her father obviously itching to go. They could at least have come to her room and cuddled her good night. But still, that was their way.

"We're going now, dear, so don't be long and see you in the morning." The sound of a rather fake, blown kiss wafted up the stairs.

Ben was in his very small magnolia painted bedroom, about the size of Laura's bathroom, just waiting to drift off to sleep. He just had one old free-standing wardrobe and a couple of storage boxes for his things. Will he or won't he? Will she or won't she? He was imagining what the audition for stage school would be like. He so wanted to be able to leave his very ordinary school for something special. Laura would go to some posh school whatever happened, so Ben felt it was all the more important to him. Suddenly there was the sound of raised voices.

"Why does he want to go there?" shouted his father from the room below. Ben could hear it and so would his neighbours. Ben cringed as he thought of the reaction of the kids up his road. He lived at number forty one Macey Avenue and the McAllisters, who were a rough, troublesome family, lived at number forty-five, just two doors away in the same terrace of houses. They were 1930s houses, all threebedroomed terraced and no wider than four metres. If there was shouting, then you could hear it through the party walls and sometimes even if it was the next house but one.

"Of course it's a waste of time. But if it's really what he wants I'm not gonna stand in his way," screamed his mother, in response.

Ben prayed they would not mention WISPA during this argument. He did not want the matter to come between him and his parents, but was unprepared to change his mind to suit them. Why should he? It was his life he was living and not theirs. All he wanted was that scholarship because he knew his parents couldn't afford to send him to stage school even if they had wanted him to go.

"He'll be jobless and penniless at thirty and still living here if we let him go to bloody WISPA," his father bellowed with more than a hint of disapproval.

Ben's heart sank. He was sure the neighbours would have heard the all-important title. He could only hope they didn't know what it meant.

"No he won't coz they do all the exams as well as prancing about and dancing around the stage singing 'n stuff."

Ben's mood lowered again. His mother had blurted out everything anyone needed to know to realise it was a stage school causing disagreement. Strangely, his mother was now defending the idea of going, when earlier she had said otherwise.

"He needn't think I am going to help him with it. He's turned into a right dreamer that one," stated his father with a distinctly different mood. He had blown out his anger and was accepting it. He would not help but he would not prevent.

"I bet he won't even get a look in. It's an audition and hundreds of posh kids come with pushy mums knowing all the right people. What chance has a kid like ours got, eh?"

It was all calming down. Even so, Ben did not want to hear anymore of this hurtful banter. He pulled the pillow over his ears and just prayed he would get a fair go. His feeling of hope had been severely tested. Laura was so lucky to have supportive parents who wanted her to go to WISPA!

The following morning Ben woke early. Despite last night's episode, he'd slept well and felt ready for the day. It was nearing the end of term and he was looking forward to a break. He washed and dressed quickly. Packing his carefully prepared WISPA application in with his ordinary schoolwork, he took himself and his bag down the small staircase to the kitchen below. His mum and dad were already seated, eating their respective breakfasts in complete silence. You could feel the air of complete disappointment. Ben attempted to stop this atmosphere.

"Are you all right? It's just—"

His father interrupted immediately. "Ben, your mother and I were discussing things last night."

It was hardly discussing thought Ben, when recalling the shouting and anger. He felt very nervous about the coming speech. "Your mum says you want to go for the WISPA audition." Ben could barely nod. "As far as I'm concerned son, you go for it if that's going to make you satisfied. But—" Ben did not want to hear a 'but'. He had only just heard the first positive remark from his father in years. "I'll say it once. If you go to that school, you must promise me that you'll keep up with all your other lessons apart from singing and dancing. You may still want to be a plumber you know." His father, Jim, was convinced nothing would come of it, but he would stand by his son.

"Thanks, Dad and I will," was all Ben managed before turning to look for his cornflakes. What a relief! His mum said nothing but her lips could not help curling upwards a tad after hearing her husband changing his mind from last night. It was a mother's knowing kind of smile. At least she wouldn't be having that argument again!

Quick! It was nearly eight o'clock and Ben's school bus would be coming soon. He gobbled down his breakfast, collected up his things and said goodbye to his parents.

In his excitement leaving the house, Ben blinked quickly as he looked towards the hallway mirror and rushed past. It swung on the wall and just fell on the floor breaking instantly into shards of sharp glass. It was all over the hallway floor. Both his parents peered into the hallway to see the mess as Ben put his hand towards the front door. They looked on in astonishment. Ben knew he hadn't even touched the mirror. Something very strange indeed was going on.

There was a very tense silence as they all stood still. After a few seconds Ben blurted out, "Sorry". He swiftly left mumbling about catching the bus.

"Blimey, that'll be seven years bad luck straight away won't it?" said Ben's mum. Jim nodded in amazement.

Luckily the bus was late. Stood at the bus stop were about a dozen shabbily dressed kids from his road, being mostly boys and a couple of girls. Most were listening to music and some using mobiles to pass the time. A hectoring voice came from behind.

"Now we know why yer always going down yer garden and moving round in the bushes, don't we?" he smirked. It was Robbie McAllister who was about fourteen. His appearance was very aggressive. He had unkempt dark brown hair and spotty skin. He was taller than Ben and liked to train on weights in his garden.

The rowdy crowd shouted at Ben, jeering in a group that made him feel very uncomfortable. It was not yet clear what they knew. Suddenly it became a chant amongst the small crowd.

"Ben is going to stage school, and he's going to be dancing with gi..irls."

"Oh, come on. Get a life," Ben shouted. The only thing worrying him more was the thought he may not get a place at stage school and he'd have to carry on catching the same bus next term.

He did not bother to respond any more. It was obvious his parents' argument had been overheard. The bus drew up and they all scrabbled on leaving Ben to be last.

He had far more important things on his mind. On the journey, Ben had to sit at the back of the bus dead centre, looking up the aisle. No other seats were left. He caught sight of Robbie McAllister's bag, which was on the floor by his feet in the centre aisle. It was blue with a black strap. Immediately the bag swished towards the back of the bus just as if the bus had gone up a very steep hill or round a corner too fast. It landed up just in front of Ben's feet at the end of the aisle and Ben could see a small rip literally appearing without anything touching it! There was a howl of "Ooohh" from about half of the passengers who saw this strange bag movement. Ben was shocked.

The bus driver, who had seen nothing, called for calm. The bus had not been up a steep hill nor turned a corner sharply enough to cause this motion and certainly not a rip. Ben had seen the bag move as his eyes followed it. He knew instantly something weird was happening. Somehow he suspected it was something to do with him. First the mirror falling off the wall on its own and now a mysterious moving bag!

Laura on the other hand, had started her usual short journey to school courtesy of her mum. They listened to Vivaldi or Beethoven or sometimes Michael Bublé on the way, comfortably nestled into their leather electrically adjustable seats. The electric gates opened on call and out they swished onto the Upper Beeding Road. Laura's mother waved at the postman in a withering way. Even for the school run her mum had to dress up as if her life depended on it.

She was wearing beautiful couture clothing as if ready for a high-level business meeting, but was more likely to be seen at an expensive café bar within the hour.

"Do you have to drop me right outside school?" Laura asked. As usual she was rather embarrassed about the size of her mother's car and her dressy appearance.

"I just need to see you off safely for the day. I could drop you in Tenby Row if you like?" It was an adjacent road with a side entrance to the school. Her mum had spoken very warmly, knowing her daughter worried about her 'street cred'. "I might even get a kiss out of you," she added with a polite giggle. They turned the corner and found themselves behind the school bus.

Meanwhile, Robbie looked at his bag sitting in front of Ben's feet and opened his mouth to shout towards him. He noticed the rip in the side, but didn't know how it could have happened.

"Hey—" Robbie was stopped in his tracks and his mouth opened much wider. The bag had begun a sudden movement back up the aisle of the bus, neatly landing just about where it started. The bus had been turning a corner quite sharply this time. Nevertheless, no one seemed too sure what had happened. Their natural senses made them glare at Ben, who still wanted to believe it was nothing to do with him. He tried to persuade himself the kids were acting up and teasing him and nothing else was going on. But Ben knew inside himself that it was probably him causing it.

Robbie looked at Ben turning his head slightly to one side and rolling his eyes in a knowing sort of look. Ben looked back at Robbie and the bag began to move again.

"I'll have you for this, Ben," Robbie threatened. This time Robbie grabbed it and took it onto his lap. There was a feeling of awe developing on the bus. It fell silent and the kids all behaved as if something unreal had occurred.

The bus driver smiled as he enjoyed the best behaved school bus he had driven for many years. The bus arrived. Ben looked down the aisle once more and caught sight of Robbie lifting his bag. As Robbie left his seat he felt a strong inexplicable tug from his bag towards the back of the bus where Ben looked at him. Some of the surrounding passengers, who had risen to their feet, quickly covered their faces as if the bag was about to move on its own again.

"Watch it, mate!" barked the nearest boy behind Robbie. By now Ben began to feel even more sure that he must have caused the strange happenings, but how?

At break, Ben was seen talking to Laura outside the tuck shop.

"Then I looked down the aisle and the bag went and moved again," he explained slowly and intensely. "It even got a rip in it!"

Laura assumed that somehow the bus movement made it happen by some fluke. She didn't believe Ben could have done it. However, Ben was nervous and upset because he knew he had caused it.

"Look, I'll be around this afternoon if you want a joint practise session," she whispered changing the subject somewhat.

"OK." With that Ben gave his beloved stage school application to Laura who promised her father would pick it up with hers at reception sometime later that day. Suddenly from behind the tuck shop about ten rowdy pupils emerged all pushing and shoving Ben in a very unpleasant way.

"What's this WISPA place all about then?" demanded Stewart, their self-appointed leader. At least half of them had been on the bus that morning. It was clear now the whole school was rapidly becoming aware of Ben's plan. Laura bravely intervened.

"Look, it's none of your business and if you don't cut it out I'm going to the head mistress." With that a long, prolonged, rising Ooooohhh, came from the entire crowd in unison. "Pathetic," Laura announced and beckoned Ben away. The crowd dispersed but there was much muted whispering amongst them as they went.

Some days later, term had ended. Ben and Laura awaited their fate. Ben just wanted to know; will he be asked to audition or not? Was that so much to ask? It was 16th July and there was only one day left in which he could expect to be contacted. He was really worried now.

That evening, he went downstairs to his living room and cast his eyes about at the boring arrangement of old furniture. As he swished his eyes around he heard his mum calling from the kitchen.

"Can you peel the carrots love? I'm just going to get the marrow stuffed."

Not marrow again! He sighed heavily to himself, under his breath.

"I love marrow, don't you?" spouted his father as he entered the kitchen from the garden, excited as a schoolboy going on a trip.

"Yeah OK, Mum, I'll come in a min..ute." As he finished the sentence, slurring the last word. "It's moved," he muttered. Some of the room's furniture had rearranged into different places. That was scary! He gave a little scream of about half a second in a high-pitched tone. He suddenly wanted to know what was happening. Was he going mad?

He ran out the back of the dining room into the garden and down to his concrete square at the end of the garden. His parents were now calling out.

"Where are you going?" and "What are you doing?" in unison.

He was choking with fear. He felt a huge adrenalin rush through his young body. Then he began to calm. Something was definitely going on.

"I need the carrots peeled, not a blinking dance routine, Ben. Get your bum down here at once," bawled his mum.

"Kate, leave him. He'll be back in a minute," his dad pitched in very sensitively.

Ben shook off his feelings and returned to the house. What would his mother say about the furniture?

Carrots peeled and cooked, supper began. The taste of stuffed marrow did nothing to lessen Ben's unease over the strange happenings. He had just put a large fork full of food into his mouth when the moment it hit his tongue, he was saved from the awful taste.

"Aaaargh, oh my goodness!" his mother screamed. The food fell straight from Ben's mouth onto the plate. She had noticed it.

"What on earth have you done to my furniture, Jim?" she pleaded, believing it must be him. He looked up and nothing much registered.

"What do you mean?" he asked.

The disturbed look on his wife's face made him look around the room.

"Well, it's you that's moved something, not me," she screeched. Her glower demanded an explanation.

"I didn't move anything in here. Why would I?"

"Ben?" She stared, her eyes widening in disbelief.

"Mum, I didn't touch any of it. I couldn't have," Ben stated truthfully with a hint of apprehension. It was kind of true. His hands had not touched the furniture. The large single armchair and sofa, the standard lamp and a heavy wooden storage box had all swapped places very neatly.

"I saw everything in its usual place only ten minutes ago," was his mum's confused announcement. All three of them looked inquisitively at each other. The only thing was that Ben had more than a sneaking suspicion it was something to do with him. He was there when it seemed to happen. The incident on the bus that morning had been the start of a very strange day. Surely they had not just forgotten where their furniture went?

"I reckon it's still where it was before. Don't know why you're so jumpy all of a sudden," Jim asked. Like many dads, he never noticed anything. He never even showed a flicker of recognition when Kate had her hair done. "It looks the same" he once made the immense mistake of saying, instead of just thinking it. "The lamp and the sofa have been there for years. The box is just on the other side and you've forgotten you moved it," he scoffed.

"I don't think I moved anything?" Kate queried, less sure than before.

After debating the position of each piece of furniture for some time Kate began to wonder where any of them usually were. Ben kept quiet.

"It looks pretty much the same to me love. It's only been pushed around a bit when you cleaned, that's all."

It was true, all of it was adjacent to the former spot, but equally true several pieces had moved. In the end they just cleared up and all went to bed convincing each other they had been confused. But inside, Ben's mum knew she was not mistaken. Something very bizarre was happening!

Ben just wanted to put it out of his mind. He barely wanted to sleep; his hope of going to stage school was still burning alive so strongly in his stomach. Tomorrow was the day he would know.

Ben awoke with a start at eight – later than he thought. He rushed out of bed and straight to his post box. It was 17th July. He had to hear today. He found nothing. He felt like a lead weight had just been added to both feet. His head and shoulders shrank back and a piercing thumping pain developed in his head. Had his whole life been a waste of time? He had so wanted to audition for WISPA.

"I'll do bacon and eggs for those that want them." His mother saw Ben's face as she finished speaking and she knew. It was the most despondent look she had ever known on the boy. She bent down and put a motherly arm around him.

"Life's very hard to take sometimes. We all have lots of difficult times. You just carry on and something turns up if you keep trying love." Her comforting was kind but having little effect. Ben found tears rolling down both cheeks.

"What will I do, Mum? It's all I ever wanted, just a chance to show them, that's all," he whimpered.

"I know love. Can I see the letter?" she sighed putting out her hand ready.

"Letter? That's the trouble, Mum, I haven't got one!" There was a gasp. Kate took a sharp breath.

"How do you know it's a knock back then?" she reasoned.

"The ad said if you're getting an audition you will be told by today. The post has been and there's no let—" He could hardly finish the sentence without his face snarling and curling into a screwed up ball.

"Look, let's—" The phone rang and interrupted this display of despair. She moved to get up saying, "Hang on love, I'll be right back."

"It's OK," roared his father from upstairs. "I've got it."

"Look," his mum reasoned, bending down again; "If you want it bad enough there must be another way."

"It's for you, Ben," his father called out. "Something about collecting your school report or something?"

28

Ben was not in the mood to speak with anyone from school. It was the holidays! He took the phone.

"Is that Ben Street?" the polite, softly-toned female caller enquired.

"Yes" he sniffled.

"Well, this is Danni, Mr Goving's secretary. Now you sent in last term's school report but I have been asked if you could bring *this* term's school report to the audition. Have you got it yet?"

"Audition? Are you from WISPA?" he pleaded, perking up instantly.

"Yes, of course. We are expecting you Saturday at twelve noon. Haven't you received the letter?" There was a stunned silence. It had just registered.

"Wahoooo", Ben squawked. "I can't believe it. Thank God you called. No letter has come here."

"I sent it the day before yesterday by recorded delivery. Well, can you bring the last report on Saturday then?" Danni laughed, joining in Ben's sudden happiness. Taking the phone away from his ear and covering the microphone he looked towards his mum.

"Where is this term's report?" he chanted.

"Uhmm, I am sure it's here, Ben," his mum stuttered, ripping through the nearest pile of untended mail from the last few days. They didn't normally care you see. There was a large yellow envelope, which she forcefully pulled opened to ensure it would be the right document. It was!

"Yes, it's here. I'll be there for definite," Ben announced to Danni, so excited he could hardly contain himself. He threw the phone down and flung his arms around his mum in the greatest show of affection she had received for years.

"I got an audition!" he cried out, wiping away the few remaining tears.

"Well, I'll be darned," chortled his father as he walked down the last step of the stairway. "Life is unpredictable, eh?"

Ben rushed upstairs to start his preparations. Then it struck him. Oh no, what about Laura he thought? Shall I phone her and what if she hasn't got an audition? Should he ask his dad's advice? Not something he did much anymore. The nearer he was to being a teenager, he was that bit more sure he knew almost everything. Parents are always old and don't know much really, he told himself.

"Dad, can I ask your opinion?" After a short pause the answer came.

"Are you sure now? Am I going to know?" questioned his father in a knowing manner. He had guessed the conundrum already.

"Well, if you were me, would you phone Laura?"

"Actually, I would. She hasn't phoned you and she may be in the same predicament. You'll both have to know about each other anyhow. Why not now?"

Ben lifted the portable phone whilst thanking his dad for the tip and went into his bedroom. The butterflies were in his stomach and now Laura's phone was ringing. The anticipation was unbearable!

"Hello," said a lady's very well-spoken voice, but not Laura's.

"Hi, it's uhmm, Ben, a friend from school. I am calling for Laura please."

"Oh, Ben! This is her mother speaking. I'm afraid she's already gone out early, shopping with her father. She has to be ready for the big day on Saturday." She slowed to a sudden halt remembering she knew already that Ben had applied for a WISPA audition.

"Did you have any news, Ben?" she asked, not wishing to be too direct. Ben plucked up a little more courage in view of the reference to a 'big day'.

"Is she going to audition at WISPA on Saturday Mrs Munday?" Ben enquired, avoiding the question.

"As a matter of fact she is, Ben." Thank God, Ben thought, with another feeling of relief coursing through his body.

"I was phoning to say I'm auditioning too. And please tell her I hope to see her there."

"Yes, of course and I am so glad to hear about you as well! Good luck with yours, Ben," she replied putting the phone down at almost the same time. Laura hadn't spoken about Ben very much to her mother and Ben had only seen their opulent home from the road.

Ben turned around. His case of audition items he knew he had placed on the storage box, had moved themselves to his bed. His bed had turned around to face precisely the opposite direction. He sighed and putting his hands over his face vowed to put these strange incidents out of his mind.

Ben felt out of control. It didn't matter how hard he tried to convince himself it must be the excitement or that he was mistaken. No matter what, nothing would get in the way of his audition.

He had a hurried breakfast and strolled to his beloved concrete slab where he practised his hip hop or tap and jazz dance routine, humming the music to accompany him. The singing could not happen at home.

The next two nights passed without further ado. Ben woke to a cool summer's morning. Just one more practise, he muttered to himself. Off to the concrete slab again. He hip hopped and danced hard. An occasional 'tap, tap, tap', was all that could be heard in the Streets' garden.

His father amused himself in his greenhouse. Eventually he came out washing off his hands with a hose.

"Come in now, we have to go soon, Ben."

"I can't find a hairbrush anywhere," shouted his mum. "Who's got 'em?"

"Not me," Ben and his father chuckled together in unison. Ben went in to find the dining room mirror had put itself on the opposite wall. This joke was wearing thin. He looked again moments later and it had returned. Now he was worried his mind was playing tricks.

"Let's go," said his mum who had not seen anything. They went out to their ageing Volkswagen Golf with Ben both confused and excited about this extraordinary day. WISPA was thirty minutes drive away, on the edge of a town called Filtrington.

Ben arrived outside the school at about ten minutes to twelve; dance shoes and kit in his bag, more nervous than ever. He knew Laura must already be there as he spotted her father's parked Bentley.

"Ben love, me and your dad want to do a bit of shopping while you do your bit. I'm sure you don't want us there do you?" Ben did not want his parents to stay and watch, but would have appreciated some sign of interest in his special day.

"No, Mum, I don't need you for this. I'll call you when it's over." With that he hopped off in the direction of the large double-fronted entrance hall.

The main building was a beautiful old stone and brick affair, probably built for someone wealthy in the past as their home. He reached the hallway and saw about fifteen people aged about eleven to thirteen anxiously trying to see their name on the timetable for audition. A few current pupils passed by giggling and joking.

A teacher approached, smiling broadly. "Now, have you all found your names and times?" After noting the sea of nods, he added, "Just make your way through to the Peter Phelps Theatre and you will be able to use the changing area if you want. Then wait to be called. Listen out because they won't wait."

Ben had seen his name and made for the changing area, returning at about two minutes to twelve. He sat in the group of nervously waiting hopefuls. He heard people reciting Shakespeare: "If music be the food of love play on—" Then poetry: "—in the light of a blustery day—"

Ben had come to sing and dance. The panel of judges did not look as though they would like hip hop or street dance. He suddenly felt his stomach drop and his heart pound. Had he practised the wrong type of audition material? He looked around to see seated behind the hopefuls were rows of mothers and fathers smiling intensely at the spectacle.

Through a little light clapping he turned back to hear, "I have a song and dance to show you." Ben saw music handed to the pianist.

"All right, Heidi, when you're ready, signal to the piano."

Ben sighed with some relief that someone else was performing song and dance. He noticed the big clock said five past twelve. He couldn't have missed his turn could he? His worry became intense as he moved into an almost dreamlike state and he barely noticed that Heidi had finished. Where was Laura?

"Ben, go on, it's your turn next," he heard from behind him. It sounded like Laura, but he could not see her under the dim audience lighting. Ben came to and distinctly heard the panel judge calling out.

"For the last time, we are calling Ben Street. Is he here please?" Ben leapt to his feet and nearly stumbled over in his excitement to put himself on that enormous stage. Handing his music to the pianist he calmed himself and awaited the instruction.

"OK, Ben, when you are ready, signal to the piano."

Ben signalled. He mustered up his dance routine and started to sing his song. He began tentatively and warmed as he went, confidence building all the way through. The pianist was fantastic, so it was made all the easier. As he reached the home stretch, his comfort grew with every step and movement.

He knew he was moving well now. Smile and enjoy it he told himself. Throw yourself into it and relax was the way to a good performance. He moved on to his hip hop and street dance routine almost seamlessly. The bright lights were on and the heat beat down as he reached his crescendo of steps. Time was standing still and he completed by singing out the final notes of his song. There was silence.

He could hear nothing and barely see the panel of judges due to the intense stage lighting. He didn't even notice if anyone clapped such was his feeling of tension. Suddenly he heard a little applause and voice shouting, brilliant!, somewhere in the audience of parents. Ben looked towards the panel and saw a hand beckoning him over to them. It could only be for good or bad news. He hadn't seen anyone else doing this.

"I have a note here to ask you for last term's school report, Ben," the panel judge said leaning forward.

"It's in my bag. I'll get it for you," Ben panted, out of breath after his energetic show.

"You will hear within two weeks, but I am afraid there are only four scholarship places this year. Good luck," he added. Ben could not find the remark positive or negative. It would be the longest wait of his life; worse than the wait for his audition letter that never arrived. Ben moved away towards the watching parents when an arm grabbed his wrist.

"I thought you were great, Ben," stated the over-dressed lady. Ben recognised the voice and then saw that it was Laura's mother who was sitting next to her husband and Laura. She waved and leant across her father's lap.

"Hi, Ben," she whispered cheerfully, wearing a huge smile. "I did mine just before you arrived and we're staying to watch the competition. You did great, but it's pretty tough I'd say."

"Thanks, Laura. Let's speak when the result comes."

With that Ben looked across to the pool of waiting contestants and saw one of the bags begin to move across the floor. He looked away sharply. Not again, it can't be me! Looking back there were two contestants who had caught it before it went too far and they were pulling at the bag that curiously appeared rooted to the floor. As he blinked, Ben saw it become free and he sighed. He knew that he would have to find out what was causing these odd power surges. Had he developed mind over matter?

Jim and Kate Street were in Filtrington town centre in a supermarket, oblivious to their son's audition experience and neither did they care.

"I bet they'll just choose kids that have been to loads of dancing and singing classes already," said Jim to Kate, who was at the deli counter.

"You never know though. May be they'll like him if he's different," replied Kate being positive. Jim pointed towards some expensive ham.

"I'm not paying for organic nonsense. Can't afford it on your wage anyhow," Kate sternly pointed out, so the entire supermarket could hear her business.

"Just keep your voice down please, it's embarrassing. No harm looking is there?" Jim half whispered irritably.

Their mobile phone started to jingle. Kate pulled it out of her bag just in time to answer.

"Hullo, Ben love, how did it go?" she said in a nauseatingly insincere way.

"It was fine and we hear in two weeks. Can you pick me up now?" asked Ben. He was imagining his mum with her rather old mobile phone in her hand, the shape of a bar of soap.

"Ooh, what was that?" he heard, as if his mum was startled.

"Can you pick me up now please, Mum?" he reiterated in a miffed tone. All he could hear was a shuffling sound as if someone was moving items around. In fact his mother's mobile had flown out of her hand. A strange force had thrown it in the air landing it on top of the food aisle. He heard a distant voice saying, "Got it," through the rather old earpiece in the school's phone booth.

"What the heck are you doing throwing it away up there?" chided Jim.

"It went on its own," Kate replied firmly. She put it back to her ear, put out that Jim did not believe her, giving no thought to the supernatural power at work. Ben did not yet have his own mobile. His parents 'couldn't afford it' and claimed it was bad for him, being so young. His mother resumed the conversation.

"Oh, Ben, sorry love. The phone quite flew out of me hand on top of the cereal aisle. Heaven knows how. We'll just finish our shopping and be straight back. About twenty minutes?" she puffed.

Ben knew his thoughts had caused this incident. But he seemed less worried now the audition was over.

Later that afternoon, as Ben and his parents went through their front door, there on the mat was a crisp white envelope. On examination, it had already been opened.

"It's for you," his disinterested father mumbled. Ben opened it to find it was the audition invitation letter from WISPA dated 15th July. A note had been hurriedly scribbled onto the front of the letter itself: It came to us by mistake. It was signed 'Paul McA'.

It had been correctly addressed to number forty-one. None of them could see why this had occurred. Ben was suspicious of the McAllisters and did not trust them. After all, they must have had the letter for about three days and only brought it round on the audition day, after Ben had left the house. They must have seen what it was about and that was truly mean. He wouldn't forget it easily.

"We'd best get packing for Aunt Junes. It's only the day after tomorrow we go on holiday. I've got all that washing to do. You lot never lift a flipping finger to help," complained his mum.

Ben was forced to go to Blackpool every summer holiday to stay with Aunt June. He did not have any desire to go this year. There were no other kids staying with them and his parent's idea of fun was reading the newspaper and having a coffee in a seafront café. It was just so boring! He had so many other things on his mind didn't he?

CHAPTER 3

Strange happenings

Ben hopped out of the car and ran for the house without even offering to help with the bags. All he knew was, he must have the answer and have it now. He'd been away far too long in Blackpool and could wait no longer. He opened the front door to a near mountain of post. It was the first week of August. Surely WISPA had written to him?

He found himself going from letter to letter looking for just one, addressed to him. In fact there were two. One handwritten and one typed. The official looking letter was from WISPA. It had their logo franked on the front. He suddenly had to put off opening it. He wanted to carry on hoping he had a place there for a few moments more, before his dream would perhaps be cruelly dashed.

The handwritten letter read: Dear Ben, you didn't answer the phone, so I decided to write instead. We are off to Greece tomorrow for three weeks. I am afraid the audition at WISPA did not work out for me. I got a commendation but no scholarship. I do hope you got in because Daddy enrolled me anyway and they accepted me as if the audition was my interview – well, I am lucky because he can afford it. Catch up soon. Laura.

The three weeks seemed to have started about two weeks ago according to the postmark date. Ben did not want to open the letter in front of his parents and rushed away upstairs to do it privately. They guessed what he was doing and brought in the cases, one by one.

"Kate, I'll put the kettle on," mumbled Jim, not knowing what to expect next.

"OK, love," was the calm quiet response. They sat themselves down at the dining room table in silence with their Wallace and Gromit tea mugs in front of them. His mother couldn't find the sugar anywhere. She was sure the empty flower vase had been on the sideboard and not on the trolley.

Ben entered the room, with his head bowed, looking at neither of them. From the still visible top of his cheeks, a few signs of dampness showed in the late afternoon sunlight. He was clutching the letter rather tightly. He looked up and tearfully spoke, "Mum—Dad—" He swallowed almost audibly. After a moment he spoke with his voice trembling.

"It says: Dear Ben, following your audition on Saturday 19th July, the Scholarship Committee met to discuss your performance. After lengthy deliberations, I am pleased to advise that you have been awarded a full scholarship. This will last until you are sixteen in the first instance and is renewable for a further two years thereafter if deemed appropriate. I've done it!"

Ben's face was a collage of different emotions; he was overcome with the situation. For a few brief seconds tears welled up in both his parent's faces. Perhaps they did care after all. They just didn't know it. The slow motion scene ended suddenly with his mum and dad jumping to their feet in complete syncopation.

"Well done, Ben," Mum chanted.

"Fabulous news, son," his father laughed. They all laughed out loud as a kind of relief.

"Well, we must celebrate," Dad announced. "You don't want to be a plumber then, I take it?" he added tongue in cheek.

"Not today, Dad, thanks," sniffed Ben regaining his composure.

Ben turned to see their tea trolley was now in the garden just outside the dining room window, complete with vase. The door was shut to the garden. How did that happen? All of them looked aghast.

"There's something funny going on here you know. I don't like it. I bet it has to do with them McAllisters," Mum offered. No one, not even his mother was happy with this explanation. Ben withdrew to his bedroom to consider everything that was happening.

He sat up on his bed and looked at the WISPA letter again. Each time he looked up, with the click of an eye he saw that the object he focused on actually picked itself up and looked for an alternative resting place. Ben knew he had discovered some bizarre kinetic power. How had he received it and what on earth for?

He practised with his eyes in his room, moving little objects for an hour or so. He could easily lift pens and pencils or books just by concentrating on them, clicking his eyes and thinking of movement of some sort. Now he had learnt what caused it, he thought back to the incidents of the last few weeks. Could he have caused them all?

The McAllisters sprang to his mind. He would like to pay them back for the shabby way they treated him. They let him down with the WISPA letter and Ben wanted to get them back in a quite different way.

Ben decided he would sleep on it. He had only a few short weeks to wait until he could go to his new school. It would be a different bus, with different school kids on it and he was thankful for that. Before going to bed, Ben wanted to see all the photos on the WISPA website. He hurriedly booted up the computer whilst his parents watched television. As he flicked through the section on school trips, an old newspaper article appeared on the screen. Ben looked at it carefully.

It concerned a school trip to Stonehenge in 1946; the day an almighty meteorite fell to earth nearby. Mysterious it should be on the website section about recent trips. It did not look as though it was meant to be there and slowly faded as Ben read it. That night Ben slept like a log, exhausted by the excitement.

In the morning, he woke up late to the sound of small gravel stones being thrown at his bedroom window. What now? He sat up on his knees on his bed and peered out of the edge of his thin curtains. They caught sight of his face.

"Come on out. Show us yer stupid dance then," blurted out the sarcastic voice. It was Robbie McAllister. To their surprise Ben opened the window.

"Yeah, all right then. I'll just get into my clothes and see you in the park out back."

He donned his white singlet and black dancing trousers. He rushed out through the kitchen door.

"Hang on, you haven't had your breakfast," squealed his mum.

He ran up the garden path, mini music player in hand with his dad waving to him through the greenhouse glass. His marrows had called him into service straight after morning tea.

"You're a bit keen aren't you?" his father mocked through the open window, as he saw a pair of dance shoe heels running up the path and into the bushes. He shook his head, not in disapproval, but in disbelief.

Ben left his own garden through the rear gate and saw five boys including Robbie McAllister making their way towards him in the park behind his house. He wasn't any longer so sure he could suddenly use any kinetic power that he had planned in his head and felt quite unsafe. He put the music player down switching it on, hoping for the best. He started to dance one of his routines with the boys jeering and chanting at him.

As they came towards him, he stopped suddenly. He paused, looking at Robbie intensely. Ben's eyes lowered to Robbie's sneakers and with a click he pulled them forward with a quick jerk. Robbie fell over backwards to the ground. As the other four started to move forward he locked his eyes onto each of their pairs of shoes and clicked. One by one they all fell down and then sat up confused.

Ben then picked up his music player and danced the short distance back to his garden gate and disappeared from their view. All he could hear was muffled disagreeable comments coming from the park behind him. He looked back to see waving fists but he didn't care anymore.

His fear left him and now he believed they would never bother him again. He felt a sense of power and freedom he had never experienced in all his short life.

"Ah, there you are, Ben," his startled father laughed merrily. Ben trotted along the garden path towards the house. "Come and look at this amazing marrow. I bet you've never seen one like this—"

However, Ben had other ideas and passed the greenhouse without a murmur. His new life was just beginning. He still had no idea how or why he had acquired these strange powers and he couldn't mention it to his mum or dad. They would never understand anything at their age.

That night he dreamt he was floating in a school playground and all he could smell was jasmine flowers. All he could hear was a constant faint buzzing sound like that from a disturbed wasp nest. This was a dream Ben remembered having a couple of times after his audition back in July. Why was he having it again, he thought?

*

As Ben drew up to WISPA on his first day that September, he felt so excited and nervous his stomach ached. For this first day of term, his mum had brought him in the car.

It was a cool day with a little sun appearing from time to time behind the patchy clouds. After walking him through the front door, his mum kissed him goodbye. It was an act that he moved to avoid but failed, as she planted her sloppy lips onto his cheek. He skipped enthusiastically into the main foyer of the school entrance hall and went in line to be checked off for arrival. A senior pupil was dealing with it.

He found himself next to another lad also on his first day, and probably about twelve as well. This lad tentatively introduced himself to Ben as Hitti Singh. Hitti was short for the name Hittendra, but no one ever called him that. Once they checked in and found they would share most of their lessons, they agreed to look out for each other. Hitti was of slim build and average height. He had very dark straight hair and was impeccably clean. His mother and father had come over from India when they were kids themselves.

"I do street, jazz and tap," he announced to a delighted Ben.

"Wow! I do all those. I love a crip walk, knee slide combination.. I'm really into routines and a bit of singing."

This sealed the possibility of friendship. They separated, not realising they both had to find the same classroom that morning. Ben was directed to his class along a corridor, up some steps and across a landing area. The smell of school cleaning fluid was quite overwhelming. Ben peered into a classroom.

"Is this Mrs Rigging's class?" appealed Ben to some of the kids already there. A large burly woman came from the side to stand astride the doorway.

"Who's asking dear?" she responded in a mild-mannered, low sounding voice, with her nose twitching like a rabbit.

Her vocal sound was soft but otherwise seemed in tune with her fit, stocky, rather masculine look.

"I'm Ben Street. It's my first day here."

"Ah yes, you're on the list," she reflected. After a few seconds she continued. "Come on in, but just put your bag in the locker out there first." She pointed to the corridor. "Yours is number five. Remember that because you'll be number five in this class for all purposes."

Ben was invited to sit at a desk almost at the centre, but quite near to the front of the classroom. There were about twenty of them there and just a few more to come. More than one fellow pupil frantically informed Ben in semi-whisper that Mrs Rigging was known as 'Ropy'. It didn't dawn on Ben for some time how she had acquired this funny nickname.

"Good morning, class. I am Eve Rigging." Barely a soul there could contain their giggles and Mrs Rigging was treated to a sea of smiling faces.

"Good morning, Mrs Rigging," chimed the class. She knew all along exactly what was being muttered, but the tradition in the school was to accept and applaud the ingenuity of the nickname rather than take issue with a bit of fun. Ignoring it, she carried on.

"I am your form teacher so you'll have me for maths and English and I also teach choreography along with Mr Wood. Some of you will have to put up with me for several things I expect," she chortled. "I am quite flexible with most things, but there's one thing I will not tolerate and that is incorrect clothing. Simon and Ben can you come up to the front please?"

This did not feel like a good start. Ben could feel an irritation developing with this teacher already. Simon Burns was a stocky boy of twelve with wavy dark brown hair, grey piercing eyes and large, prominent ears.

"Now, Simon, can you tell the class what sort of trousers you are allowed to wear?"

"I know they are either corduroy or cotton, but my mum couldn't get the right size."

"Enough, Simon," she snapped. "Please make sure you are properly dressed by Friday. Ben, why are you dressed in a non-regulation shirt?"

"I didn't know Mrs Rop—I mean Rigging." There was a loud guffaw from the class who all realised Ben's mistake. Mrs Rigging was beginning to turn a sort of pink verging on red, but held her self-control and spoke in a remarkably friendly tone.

"Just get it right by Friday please. And clean your finger nails, Ben."

As he turned to go back to his seat, Ben noticed the familiar face of Laura at the back. She must have been last in as he hadn't noticed her before. He was so pleased he lost concentration, tripped and stumbled on his way. Laura and he giggled a little too much and Mrs Rigging gave them both a warning.

"For English we'll be learning about the great playwrights this term, from Chaucer, through Shakespeare to Tom Stoppard."

They listened to this for about fifteen minutes and were handed various assignments to carry out for the term. It all seemed very advanced to Ben. Suddenly there was a knock and a man entered.

"Mrs Rigging, can I have a quick word?"

"Class, read the first passage through and we'll talk about it in a minute. By the way, if you're new, this is Dr Metanite who will teach you science. Excuse me for a moment please," Mrs Rigging pleaded.

They withdrew to the front of the classroom and were speaking softly so no one could hear. Dr Metanite was a slightly strange looking man. No one seemed to remember his first name, although he did have one. It was Samuel. He had to be addressed as 'Doctor' or 'Dr Metanite'. His eyes seemed very wide apart and he had an unusually expansive forehead. His fifty or so years had left him with thinning grey hair that was straggly and unattractive. However, he was always smartly dressed. He wore a well-tailored jacket with velveteen around the collar and a clean white shirt. He had one button of the jacket done up and a wide tie of dark blue silk.

Ben was to learn that almost all teachers at this school were referred to by nicknames, some happy to accept it to their face. Dr Metanite was an exception. He was known on the quiet as 'Metatarsal', the actual word for a set of foot bones, on account of the fact that he had long spindly fingers, which looked more like the skeleton of a human foot. Luckily they were covered in flesh. He did not appreciate his nickname and people occasionally referred to him as 'Meti', but never to his face.

As the teachers stood speaking, Ben was distracted from his reading by a feeling of brewing cold air in the room. He almost shivered as it wafted across him. It was accompanied by the slight smell of chemicals. Could it be some strong cleaning fluid? Ben had a sudden eerie feel and a huge sense of power in his stomach. He looked around him to see his fellow pupils almost motionless but still reading or quietly whispering to one another. None seemed to be experiencing what Ben felt!

A sunlight shaft shone strongly through the classroom at an angle right across Ben's desk. It was streaming at him alone. Apart from that, it looked like normal light. It intensified for a millisecond and went across Ben's mouth. He had weird tingling sensations across his face and could not speak. This held for a few moments.

The stream of light subsided, spreading out to a normal intensity. Ben gasped at the shock. Only the chemical smell and a cool feeling remained. Whatever was happening was mighty weird! He looked down to see goosebumps across his lower arms and felt his legs to be quite twitchy.

It had slowly sunk in that wherever Ben looked around this school there was information and pictures about insects. The classrooms, the theatre and the corridors all had some form of insect representation. Even the school tie had a blue background with yellow stitched dots on it. Look closely and the dots looked like insects with six legs. Dr Metanite turned to leave and opened the door.

"Well, I look forward to teaching you the science course starting next week," he announced with a slight smile. He then left the room. Gradually, after a few seconds the cold air and the smell of chemicals subsided. Ben started to feel the power in his stomach again. Almost like a wave of intense sensation, it returned every few minutes during the lesson.

"Ben, please read the next paragraph," ordered Mrs Rigging. Ben had been away in his own world, which did not please his new teacher at all.

"Uhmm..oh," struggled Ben, looking across to his neighbour's open book. There was a very short silence followed by giggles from the back.

"Laura Munday, I've warned you already today. You will do thirty minutes detention on Friday afternoon. Report to the theatre front desk at three fifteen." Laura's smile vanished. She hadn't even wanted to laugh at Ben. She just couldn't seem to help herself and then regretted it.

"Ben, well—? I'm waiting," came the hectoring demand.

"I'm sorry, I lost my place," Ben tried, hoping the truth would calm her. The classroom was filled with strained chuckles. Mrs Rigging paused and paced up and down the class between the desks showing she was in charge.

"You will join Laura in detention on Friday, Ben. We are here to learn. The schoolwork is just as important as your stage work. See me at the end of class."

That sounded ominous. Ben was mortified. How could he make such a mess of his first day? A few minutes passed and then the bell went. Ben made his way to the desk at the front. Mrs Rigging smiled at Ben and was surprisingly pleasant.

"You know, Ben, I have taught here for ten years and every other year or so I am lucky enough to have a pupil like you." Ben had no idea what she meant. "I have seen your last school's report. It was excellent, given the general school standard. I was there to see your audition. It was one of the best auditions for song and dance in years."

Ben had never been told that. He was thrilled with the news.

"You were awarded a scholarship to come here. That means others are paying your fees. So why are you behaving like a prize idiot on the first day in my class?"

There had to be a sting in the tail. Ben was speechless. He calmed himself and squirmed a little.

"I'm very sorry. I just haven't been to a place like this before and it's all been a bit much to take in."

"Look, you are obviously a talented young man. We have a high level of discipline here you may not be used to. Don't spoil your opportunity. Do your detention and we will start afresh, OK?" urged Mrs Rigging. "Now, off you go."

"Yes, Mrs Rigging. Thanks," said a relieved Ben as he slid off out into the corridor with his schoolwork bag. There waiting for him was Laura.

"Am I glad to see you," sighed Ben.

"What did Ropy say then?" enquired Laura, a bit keen on some gossip.

"To be honest, she was quite nice and kinda said we could start again, but I still got detention though." They started to walk to their next class whilst chatting. It was to be 'Theatre Management'.

Meanwhile, there were some strange high-pitched wailing noises coming from somewhere nearby. Wherever they walked through the school, Ben could hear it just the same.

"Laura, did you hear that?" questioned Ben intensely every so often. But Laura heard nothing and began to worry if Ben was becoming troubled in some way. He decided to keep quiet about it.

Just as they caught up with the tail end of their classmates entering the theatre door, there was a loud squeak. Some turned. Some thought it was the door. Laura and Ben looked at each other with puzzled expressions on their faces. It definitely wasn't the sound of a door, thought Ben. He was becoming even more puzzled by these events. He was not just 'hearing things'. Whatever it was, it was for real and very worrying.

"Come on, it's time to begin," called a stern voice from within the theatre, with a distinctly strong Welsh accent. It was Mr Euros Wood, happily known to everyone by his nickname of 'Splinter'. He was one of those schoolmasters who did not mind if you used his nickname directly to his face, even in lessons. He actually had a brother called Aled Wood, working in the school office referred to by the nickname of 'Branch'. Mr Wood was strict but fun. Ben soon found out that people applauded his firm, friendly style.

"Now, I'll be teaching you for this year. Mr Wood's the name, but call me Splinter coz everyone does. Anyone who chooses the Spanish language option or cycling club will have me for that too." Ben and Laura just managed to be seated in time.

He started handing out a manual to all pupils. When Ben's copy arrived in front of him it seemed to be a rather old tatty book, unlike anyone else's. It clung to him like a magnetic force had attached it to his lap. Mr Wood noticed Ben wriggling with it.

"And you are?"

"Ben Street."

"Oh, well I've heard of you. I think you're doing detention with me on Friday."

How on earth did he know that, wondered Ben? He had come straight from one class to another! "That manual needs replacing. Hang on to it for now and I'll have another next week." As the class continued, the manual seemed to change colour slightly several times. It was at least five shades of red during a few minutes. Even Laura could see its cover was strange.

"Open up the manual at page fifty four please and we can see the likely job role of a Theatre Manager. Most of you think you will be stars of stage and film. Some of you will—"

The words were lost on Ben. Page fifty-four didn't have writing on it at all. There was no print, but just a handwritten message: My darling girl, I will miss you forever. You were my world and my life. Until we meet again. Dad. 29th September 1949. Before Ben had even

48

thought much about this sad sounding message, he put up his hand and interrupted Splinter.

"Sorry, Sir."

"Call me Splinter, Ben."

"My page hasn't got the job role on it. Just writing," he said lifting up the manual to show him. The page was facing away from Ben but most of the class could see it. Splinter screwed up his eyes a little and walked towards the manual.

"Are you a joker, Ben? The page is identical to all the rest of them." As Ben began to mumble that it wasn't he turned the manual back to find a printed page fifty four with the full theatre manager's job role printed on it! Quite startled, he dropped the manual and it stuck to his ankle area. Splinter just carried on with the lesson taking no notice.

Ben felt a slimy wet gooey gunge spread around just above his foot. At least that's what it felt like. He pulled at it, but could not shift it. Laura noticed it and at first thought Ben was playing about. But she could see the sticky goo-like substance stuck to Ben's leg. She began to feel alarmed.

Ben decided to take a risk. What if he used his kinetic power? He looked at the manual sharply and blinked, bringing his eyes straight to the floor. It bounced off as if it had fallen from his lap and no more. It made a noise and the class all looked at Ben. He looked around as if he was joining in. Those near him were not fooled. Suddenly there was no sign of sliminess anywhere. He hadn't imagined it though!

At much the same time, Mrs Rigging was in the staff room and could be seen putting two names on the list for detention. The headmaster, Mr Michael Keith Goving was pouring his tea to take into his office next door. He was occasionally known as 'MK' to some of his colleagues but most called him 'Mr Goving' or 'Headmaster'. Pupils and parents alike were all fond of him. He was a drama teacher and now head of the renowned school.

"Not on the first day, Eve," moaned Mr Goving, frowning and casting his eye at the list. "It's Ben Street. How disappointing. He's on a new scholarship."

"I know, MK. I tried to avoid it, but it was necessary to set the standard," she lamented.

"Hmmm, send him to see me would you? I saw his audition and we don't want him off the rails." With that Mr Goving whisked himself away to his office, cup of tea in hand.

Ben was nearing the end of his first lesson with Splinter. The manual was back on his lap but now looked a green grey sort of colour. Suddenly there was a short sharp knock at the door and a small lady entered handing a note to Splinter. He continued speaking for a few more moments then the bell went. It was a relief. Ben found Splinter amusing, but he was worried about the manual. He lifted himself up to leave, when Splinter came over. Laura left with the rest.

"I have a note here that you are to see the headmaster this break. Are you OK, Ben?"

"I thought I was," came the puzzled reply. Ben felt a sense of trepidation come over him.

"I know we've only just met, but you seem to be in a world of your own. Here, have my manual and I'll take that one." Ben didn't know whether he should want the strange behaving manual or not and slowly released it.

"Mr Goving is a lovely fellow. Just talk it out with him. That's my advice," said Splinter kindly. With that, Ben made his way out and wandered along the corridor alone, seeing only older pupils passing. He did not actually know where to go when he bumped into Hitti.

"Hey, Hitti, how are you getting on?" he said in a very upbeat manner. It was not how he felt just then, but he was pleased to see a friendly face.

"Yeah, I really like it. You're in my dance class on the list." A hand landed on Ben's shoulder.

"Hi, Ben. Tom Cortazzi, drama group." Tom was one of the most talented actors and dancers in the school with a habit of landing plum roles in school performances.

"Don't think just because you've got a scholarship that gets you anywhere around here," he growled in a hostile way. Ben and Hitti both caught each other's eye in surprise at this intrusion. How did Tom know who Ben was?

"OK, Tom, just don't threaten me. I can look after myself," Ben stated firmly, not really believing it. Tom walked on.

"What's his problem?" Ben murmured.

"Dunno." Hitti was as confused as Ben.

"I need to find the head's office. Which way is it?" Ben set off as instructed. There was a separate corridor Ben had to make his way through. As he approached the door, the feeling in his stomach he'd felt earlier returned. He wondered if he was ill. After a few moments it subsided. "Oh well," he muttered to himself, "here goes."

He lifted his knuckle up to the solid wooden door and was about to knock when it opened. Out came Dr Metanite smiling and suggesting full agreement about something he had been discussing. Before the door began to swing back by its own weight to close, Ben knocked twice.

"Come in, young man."

"Ben Street Sir. You asked me to see you," Ben uttered nervously.

"Ah, yes, I remember you all right. Sit down over there." He was ushered to a sofa opposite the rather imposing desk. "I just wanted to welcome you to WISPA as one of our four new scholarship entrants. Do you have any idea how difficult it is to be awarded one of these?"

Ben clearly hadn't a clue and although his mouth opened, nothing came out before Mr Goving continued. "There are only four to six scholarships out of a total intake of eighty pupils each year. I was one of the guys on the panel at your audition. Your audition stunned us, Ben. Afterwards, it was your name everywhere. You were the first one picked out for an award. We had to wrestle our minds for hours over many other worthy applicants, but you—" He stopped mid-sentence as if he had nearly stunned himself into silence, let alone Ben.

"I am so surprised," Ben said softly.

"Well, I called for you because I had the shock of finding Mrs Rigging putting your name up for detention in the staff room. I want you to be quite clear that we welcome you, but at the same time expect a high standard of behaviour. By the rules of your scholarship, you have your fees paid and I am meant to report any behaviour issues to the Board of School Governors who approve it on a termly basis. It can be withdrawn in certain circumstances."

Ben had little knowledge of this but guessed you could be kicked out of school if everything went too pear-shaped.

"Yes, Mr Goving. I will do better in future."

"I will be mentioning you at assembly next week along with the other scholarship entrants. Don't let me down and I'll just overlook putting your detention down in the scholarship file this time. Run along now."

"Oh, thank you, Mr Goving," Ben said very relieved as he left quickly.

A few days passed. Ben was getting used to the school and had no further stomach pains to his relief and put it down to the excitement of a new school. But he still heard wailing in the corridors and his dreams at night were awesome in their clarity; like watching a movie, he thought. It was always the same; he floated around a playground, with the smell of jasmine and the faint sound of wasps or insects buzzing like a summer's day in the countryside.

It was Friday afternoon. Ben wandered along towards the theatre reception to do his detention. There was Laura already waiting at the desk. Within seconds the slim frame of a teacher calling herself Mrs Mudge arrived. She had a large mop of nearly ginger hair, not particularly well kept. She was carrying a large bag full of schoolwork. She wore a striking engagement type ring, with a single, very large cut diamond. Most people remembered her for that. She was never seen without it.

"Come on in, guys. Splinter was coming today but we swapped. It'll all be over quickly if we get on with it. I have a sheet of work here I'm supposed to give you, but I think we'll use the theatre for some singing practise instead," she announced unexpectedly with a smile on her face.

"Call me Smudge won't you. They all do here." Her first name was Sally and long ago at this school it was beyond temptation not to add her first name initial to her family name, making it into Smudge. Smudge sat down at the piano and looked in her bag, producing a large songbook.

"Let's start with this one," she puffed, handing them both a sheet of words and music. Neither of them knew the melody, but soon picked it up as Smudge banged it out on the piano. "Now, Ben, you start and Laura do the second verse and the third you can do together."

It was all going well until the third verse was reached. They both sang together, but somehow there was a third voice in there. Was someone else singing too? Ben and Laura looked at Smudge, but she was just playing the music. As soon as they stopped, so did the third voice. When one of them sang alone there was no extra sound.

"How ever did you two produce that amazing sound when you sing together? It seems to have a really unusual resonance. It's almost like three of you are singing," Smudge said with her huge expanse of hair flopping about.

"Is it this theatre?" asked Ben. Neither had a convincing answer. As it was being discussed, Ben noticed a misty form hovering at the back of the theatre. He nudged Laura and pointed when Smudge was looking away at her music. But Laura saw nothing. The misty form faded away. Ben stood quite still contemplating it.

"We'll have to see what we can do with you two in a show one day. Let's try another song," she smiled, rifling through her book of tunes.

53

The staff room, unusually for a Friday afternoon was still jostling with teachers either having a quiet tea after lessons, or quickly working through the first week's homework to have it marked ready for Monday.

"I'm not sure about some of my new form pupils this year, Mr Goving," spouted Mrs Rigging in a jovial manner. "I think one or two of them are a little ill-mannered. Still, we need our young stars to have no fear of their feelings to get on here I suppose," she suggested.

"You'll get used to them. Remember three years ago and you had all that trouble with Tom Cortazzi? He was a handful at first; look at him now," chuckled Mr Goving.

A few minutes passed uneventfully. Ben and Laura had finished and set off up the corridor to grab their things and hopefully catch the last school bus.

"Can you feel that?" Ben asked.

"Feel what?" replied Laura.

"It's just—Oh, forget it." Ben knew it was only him seeing misty forms, feeling strange surges and moving objects.

Ben started to run and looked towards the school offices and staff room as he flew along and out of sight. As he was running he felt like the world had moved into slow motion. It was like leaning on a strong wind. There *was* no wind, was there?

At the same time, the sideboard in the staff room, upon which all the tea mugs and kettle stood, made a sudden creaking sound and everyone turned to see it moving sideways along the wall at a snail's pace. It ground to a halt after a few centimetres and about five seconds later.

"Well, what the devil—?" exclaimed Mr Goving, shocked to see his faithful old sideboard part company with the spot it had inhabited for as long as he could recall. Dr Metanite intervened and leapt from his armchair in the corner, putting his files to one side.

"It must be a failing floorboard or joist. It's very heavy with all that crockery in it," he offered, as he made his way over and bent down for an examination. The building was at least one hundred and eighty years old and certainly given to creaks in the floor. "Hmmm. Very strange. Nothing I can see here. There is no angle sufficient for gravity to have that effect," he explained.

"I'd better have it checked by the clerk of works," Mr Goving pontificated. He had no idea what would be found. There was a severe doubt amongst the staff that the sideboard had moved itself without some prank being involved. No one said it, but Ben Street's name seemed to pop into their minds.

CHAPTER 4

Join the club!

The second week at WISPA was going to be very different, especially for new pupils. It was just before nine in the morning. Ben was in a sea of fellow pupils filing into the Peter Phelps Theatre by the huge old double doors as high as two grown men standing on each other's shoulders. They flowed like sugar through a sieve, arriving rather squashed on the other side of the doors and grabbing seats alongside their teacher.

There was loud chattering and the sound of shuffling. Without notice there was an immense banging sound. Ben turned towards the front to see a senior pupil banging an enormous spoon onto a battered desk near to the headmaster.

"Quiet please for the headmaster," he was shouting. Mr Goving was smiling and moving up and down slightly nervously on his feet. He was wearing his full black cloak and mortar board regalia. All the other teachers dressed very casually, Ben noticed. The shuffling and chatting subsided rapidly to a complete hush in the theatre hall.

"Good morning, everyone. I would like to start this assembly by warmly welcoming our new intake. We have some talented young ones joining us this year. I must announce particularly that four scholarships were awarded to pupils of outstanding promise. Those were: Amelia Montague, Richard Lund, Lauren Bonnay and Benjamin Street."

A loud roar of applause rang out like the encore at a theatre production. Ben felt happy and excited by this reaction. "I have some notices to read out about forthcoming events. Before I get to that, I would just like to speak for a moment about your Club Festival next week."

Ben was watching the headmaster intensely. He was standing to one side of the platform. As Ben looked, his eyes started to blink a little. Something was in his eye. He wrestled to remove it with one finger in the corner. His vision cleared and almost at once there was a loud crash beside the headmaster. The large oil painting of the school on the side wall had detached itself and fallen. The surprised head stepped away from the crashing frame just in time and then continued, trying not to be put off.

Ben had more than a suspicion this was his kinetic power at work when he hadn't wanted it. He had hoped he was in control of this power and not the other way about. He craved answers now more than ever. But where would he find them? He had no idea where he could start, yet he knew in his heart there must be an explanation.

"So I urge all of you new ones, to join at least two clubs and even three. These are all part of your education and will help you in many ways to develop your skills and all round knowledge—"

Ben was not so relaxed now and drifted in his thoughts. What if he was going mad? He so needed to talk to someone, but who could keep a secret this important? Who would even believe it?

"Come on, Ben," said Mrs Rigging. "We have work to do!" Ben realised the assembly had ended without him noticing. He moved off and waved to Hitti Singh across the hall as he made his way to his form classroom.

*

It was a Wednesday and the Club Festival was due to start in about ten minutes. Ben and Laura had agreed to attend

57

the theatre hall together. There were small collapsible table stands with bunting attached to each showing the club name.

"What's this club like?" asked Ben as he stood at 'The Ventriloquists Club'.

"It's really good. You learn to talk without moving your lips like this," Josie demonstrated. "Or otherwise throw your voice like this," she continued, showing off her skills. Ben and Laura looked behind for the voice but it was Josie in front of them.

"Over here, over here" a dog-shaped puppet kept saying, imploring a visit from anyone interested. Ben was not sure, but saw Hitti signing up shortly afterwards.

Next he noticed 'The Juggling Club', and someone throwing three balls around with another pupil. It was impressive, but that was a circus act and not for him he thought. Ben and Laura wandered along together. They passed diving, costume sewing, mimicry, current affairs, illustrators and clay modellers clubs. Mimicry, Ben mulled over in his mind. That would be brilliant.

"I'm sorry but there's already a waiting list to join because it's one of the most popular clubs," said Lucy. "If you want to join it's quite a lot of watching at first."

"I'd like to put my name down. Who do you learn to mimic?" asked Ben.

"It could be anyone, but mainly all the stars and some teachers. We just use a few props like hats or wigs."

There was always a mimicry section in the end of year show and a prize for 'Mimic of the Year'.

While Ben was chatting, Laura slipped away unnoticed and joined the illustrators club. You learn to take the theme of a book and provide really good sketches and watercolours, or make clay models of the illustrated characters. Some writers asked club members to provide illustrations to go in their books. If they actually used the drawings you might even be paid! Laura loved art and felt at home right away with the idea.

As Ben wandered by he felt drawn to a club table, the sign for which he could not make out across the hall. It had a very old piece of bunting attached to it with some rips on the edges. Why am I walking this way, he chewed over in his mind? Laura had been left behind. His legs just went there without him wanting them to and without stopping. He arrived and was placed right in front of the desk. No one else seemed the slightest bit interested. All he could see was other pupils passing it by.

There was a strange young boy behind the table with a gaunt look on his face, rather scruffily dressed. He didn't look well. He was somehow out of place and Ben suspected he was a loner type. He seemed rather withdrawn for someone at a stage school.

"Hi I'm Ben," he found himself saying without hesitation. There was little response. The older girl behind him was also unusual. She had extra long dark brown hair, an unfortunately large nose and spots on her forehead. She stepped forward.

"Oh, Ben, take no notice of him; he's Matt Fingle. In a world of his own, that one. Marvellous at trumpet and ballet, but otherwise…well." She described him, just as if he wasn't present.

"Is this local history?" Ben's mouth said without him wanting to speak at all!

"I'm Fiona Payne and local history is our thing. Are you into that Ben?" She enquired with a hopeful tone. She was putting very old pages of broken books together. "This'll tell a story. They all come from an old store of stuff someone discovered about five years ago in one of the school vaults. We've been working on it because it's got local history as well as school history in there. The idea is to bring out a book eventually."

Ben didn't answer. His lips had frozen at the moment he had noticed something. On the table was that same old newspaper article he'd seen on the school website about the

1946 trip to Stonehenge. His lips came free and began speaking on their own.

"Can I join then?" Ben stood there feeling as though someone was working him like a puppet. In his head rang out the words, join and search, join and search, join and search, over and over again. It did not seem an unpleasant calling, but weird.

"Yes, of course. We need more help." Ben remained quite calm and tried persuading himself it was just his own thoughts. He knew he didn't want to join, but his mouth was out of control!

"Well, what do I need to do?" he heard his own voice spouting quite against his will. He didn't feel spooked, just confused.

"Just pop your name down here and we meet after school at three fifteen on Thursdays in the Local History Club room. Corridor six, fourth door on the left," Fiona trotted out like a rehearsed script. "See you there," she beamed.

Ben looked down at the joining list and saw no one's name but his own. He didn't remember writing his name there either. It was his handwriting, so he must have. His legs relaxed and felt like his own again. He turned to leave saying, "Great, three fifteen, Thursday." His mouth spoke without permission again!

Where was Laura? Ben had not seen her leave his side in his preoccupied state. On his way around to find her he joined the diving club too. He was already a good swimmer and had heard much of the mosaic pool at the school. A short while later she was to be found sketching merrily at the illustrators club table. Laura had already sketched a pretty girl in an old-fashioned school uniform.

"Hey, that's really good, Laura!" Ben enthused. "Where did you learn to draw like that?"

Laura's drawing hand was moving in an animated way as if slightly out of her control.

"I don't know. It's just seems really easy today," Laura replied excitedly.

That night Ben lay restless in his bed with his bedside lamp on, churning over all that was happening in his new life. His heart raced as he remembered the strange kinetic energy he had acquired. His legs moving themselves and his mouth speaking on its own worried him. What about this wailing he kept hearing in the corridors and why did his manual in Splinter's lesson take on a gooey form, let alone have a weird message in it? Was someone trying to tell him something? He worried what may happen next.

Nobody would believe a word of it! He turned over and decided it would have to be Laura. That's it! Whether she believed him or not, she was going to hear about it. He just had to get it off his chest. She had seen a bit of it anyway.

"Hey, I was watching that," cried out the muffled voice of his father from downstairs.

"You ain't watching that rubbish while I'm here," shouted his mother in reply.

Ben pulled up his duvet over his head. What silly parents. Can't they agree about anything, not even a telly channel?

"Well, I can't stand any more of those cooking programmes," lamented his dad. "They've done *you* no good anyhow," he screeched cuttingly.

"Well, if we didn't have to eat marrow with everything then—" She retorted angrily.

Ben switched off. He knew life was complicated enough without arguing over telly and marrows. Other people's parents always seemed so normal compared to his own.

Laura had gone home really happy. She fitted in at her new school and saw it as the beginning of her career. She put her electric toothbrush away on its solid brass stand and it clicked itself away in a cupboard in her bathroom. The lights automatically dimmed as she left for her connected bedroom. The sumptuous carpet ruffling between her toes was as soft as washed fur. She grabbed a remote controller and drew the curtains. The air conditioner blew warm air across the room silently. She hopped onto her peach coloured silken sheets in her queen size bed, lay back on her duck down pillows and pressed a further button. An entertainment unit gradually withdrew from the fitted furniture unit and Laura chose from a list of movies. Frankly, she might as well be living in a world-class hotel penthouse suite.

Ben pushed his hand out of the side of his duvet, nestling on top of his old divan bed. He reached for the old wine bottle that was now filled with sand, topped with a light bulb and used as his bedside lamp. He felt the cool, damp air on his hand as he switched off the light. Ben lay still, trying to sleep. A few minutes passed. He sat up, bolt upright, with a start. Something was dawning on Ben.

"I'll bet that's the answer, he muttered." He was so tired he fell back like a plank of wood and drifted off until morning.

CHAPTER 5

The 'top secret' promise

Next Thursday came and Ben had PE first followed by double stagecraft. His class and others were to receive a visitor during this lesson. They all took their theatre seats expectantly.

"Today we have one of our most famous former pupils visiting. Give a warm welcome to Dame Sarah Puttock," announced Mrs Rigging.

The Dame was a revered actress of the stage and an eccentric endearing soul who could speak for as long as you wanted on her experiences and the stagecraft she had learnt over the years. Every twenty minutes or so, she would pause and address the teacher, Mrs Rigging, in a very theatrical manner.

"Have I gone on long enough yet, Ropy? Do stop me when you've had enough, because I can just go on for hours." The teacher waved her on to continue each time. It was nearly two hours of the funniest stories about her life and career you could possibly imagine.

"One of the funniest incidents I can recall was when many years ago I was in a play on Broadway. The main actress failed to turn up. I had a small part but was asked to do both at the same time and with just a moment's notice," the Dame recalled. "It was all going well until I realised both I and the director had overlooked one scene where both characters appeared at the same time!" The theatre was full of muffled laughter already. "I was forced to jump from one position to another whilst saying the lines for both parts."

The Dame demonstrated how she carried it off in her eccentric way, changing her accent and expression for each part, to the complete amusement of her audience. She could still remember the words from over thirty years ago! "In all honesty the play was far better that night—"

Through all the laughter, Ben felt a cool wind come across him. He caught sight of Smudge peering through the side of the smoked glass of the lighting box. She appeared to be speaking, but Ben heard nothing. Someone knows something they shouldn't, he thought. It's all connected to my theory.

One of the boys, Ned Elliot, was sitting just below the lighting box and heard some comments. Smudge was almost whispering into a telephone.

"Have you come across this new boy, Ben Street, in science yet?"

"Yes, I have. But the way you said that, it sounds like trouble. Is there a problem?" Dr Metanite asked, sensing her tone.

"Well, there's just something about him. I had him in detention and he's very talented. Just watch him. I think he thinks he's too clever by half," she replied, not really offering any concrete information.

Ned was not into gossip and thought nothing more about it. He was just a normal fair-haired twelve-year-old, who only enjoyed school sometimes.

"I was here about sixty years ago you know. I can even remember the old drama teacher, Tim Dreante. He was absolutely marvellous," the Dame enthused.

"Any questions?" Ropy called out. With that, Ben found his mind clicking into action as if someone else had taken over his voice.

"Did you go on the famous school trip to Stonehenge in 1946 when the meteorite came down?" Ben asked.

"I'm amazed at what they teach you here. That story is as old as the hills! I didn't actually go, but my best friend Sonia did and I'll never forget her. She later died in a terrible accident in this theatre. Before the safety cages were installed," she indicated pointing at the backstage." There was a loud intake of breath at this news.

Ropy knew she hadn't taught anyone about this episode of school history. Smudge caught her eye and scowled. Her suspicions about Ben had just gone up a notch. The session ended with huge applause and everyone filed out happily.

"Laura. Over here," called out Ben, waving like a traffic policeman. Laura pushed her way over to Ben in the crowd politely. "I really need to tell you something, Laura. I don't want anyone to see or hear us though. It's top secret," Ben said.

"What about straight after school?" Laura queried.

"Yeah. Great. Uhmm..oh, I'm going to local history club then." Ben paused. "But you could come too and we'll find a quiet place somewhere."

"Uhmm, I don't think I want to join—"

"Just say you are thinking about it?" Ben interrupted sharply. Laura nodded agreement. "Just one thing, Laura. You must promise me not to tell anyone about it," Ben poured out like some strict teacher. He was fiddling with the buttons on his jacket in a nervous, twitchy way. Laura knew he meant it. Somehow the words 'top secret' were so attractive weren't they?

"You've got it." Laura saluted as she spoke. It all seemed like a military operation and she almost giggled imagining Ben in a General's uniform and she, dressed as his lieutenant.

"Meet me at the quadrangle, by corridor six."

They went their separate ways until the end of the school day. Ben had to help the stage crew. There was a rota for that. Laura was going to do a first aid class.

Meanwhile, Dr Metanite was spending the afternoon preparing all sorts of experiments during class.

The science labs were on the edge of the school grounds and he lived in a terraced house very close by and would walk to work. He never drove anywhere and didn't own a car. He had been at the school longer than any current staff member, over twenty-five years. The story went that his wife had apparently died before he started at WISPA. In his lab, or indeed anywhere, he would frequently hum to himself. People used to comment on his noisy humming. It was even heard outside his house sometimes by the neighbours.

Today he seemed wildly engaged in an experiment of his own and teaching his class something entirely different, at the same time. The door of his classroom opened and Dr Metanite locked his desk drawer almost simultaneously.

"Ah, Dr Metanite. I am showing prospective parents around," announced the headmaster. The whole class rose to their feet in unison.

"Good afternoon, Mr Goving," they all chanted slowly.

"And what are you working on today, Doctor?" asked Mr Goving innocently.

"Me? Uhmm..oh the kids," he corrected himself. "They are working out what element metals may be in the example substances."

"Good, good," the head smiled, having little idea of any scientific matter. "So you see," he went on, turning to the parents and ushering them out of the door.

"Come over here, Ned," Dr Metanite demanded, curling his long index finger back and forth. "Can you hold this still while I have the contraption operate?"

"Yes, Sir," Ned obeyed. Dr Metanite lit his Bunsen burner and applied the heat to two test tubes of liquid attached to four tubes and three other receptacles, humming as he went. The heat quickly attacked the substances and they started to thicken and flow through the tubes. A dark green goo began to emerge into the receptacles.

"Excellent, excellent," puffed Dr Metanite as he saw the process through. He was excited and twitchy, quite unsettling poor Ned.

"Can I go back to my seat now, Sir?" Ned requested, in a fearful voice. There was an unlikely pause, whilst the doctor fed the goo into a final jar and put a lid on it and put it in his desk drawer. He suddenly came to life.

"Yes, yes and thank you, Ned." He had sounded insincere in his thanks. Ned knew it had nothing to do with their lesson. Dr Metanite was the kind of teacher who knew all the answers, but at the same time everyone thought him odd. What on earth was this goo for, thought Ned?

The bell went, thank goodness! Ben made his way up the passage towards the quadrangle. Laura met him at the entrance to corridor six and they made their way up to the fourth door on the left. Fiona Payne was there alone, putting out some boxes of items to be examined.

"Hi, Ben. Have we another new recruit then?" she smiled looking at Laura.

"Well, I'm thinking about it and just want to try it out please," replied Laura spitting her words out quickly.

"That's fine. You two choose a box and spread it out on a table where you like, over there somewhere," Fiona suggested. "I'm in the middle of this one. We'll chat about what you uncover in about half an hour and go from there." Fiona pointed at a large trunk full of dusty looking paperwork and even some photos.

Ben and Laura glanced at the contents of the boxes. They looked at each other as if to say, what are we doing here? Ben just wanted to get Laura away to tell her his secret.

He picked a medium-sized container because it had old photos on the top. They moved it to a table away from Fiona and quickly spread some out to look like they were doing something. Ben whispered.

"Laura, you know how that school manual went gooey on me in Splinter's class?"

"Yes," said Laura waiting for a secret she didn't already know.

"Uhm, other things have happened, like hearing wailing in the corridors and things have started moving about when I look at them. You must believe me," Ben added responding to her frowning expression of disbelief. He stopped.

"Don't you think there's some ordinary everyday reason for this? The manual was probably on the top and left to melt in the sun. The wailing; well, could it be some wind noise you heard?" Laura reasoned.

"What about being able to move objects then?" Ben answered, rather restless at Laura's attitude. With that, Ben looked across to Fiona and saw her deep in thought. "Watch this," he commanded. Ben locked his eyes onto the tea chest in front of them and blinked like a clicking motion. He looked to see but nothing happened. Laura was looking like she might get up and go any second. Surely his powers had not just gone?

"Laura wait," Ben implored. Fiona looked in their direction and then gazed back at her work. He tried again with just the pile of photos in front of them. Blink and click. The photos hopped up and landed on a very shocked Laura's lap. She nearly choked as Fiona came over to see her spluttering. In fact, she was in a state of semi-belief.

"It's OK. Dust I expect," she told Fiona, regaining her composure.

"Are you sure you're all right?" questioned Fiona.

"Yes, I'm fine thanks," coughed Laura, determined to keep the secret now it had been revealed to her. Fiona moved away.

"See?" said a relieved Ben. "I've moved furniture and all sorts," he laughed with self-satisfaction beaming through. Laura was still not sure.

"That's incredible, Ben. How come you can do it?" a puzzled Laura asked.

"Exactly," said Ben. "That's what I need to find out. I get the feeling someone is watching or giving me signals and I don't know what for."

Ben told Laura all he could about the strange happenings, whilst emptying the old container. As he put his hand in for more he suddenly pulled back. An old wooden-handled screwdriver had put a pinprick into his right palm. The tiny bloodspot began to glow like a miniature, but powerful light. Ben pointed his hand away from Fiona. Only Laura saw it. Fiona was putting things away and called out.

"I've gotta go early today, guys. Just put the box back when you've done and we'll chat about it next week. OK?"

"Fine," replied Ben, worried about his hand. It was more strange happenings and now, at last he could share it with someone. Laura was about to change from undecided to firm believer!

As Fiona left, the temperature plummeted. Moments later a ghostly form of a schoolgirl in uniform appeared, floating slightly with her feet at normal floor level. An adult-sized male ghostly spirit was holding her around her neck, dressed in trousers and long-sleeved shirt. The foul ghoul roared. Ben and Laura stood back in horror! They were like real people, but just vaguely see-through!

Ben was so close he had touched it when he jumped with fright. You couldn't feel the ugly ghost but the clothing pressed in to the touch!

The male spirit spoke in a normal voice but which echoed and buzzed with interference like it came through a long tunnel.

"I suppose you think this is funny sticking your nose into my business?" Ben and Laura had struck the word funny from their thoughts. "If you carry on meddling it can only lead to one thing," howled the ghostly form holding the wailing girl.

Was this spirit form addressing them? They froze with fear. "I'm talking to you two over there. Don't interrupt me with your thinking." Could the ghost tell their thoughts too?

Ben and Laura felt sheer terror. Ben's hand was throbbing with the tiny light pulsating on his palm. As the light moved around with Ben's hand, it inadvertently pointed at the ghosts. When the shaft of light struck the spirits, it put a hole through them the size of a small coin, which repaired seconds later. Ben tried anxiously pointing it all over the ghostly bodies and it looked as if he had scribbled a picture.

"You will be cursed if you try to help her and it will never leave you. Meddling will lead to the curse of the Scarigus. That I promise you."

Scarigus meant nothing to Ben or Laura. The voice and the apparition faded gently away, whilst the schoolgirl spirit struggled in the male's grasp. A pause of several seconds took place whilst the two friends calmed down.

"Ben. I don't want to have any more to do with this. I'm sorry but it's frightening me and—" Laura made to get up.

"Don't you see, Laura?" Ben said excitedly, holding Laura's arm. "You're getting messages too. That sketch you did at illustrators club the other day; the moment I saw that ghost girl I knew right away. You drew her," Ben said slowly, satisfied he was finding the answers.

Laura turned very pale as she took in the enormity of her new world. She looked around the room thinking and frowning, playing for time. She could see Ben was deadly serious.

"Hey, Laura. The light on my hand. It's gone!" Ben piped up enthusiastically. They both immediately noticed, as he was speaking, a light coming from inside the old container. With a sharp intake of breath, Ben peered over the edge. The container was almost empty. Sitting in the bottom was a rectangular envelope. It looked perfectly normal except it was bright like a light was shining through the paper.

Ben plucked up the courage to pick it up. It was warm to the touch but didn't feel like paper; more like thick treacle that left nothing on your hands when you took them away from it. Ben started to open the letter and as he did so the light inside intensified and a little background wailing was heard. "That's the noise I hear in the corridors sometimes, Laura. I swear it's the same."

For a few short moments, somehow Ben had felt fearless. He tugged and the whole papery form suddenly became flat in his hands. There was a handwritten script all lit up, clearly very old and done with an ink pen. It was on old school headed notepaper signed by 'The Headmaster,' but with no fully readable name, just a scrawled signature.

The William Ingram School of Performing Arts
Copied to all parents – twelfth day of October 1949

Dear parents,
No doubt you were all as deeply shocked and saddened as I was by the sudden tragic loss last week of one of our finest young pupils, Sonia Bird. Her father, Dr Edward Bird, will shortly accept donations for his nominated research charity in remembrance of Sonia. The Department of Entomology where he is a scientist, are donating a plaque that will be placed at the school in her memory.
You have my assurance that following extensive investigation by both the police and myself, the matter is sincerely believed to be a tragic accident.
The Inspector is satisfied that no other pupils are at risk in the backstage of the theatre and it has re-opened today. The poor girl concerned must simply have fallen awkwardly, injuring herself in a

most unlikely manner. Even so, the master in charge, Tim Dreante, immediately offered his resignation. In the circumstances this was graciously accepted as a mark of respect to the parents.

Naturally the Coroner has been informed and I will write again in due course.

Yours sincerely,

Gareth Streeter

(Headmaster)

Ben could not read all of the signature. But it didn't seem to matter. Ben looked up at Laura who had also read the letter. When he looked back it was fading in his hands until after a few seconds it had disappeared. Both Ben and Laura sat breathing hard with over-excitement and anxiousness, until they began to calm.

"That's crazy. You just asked the Dame a question today and she remembered her friend Sonia. There it is in that letter talking about her! How come you asked that question?" asked Laura.

"I didn't exactly. That's the problem. It just came out," Ben replied.

"You aren't making any sense." Their discussion stopped at the sound of crackling and the sight of a small stream of smoke appearing from the old container.

Laura and Ben looked in and saw in smouldering letters, a message: Help me. Sonia. They couldn't see a family name but it might have begun with 'Bir' judging by the writing that ran into the corner of the chest.

Neither said another word. Ben's fear had returned for now. They just got up and ran out of the room, down corridor six and straight to the bus stop outside the school.

They stood there in near panic without talking until the bus arrived at four fifteen. They both knew that a strange mystery had been revealed and they must solve it. The male ghost had accused Ben of 'meddling'. He must have something to hide. Ben felt a huge determination to find the answer. The ghost 'Sonia' was asking for help like a lost soul.

*

"Laura, darling. How was your day?" called out her mum as Laura walked up their palatial stairway. As she ran her hand up the cast iron balustrade she sighed.

"Fine thanks," Laura squeaked revealing nothing of her feelings. After all, what could she say to a mother about *that* day? She withdrew to her bathroom for a long soak. Ben and she were in this mystery together; that she knew for definite. It was a little different in the Street household.

"Ben love, is that you?" chirped his mum. "Come and speak to me. I've got some news for you."

"I'll be down in a minute, Mum," he trotted out wearily. He quickly showered and returned refreshed to the kitchen dressed in pyjamas. His mum was cutting up vegetables for a 'bake'. It was more likely to be a flavourless mush. But still, she had a heart of gold. She didn't really like anything with herbs or garlicky tastes at all.

"Are you tired or something?" she glowered as she noticed his pyjamas.

"Very tired today, Mum. So what's the news then?" Ben expected nothing of this news. His mum, bless her, thought it interesting if crocuses were early in spring. She would be happy talking about aimless nothings, not that Ben was against it. It just wasn't for him.

"Your dad had a chat with Uncle Terry on the phone last night after you was in bed. It got on to what you were doing. Yer never guess what? He only went and said that Dad's grandad was once a teacher at WISPA," his mum smirked, nodding with her eyes twinkling.

"What?" exclaimed Ben, disbelief in his voice that it was actually news worth discussing.

"Oh yeah, he said, could've been the head even. I think Dad's gonna try and find out about him, now you're there."

His mum was so pleased about it, but Ben was having misgivings now. What if these strange happenings at school were connected to this great grandad of his? His mind whirred like a steam train moving off at top speed. He went a shade of pale.

"What's the matter, lovey? You don't look well," his mum said now becoming concerned. "I guess you're over tired coz it's all new stuff there ain't it?"

Ben was not sure if he should worry or not about this unexpected development. Was it possible his great grandfather had even written that letter he and Laura had seen today from way back in 1949? The pieces of this puzzle were always growing. But the big picture was not yet clear.

"Oh, I've grown the biggest marrow you ever saw, Ben," announced his happy father walking in the back door, forgetting about his muddy boots. "Come and see it. I'm going to put one in for the show this year."

If only his worries were confined to marrows, thought Ben! They left the kitchen together leaving Mum behind to finish making their supper. As they walked along the garden with Ben cold in his pyjamas, asked about his dad's grandad.

"I never knew him, son. He died before I was born, sometime in the late 1950s," pointed out his dad politely. "Don't even know his first name."

"Did you ever hear anything weird about him from grandad?" asked Ben.

"Why on earth would you ask me that?" His father frowned as he spoke.

"Nothing really. Just want to make sure if it gets found out I am his relation, there's no bother with it," said Ben hoping to put his dad off the scent.

"Just one thing though. Your grandad changed our name slightly." Now, that was a surprise. "It was Streeter, and my father got fed up with it and cut out the last two letters to make it Street as it is now." That's convenient thought Ben.

"Supper, you two. Come in here now or it'll be ruined," called his mum up the garden. You couldn't actually ruin one of his mother's suppers though, could you?

CHAPTER 6

The big chill

"Hey, Ben." Hitti panted, as he rushed past the moving jumble of young people making their way to class. "Could you actually work out that maths assignment for Ropy?" he asked Ben, hoping for help. Ben was preoccupied.

"Uhmm..oh, I had a go. Doubt I got it right," Ben replied.

He and Hitti reached their lockers outside the classroom. There was Laura smiling across at them putting her things away in a locker. She had just been given back her first sketch done at the Club Festival. It was that ghostly girl she had drawn. Laura was thinking it through, still smiling for the audience. It was possible evidence and so needed to be locked away for use at a later stage.

The knowing smiles between Ben and Laura were being noticed these days. The fact was, they were investigating something very important weren't they? No one else knew and their secret mystery was not going to be revealed, for now anyway. Their classmates knew nothing and saw it another way.

The chanting began quietly and slowly, gathering pace as more and more laughing, screeching pupils joined in. It grew louder:

"Ben and Laura are in love. Ben and Laura are in love," they all sang out, with accusatory fingers pointing and waving like hooligans at a football match.

Ben and Laura were not in love of course. Kissing was for teenagers and far too yucky for them. After all they were still twelve, just.

"Stop this awful noise," boomed Mrs Rigging. The chanting ceased simultaneously. "Now, get yourselves in here and let's get on with it. I'm not having any nonsense. We have to complete the term's syllabus or you'll all get holiday homework."

That settled it! The class silently filtered in through the doorway obeying Ropy without any further ado. They all sat down and you could have heard a pin drop.

"Now, that's better. Perhaps you would like to behave properly more often?" She added sarcastically. She knew they were kids and kids will play up from time to time. It's in their nature and she enjoyed telling them off anyway.

"Instead of 'mathematical functions', I have decided we're going to have a bit of fun today."

The enormous sigh of relief in class could have been heard outside. "We're all going to do what I call 'quick calc'. That means," she paused looking sternly at Ned who was clearly screwing up a very small piece of paper, "If I see one single bit of paper moving from your desk, you're going straight to Mr Goving. Is that clear?"

"Yes, Mrs Rigging," said Ned.

"It's no good pulling a face. I know what you're up to." No one was quite sure if she did. Mrs Rigging continued to explain her little 'maths done in the head', game.

Those of the class who actually listened began to wonder if it was a game, but in fact rather a cheeky way for a teacher to have you do hard work during a lesson. That wasn't fair, most were thinking.

Ned tried to conceal his hand movements. You see there was a dare on today. Many of the class in the dare had put one piece of chocolate money in a pot being kept by Jess Brough. The winner of the dare got the whole pot to go home with.

Jess was very small for twelve, with light brown straight hair about shoulder length. She had a particularly pretty face and was always neatly dressed. Her life was acting. She had a marvellous tone of voice, which bounced through a theatre resonating to every corner. It was quite surprising for one so small. Some of the kids unkindly called her 'elf', a tease that she put up with very bravely.

What you had to do, is screw up small pieces of paper, then chew them until very soggy. Next, you must remove them from your mouth without any detection, of course. The last step was to get out your six-inch or fifteen-centimetre ruler and carefully place the soggy little lump towards one end. The trick was to hold one end of the ruler lightly and pull it down bending it slightly at the other. Then you would catapult the soggy mass across the classroom to land on a wall, all without the teacher noticing. If the teacher did notice anything, it must *not* be seen to be you. The person who completed the most full 'hits' during that lesson was the winner.

It was called 'flickball'. Annie Stapleton was the flickball judge and she counted who had scored what hits. She sat in the back row so she could see everything. As she could not compete herself, she would have three of the chocolate coins as her payment.

Annie was always the judge because somehow she was respected as being fair and usually spotted every single flying soggy pellet. Annie had very broad shoulders for a girl and was extremely strong. Frankly, no one would argue with her, not even boys. She would beat them all in an arm wrestle any day. For all that, she was gentle and feminine. She had a bob of hair with highlights giving a pretty, streaky look. She was about as tall as Ben, who looked slim beside her. She was just well-built and sporty, you might say. She was a fantastic cyclist and last year she'd been one of the top competitors in the annual school cycle race.

Meanwhile Mrs Rigging had been writing up her own maths questions on the board.

"Hands up to do the first set of ten." There was a pause. However, the class knew that if they did not participate, Mrs Rigging could not be diverted whilst soggy hits were flying around the classroom.

They were to be timed performing mental arithmetic in sets of ten. The winner was the fastest pupil to complete a set correctly and the winner would get a chocolate bar, which she had appealingly placed on the edge of her desk.

"I'll have a go," agreed Marlon Huggett. He was asked to march himself up to the board and write up the answers without doing any workings out or written calculations.

They were not the easiest multiplications and divisions. Marlon had to think quite hard to get some of the answers at all.

Ned and others were carefully chewing up their little pieces of paper ready for the flicking that must follow. One of the difficult parts was to actually tear off strips of paper without Mrs Rigging hearing it. Some people coughed and tore at the same time. Some waited for the sound of speaking in the class. Some ripped their paper as soon as Mrs Rigging walked around.

Ned was the first to flick a damp ball of the stuff across the room. Mrs Rigging had turned to see Marlon's progress and Ned's timing was perfection. It flew across in an arc, landing neatly above the doorway and sticking triumphantly to the wall.

Of course all the soggy pellets were completely removable and taken away on a regular basis, so the game could continue time and again. Somehow they blended in with the off-white colour of the wall paint and seemed quite hard to see once landed. Marlon returned to his seat having completed all ten answers.

Next up for the maths challenge was Barry Trinder. Mrs Rigging only had to point and he knew it was his turn. Mrs Rigging was noting down the result for Marlon whilst he started to come forward and then she turned to the blackboard. In fact, they were all going to be forced to do the maths challenge one by one so long as there was enough time.

"Now, if you can't get the answer straight away, move on to the next one and come back to it at the end," ordered Mrs Rigging.

Barry always sat towards the back of class and giggled too much for anyone to feel relaxed near him. His teeth stuck out a little giving him a comedic and cheesy grin. He had a slightly pointed nose and often looked scruffy in even the neatest clothes. However, put him on the stage and he was electrifying. He could master a script in minutes and his mimicry was hard to beat. He was fantastic at impressions of the teachers, male or female and was well liked on account of his ability to make everyone laugh.

Barry was the youngest person ever to be awarded the 'Mimic of the Year' prize when he came to the school last year, the year before Ben. He was tipped to win it again some day. He had very short, slightly greasy dark hair, but a pleasing complexion and an angelic look about him. He had an Italian mother and you could even detect a slight accent now and again.

He trotted up to the front as Mrs Rigging finished putting up the next ten questions. Whilst she still had her back to the class, Ned scored another direct hit above the doorway. He was in the lead! No one had yet done two. Within seconds it seemed like it was raining soggy paper balls as at least six went off. At least two had to be retrieved along with a pencil thrown on the floor, all to be picked up together as a mask for the real reason to bend down to the floor.

Marlon had got back just in time to tear, chew and flick his first attempt. Unfortunately, his landed on Hitti's neck. That didn't count, Annie Stapleton decided. She was keeping a perfect mental note of the whole soggy paper saga.

"Right, Barry, off you go," instructed Mrs Rigging, blissfully unaware of the pellet stream flying around the room. She usefully continued to look towards the blackboard, standing just in front of her desk, and with her back almost exactly towards the class of pupils. She was checking his answers as he proceeded, believing the class was following it all and actually interested in this farce of a lesson. An opportunity like this rarely happened. Most times teachers spent much of the lesson facing class.

"Keep going, Barry. Just move on or you'll lose points."

Mrs Rigging was pressing hard on poor Barry. His maths was not that strong. "Don't giggle, Barry. You can't think if you're always giggling," Mrs Rigging said using her best smiling frown.

The trouble was, what Barry could see was terribly funny. There was Marlon, Jess, Ned, Hitti and the others flicking away at every opportunity. He quite forgot what he was doing. "Right. You're disqualified, Barry. You've gone over the three minute mark."

Mrs Rigging turned towards her class. Barry left his place at the board, somewhat deflated. The whole class was so slick at reacting to Mrs Rigging; she noticed nothing, except for Ben who seemed to be quite still and looking aimlessly towards the large classroom window.

She stepped quietly up to the board area and rapidly put the next ten little nuggets of her maths challenge up. All the class was silent and Ben did not seem awake at all. He hadn't played flickball this time. It was not that you had to, nor that it happened all that much. It just wasn't Ben. He carried on dreaming in his own little world.

"Ben. Your turn," she calmly stated in a normal pitch of voice. She and the class waited through silence. "Ben, come up to the blackboard please," she repeated a little more firmly. Still there was no reaction. There was no possibility of flickball now.

It was a deathly hush. Rulers were twitching, paper was waiting, pupils were salivating, all in anticipation of another opportunity they hoped would arrive any second. Surely

Mrs Rigging was not going to just stand there. They were not interested in Ben's problem.

Mrs Rigging had quietly moved herself right next to Ben. By now she was wearing a very irritated expression indeed. Her lips were snarling, her hair let loose. She behaved like a person moving in slow motion.

Then it happened. She crouched down, putting her head close to Ben's. And after waiting a few agonising seconds, the whole class heard this enormous rush of breath as Mrs Rigging breathed in at lightening speed. She shouted at the top of her voice in a high pitch.

"B.e.n. It's y.o.u.r turn." Ben leapt out of his chair and landed in a heap on the floor to the extreme amusement of the whole class. Mrs Rigging's voice returned to normal and she added, "Nobody dreams in my classes. Get yourself up there," she pointed. "Do your sums on the double."

Ben was already rising from the floor and quickly making his way to the board. In fact he had missed all of the maths challenge and been thinking about his strategy to investigate the case of Sonia the ghost. What do I do now, he thought? Turning back to the class, he clicked his tired eyes and wished it would all stop, while he gathered back his strength.

He opened them again a moment later, detecting complete silence. Oh my goodness! He was stunned into a shocked silence. Mrs Rigging and all his classmates were frozen still like statues. Ben just stood there in amazement feeling faint.

Of course, this time he did not doubt that some strange new power had visited him. Immediately, the enormity of it hit him. What if he could not unfreeze them? Worse still, what if they were all dead? A huge surge of unwanted adrenalin made his heart pound furiously for a few panic-stricken moments.

He moved forward to touch someone. The nearest was Mrs Rigging. He very nervously put out a hand towards hers. She was still warm! It was like she was a freeze-frame of herself. A feeling of relief began. He no longer thought they were all dead. He tugged at her short jacket. It moved on her just as if it were on a mannequin. It was only the body that had been affected.

"I must stay calm," he muttered under his breath. He screwed up his eyes and thought of the class moving. Click, and they were back, just as they were before, all looking at him expectantly. Thank goodness.

"Just do them as quickly as you can, Ben. I'm timing you from; one, two, three, now," chuckled Mrs Rigging. She had not even noticed her momentary freeze-framed state. Phew!!

However, Ben wanted to test how this power could be used. He could not have this happening any old time like the kinetic power, before he understood that *he* was causing it all. He had a reasonable thought that the freeze-frame must have affected whomever he saw just before he wished for the world to stop. Laura sat to the side at the back. Ben moved to one side of the board so he could exclude Laura from his vision, but no one else in the class.

"Where are you going Ben?" called out a confused Mrs Rigging as he sidled off. Look—click—and freeze-frame they went! Ben's theory worked. Laura sat very still and silent, shocked at what she saw. Ben spoke up in a whisper.

"It's OK, I know what I'm doing," he said very softly. "They're all OK. I did it just now and then for a second time but left you out of it by not looking at you. No one noticed anything, not even you?" Laura was not sure what to think and Ben could tell by the look on her face.

"Look I'll show you," he said. With that he unfroze everyone.

"You can't write the answers on the window," suggested Mrs Rigging sarcastically, as she now saw him out of place to do the maths challenge.

"Just thinking it through, Mrs Rigging," Ben replied. Then Ben turned and look—click—and freeze-frame they went again!

"That's incredible," Laura announced, her shock fading rapidly. Luckily, there were no windows into the corridor from the classroom. So no one could peer in and see this group of motionless bodies, rooted to the spot. The corridor received its light from windows on the other side, looking into a courtyard.

"Just think what we could do with this one, Laura," Ben blurted almost frightening himself at the prospect. He was moving back to Mrs Rigging's desk and opened one of her draws.

"What are you doing now, Ben?" said Laura wondering what on earth could happen next.

"Getting her calculator. Where is it? Do you know?" Ben asked as if nothing out of the ordinary was going on.

"I've got one in my bag. Catch," she called out. Laura had removed it and threw it over to Ben. She was now becoming very curious as to the next move.

"Thanks. Now, number one," said Ben. He was working out the maths challenge on the board. He quickly completed all the ten answers writing them on the blackboard. He threw back Laura's calculator.

"It's being timed, Ben, so where's it going to get you?" inquired Laura, seeing Ben had in mind to beat the rest of them. Ben stepped forward quickly and looked at Mrs Rigging's wrist.

"Oh no, you're right." Ben pressed the buttons on the side of Mrs Rigging's quartz watch. It moved back three minutes. That should do it, he thought. She'll never notice two or three minutes.

"Laura, I'm going to unfreeze them in a few seconds," Ben said. Then he moved to shut his eyes. He stopped. "No!" he almost shouted. "I've got a brilliant idea, Laura. It'll only take a few seconds and will be the funniest thing ever."

Ben ran over to his desk and took a black marker pen from his pencil case. He turned about and hopped between the desks, neatly arriving in front of a motionless teacher.

Mrs Rigging was standing straight up looking towards the blackboard, with an arm outstretched and pointing. She had been directing Ben to move back to the blackboard before the freeze-frame.

Ben removed the top of the pen and reached up carefully towards Mrs Rigging's face. It was irresistible wasn't it? He couldn't pass up the opportunity. There might not be another one. His mum had always said, grab it while you can; it doesn't always come round twice. The words were no doubt intended for other matters in life.

"Ben!" Laura cried out, as she realised his gloriously naughty intentions. "You can't," she said with fake disapproval in her voice.

"I can and I will," replied Ben. The pen reached higher until it met with Mrs Rigging's upper lip area. Ben quickly drew the most amusing moustache he could in jet-black ink. It had curly bits at each end. He jumped up, put the pen in his case and stepped back onto the raised area at the front of the class. He looked at his own watch and nodded. Suddenly Laura and Ben heard steps in the corridor becoming louder as every second passed.

"Quick," whispered Laura as loudly as she dared.

"Here we go," said Ben. Look—click—go. "Finished," Ben called out to Mrs Rigging, referring to his maths challenge answers. There was a knock at the door and Splinter entered just inside the door, holding a book.

"Oh, it was so quiet on the approach, Eve, I thought you had all gone somewhere. I've put your book back on your shelf here." He left immediately having returned Mrs Rigging's stagecraft dictionary. Wicked! He didn't even look at her and she barely turned in his direction as she worked at the answers on the blackboard.

The classroom of pupils and one teacher had absolutely no inkling of their missing three minutes. Mrs Rigging continued facing the front as she spoke to Ben.

"Well, that was quick," she said, without even looking at her watch. "How did you do that?" she asked doubting it possible. Her mind assumed only seconds had passed and she would find something wrong.

"Let's just see now. How many of them are right?" She was still checking as she spoke. "Yes, well you're in the lead now Ben, with a full house of right answers." She was very surprised, of course. Ben started to walk slowly towards his desk.

Up to now Mrs Rigging had still not turned to face the class and no one had yet seen her beautifully drawn moustache except Laura. That was about to change in the next one or two seconds.

She turned looking for the next boy or girl to come forward. Ben watched as she moved and somehow the world seemed to be going in slow motion. His anticipation was so great that he could barely contain himself; even for the short time it would take. He would be under suspicion if he let out the slightest titter. Steely faced, he took about two steps as Mrs Rigging completed her turn.

The whole class burst into uncontrollable laughter at the new Mrs Rigging now sporting her black, curly moustache. Ned nearly fell from his chair choking. Jess, was doubled up with the pain of laughter. Laura and Hitti were shaking their heads and laughing like there was no tomorrow. She had no idea why the class was suddenly in such uproar.

"What on earth is going on? Stop this instant. I mean *now*," she crowed with no effect at all, through continued unabated laughter. "Or you will all get detention for this!" she screamed, trying her best to resume command again.

She stood at the front with a pained expression awaiting the laughter to peter out on its own. "Aha," she started. "Give me that," she ordered as she marched towards Jess.

She had seen Andrea Suchet pass a note to Jess who sat beside her. The little folded note was ripped from Jess's clasp and quickly examined. The class had suddenly assumed a silent state seeing this new event.

"I suppose you all think this highly amusing, do you?" She questioned, not wanting a squeak of an answer back.

Mrs Rigging felt her control returning now and there was no way she wanted to write all her pupils names onto a detention sheet in her staff room. She would feel a failure.

She assumed this note was responsible for the uncontrolled outburst of laughter. "If I can't trust you lot not to pass silly notes about when I am being kind enough to put on a class compo, then you won't get one in future," she said more calmly.

Annie and Laura exchanged knowing glances at each other as did most of the class, realising Mrs Rigging had got it all most conveniently wrong. Only Jess and Andrea had seen the note!

"You can all get out your work books and do the answers to the rest yourselves, in silence." Mrs Rigging started to put up the next ten on the board.

The bell for the end of class went within seconds. "We'll finish next time," she bawled above the chattering, which had already begun.

Ben and Laura made their way out with the others. Ned saw Mrs Rigging screw up the note and throw it in her wastepaper basket and he whispered in Laura's ear. She nodded at him as they reached the corridor. They all put their books in their lockers. It was choreography with Splinter next.

Mrs Rigging came out into the corridor last with her bag of books and walked off towards the staff room. Ben, Laura and Hitti all huddled together chatting.

"How did she get that moustache?" sniggered Hitti. Of course, he and everyone except Ben and Laura would have no idea. One moment there was nothing, the next it appeared!

"Well, it's a long story," replied Ben intriguingly. Laura remained tight-lipped. Hitti looked at Ben with mild suspicion.

Meanwhile, Ned had slipped into the classroom and retrieved the screwed up note from Mrs Rigging's waste bin. He was hurriedly unscrewing it as the others arrived.

They all crowded around to see. Annie Stapleton stepped in and confirmed the result.

"It was Ned all the way today. You got four direct hits." She handed him the stash of choccy coins and he forced them into the nearest pocket with one hand. Annie stayed to peer at the unfolding note that Ned was holding. He started to read it out:

"I reckon Ropy is really a man. Nod if you agree." They all smiled, but no one laughed. Nothing could beat that moustache, could it?

As they moved off to make their way to a choreography class, Ben and now Laura both heard that same old wailing sound in the corridors. They wondered and worried if this was the sign for yet more strange happenings.

Mrs Rigging had walked out of the teaching block and put up her retractable umbrella to shield from the spitting rain. As a result no one seemed to notice her new face as she walked along, eventually reaching a corridor near the staff room. She put her umbrella away and continued her journey. Splinter had just left on his way to the Peter Phelps Theatre to take Ben's class for choreography. Mrs Rigging was about fifty meters from Splinter when he caught sight of her.

It must be the shadows across her face, he thought. The corridor was curved and open to the outside with small columns every three meters or so. Through this curve he had an interrupted view and he had to turn off towards the theatre. He was not sure what he had seen. He hadn't been close enough to speak to her.

Mrs Rigging carried on and trotted up the steps to the door for the staff room. She pulled down the handle and entered putting down her bag and turning to make a cup of tea at the sideboard facing the wall.

"Hi, Sally," Mrs Rigging said to Smudge, the only other teacher there. Mrs Rigging did not subscribe to using nicknames to teacher's faces. Smudge had her head buried in a book and did not look up. She could recognise the distinctive low voice of Eve Rigging anywhere.

"How are you, Eve?" Smudge replied. "I wanted to discuss the music for the show with you."

"Right, I'll just do tea. Want a cuppa?" asked Mrs Rigging.

"Not for me thanks," Smudge sang out. Mrs Rigging picked up her cup of tea and carried it over to the small table near Smudge. She put it down carefully and sat on an adjacent chair. At that same moment, Mr Goving entered and Smudge looked up. Smudge let out a small high-pitched scream and fell back in her chair.

"Good grief!" shouted Mr Goving. There was a short pause as the surprise sank in. "What on earth have you got on your face?" he ranted in a very concerned way. The black mess adorning Mrs Rigging's face had been smeared into an indistinct shape. She had no doubt blown her nose, been in the rain or done something that had disturbed the moustache into a splodge.

Mrs Rigging was speechless. She rose out of her chair trembling and made straight for the ladies rest room to look in the mirror. A second after the door closed behind her an audible squeal was heard followed by silence.

"Hmmm, I wonder which practical joker did that? And how did they do it?" Mr Goving thought out loud.

"Poor thing," said Smudge.

Ben was changing for choreography, when Tom Cortazzi arrived.

"Hi, Ben, I've got my eye on you." This sounded worrying.

"Really?" Ben replied, trying to sound unaffected.

"Yep. I've heard good things about you, Ben." Well that seemed like a change of attitude towards Ben, but he didn't quite believe it. "I'm on the team-picking panel this year and I want you on my side. So, how about it if I can fix that?" said Tom smiling.

Ben didn't feel too sure and didn't know how to respond. He pulled on his shirt, playing for time, not knowing how Tom was supposed to 'fix it'.

"I'll think about it. That's all I can say," said Ben.

"You do that." Tom left immediately without the firm answer he'd wanted.

The guys and girls in Ben's class had all started arriving at the theatre having changed, ready for choreography. Splinter was on stage doing a warm up with some music played through the theatre's sound system. He just carried on dancing a routine and the students joined in, one by one as they arrived. Soon the whole class of twenty was moving in unison to the beat.

Without warning the sound system shut down and there was silence. The dancing stopped and they all began to chatter. A second later, the booming voice of Mrs Rigging was heard over the loud speakers.

"Whoever was responsible for that black mess on my face had better come and see me straight after school today. I'll be in class waiting. Otherwise you are all going into dance detention next Friday." After a pause, the music returned. Splinter now realised he had seen the mark on Mrs Rigging's face before class. He turned the music off again.

"Now what's this all about?" There was no response. Apart from Ben and Laura none of them knew how the 'moustache' had arrived on Mrs Rigging's face. Ben was on the spot. He already felt he should own up, but how could he explain it? It was actually the funniest thing anyone had ever seen and would no doubt go down in school history. Ben knew the incident would be chattered about endlessly when it got around the next day.

"Well, you heard what Ropy said. It'll be detention for the lot of you. I'm sure you all know who did it. You might be best to have a word in their ear. Know what I mean?" Splinter explained in a friendly way.

90

After class, Ben changed and waited for Laura. When she emerged from the girl's changing rooms they sat on a bench outside the theatre.

"I've got everyone in shtook," said Ben. "I've got to go and see Ropy." Ben started to get up, expecting Laura's agreement.

"Don't go, Ben."

"What? Have you got a better idea?" Ben asked, thinking her wrong. Ben was looking in his school bag for a decent piece of paper and his pencil case. He wanted to write an apology for Ropy.

"We've got something much more important to do than worry about a bit of extra dancing. Think about it, Ben. If you tell Ropy, then one question will lead to another. You'll completely blow your cover," Laura pointed out.

"You're right," enthused Ben. "I won't go. Anyhow, we need to find out who this Sonia is and what she wants.

"Yeah, we do."

"I've been thinking about it. We've got the year she died and something about it being in the theatre. We could try school records and mags?" said Ben

"How will we get at them? The old ones are all locked up in the museum aren't they?" Laura said knowledgeably.

"There'll be a way. Let's pop in there now and work on a plan."

The school museum contained many weird and wonderful old exhibits. There were treasures discovered by old pupils of the school and usually left in their wills to add to the collection. It ranged from fossils to stuffed wildlife (no longer allowed!) and photos of the past school teams and shows. It was also a hall of fame. There was a section devoted to stars of the stage and screen that had been to WISPA. A very large photo of Dame Sarah Puttock adorned the wall. She was probably the most famous one of the last fifty years or so.

Ben and Laura walked up the wooden stairs to the stand-alone building. It was like a small colonial style wooden home you would see in parts of the USA. It stood near the edge of the school grounds on the other side of the main visitor's car park, next to the swimming pool complex. It was always open during the day and locked at night by the school caretaker. Everyone would visit the museum as a new pupil, but not frequently after that. It comprised two rooms with an archway between them.

Ben and Laura entered the front door to see the cases of exhibits jutting out from the walls. The most surprising find was a full-sized Canadian bear, stuffed and standing like a statue in the centre of the second room. At the back there were glass cases filled with old volumes of school records and magazines. There was a large and very old photograph of William Ingram, the school's founder taken in 1924, hanging dutifully in a glass frame on the wall.

"These cases are locked," Ben complained to Laura.

Laura came forward saying, "Let's just check if they are all locked." She started trying to slide the doors open. Ben let her try it while he watched.

"Why don't we just ask to look at them anyway?" Ben said.

"Do you want to be asked why you need to?" replied Laura. She had now checked about half of them and they were all locked, so far. Ben knew in his heart everything about their investigation had to remain a secret and Laura's reply had only confirmed what they both thought.

Ben had an idea. He knew he shouldn't really, but what was the harm in it? While Laura completed the task, he concentrated his glance on the stuffed bear. Look—click—move.

"They're all locked, damn it," Laura swore, out of character. She turned around to find a large furry beast, right in front of her face. With a small yelp of surprise, she stumbled backwards into the glass wall cabinets and fell to the ground.

"Oh Gawd. I'm so sorry Laura. I just couldn't help it!" Smiled Ben knowing he shouldn't. He rushed forward to help Laura up only to find her laughing.

"Just promise me one thing, Ben," she demanded, through her giggles.

"Anything," Ben replied in confusion.

"Never ever play a trick on me again. OK?" said Laura, still smiling for no reason Ben knew about.

"I promise."

"Good. You're brilliant, Ben. Do you know that? Brilliant," Laura exclaimed excitedly. Ben had no idea what Laura meant. He helped her up.

"All of them were locked," she said. "But take a look now." Ben looked along the glass-fronted casing. The lock securing the lot of them had sprung open. You could now slide any of them open just as you pleased and take out the contents.

"That's amazing!" Ben chirped. The caretaker had started his rounds for cleaning and lock-up and was heading for the museum, probably one of his first calls of the afternoon at around four.

"Look, I'd better put the bear back," Ben said calmly. He clicked away and the bear picked itself up and returned to its time-honoured place. The creaky sound of steps on a wooden stairway drifted upwards accompanied by a voice calling out.

"Lock-up time now if anyone's in." The caretaker was a Mr Bodkin. He said the same thing every day as a matter of course and always in his best west country accent. But he never expected a reply. He had his hand on the front door ready to close it and switch off the light.

"Just coming," called out Ben, to the shocked caretaker. Ben whispered to Laura and they moved the glass casing door up to the lock as close as it would go, without it actually clicking locked again. They both emerged from the back room and went towards the door to leave.

"What are you two up to down there then?" asked Mr Bodkin barely hiding his suspicion. Of course, being middle-aged like parents, he obviously assumed they'd be kissing or something.

"We're new this year and never got around to having a look," Laura replied inventively.

"Have it your own way," sighed Mr Bodkin, clearly not believing it. They were ushered out and down the steps as the caretaker's clanking keys turned in the lock. Laura and Ben made their way to the school bus stop. They both agreed they must return to finish the job.

CHAPTER 7

The pick of the bunch

At the end of the autumn term of each school year, there was a day set aside for the 'panel' to pick their teams to prepare to compete against each other in the Agent's Parade Competition which would take place at the end of the school year

The panel this year consisted of three senior pupils, appointed by the headmaster after advice from teachers. In addition, Mr Paul McKinley, the drama teacher, had his turn on the panel this year and would have the last word on any appointment to a team.

Mr McKinley was very young compared to most of the teachers at WISPA, which was refreshing. It was only his fourth year as a teacher. He was an ex-pupil himself and a talented actor. He was quite short, with ordinary, mousy brown hair and was a little overweight. He wore a wispy beard and rather ill-fitting clothes. Pupils liked his relaxed style and friendly blue eyes. He didn't have a nickname and most just called him Paul or Mr McKinley.

The Agent's Parade or 'Comp,' as it was affectionately known, consisted of a day at the end of June when theatre and film agents or talent spotters would come and sit as judges in a competition of school teams. There would be a first, second and third place for the teams. Any pupil could be given an individual 'commendation prize'. There was a tradition to give the annual mimicry prize at this event. It was the highlight of the school calendar.

Apart from Mr McKinley, the pupil panel this year were Tom Cortazzi, Fiona Payne and Gordon Munzer.

Gordon was in his last year and likely to go to university to study drama. He had very short blond hair, tiny sideburns and a square jaw. He was well-built. He was good at diving and could often be seen in the school's club practising. His strength in drama was as a character actor. Tom and Fiona we've met before.

Smudge and Dr Metanite usually did lighting and backstage between them, sometimes assisted by Ropy. She was still smarting over having to put her entire class up for dance detention. No one was sure if she'd show up, but she did.

The upper half of school attended for the morning and the lower half in the afternoon. Those that were not in attendance would enjoy one of their club activities.

Laura, Ben and Hitti made their way along the school corridors that morning. Ben asked Hitti if he would like to join in a search of school records in the museum. He wasn't told everything, but by the end of Ben's explanation, he knew there something wrong about the unexpected death of Sonia, a past pupil.

It was agreed they would all go to the museum on the day before the end of term after the school party. They reached the corridor outside the activity room where the mimicry club took place. There was so much laughter coming out of the room, the group stopped to look through the window.

There was Barry Trinder doing a marvellous impression of Dame Sarah Puttock, with no more than an old wig.

"Have I gone on long enough yet, Ropy darling? Do stop me won't you?' He said, slightly misquoting her. Then he switched and did Splinter with barely a second's gap.

"Come in. Time to begin. Page ninety-five," is all he needed to say in a wonderful Welsh accent, before the spectators fell about laughing.

All they could see of the teacher present was a pair of shoulders going up and down. He was clearly in stitches. It was Mr Stuart-Marsh looking after them. He was a considerable mimic himself. Although a very tall man, his plain features did not get in the way of some great impressions. He sported a small beard, which covered a small purple, but visible birthmark on his upper lip. He looked like a bank manager.

He was known to one and all by the nickname of 'Stewbog,' and he didn't mind a bit. Everyone from headmaster to last pupil in, would address him as Stewbog. He would even use it to sign his name for everything at the school.

"I wish I could do that," Ben said shaking his head at the wonderful mimicry.

Ben and Hitti were both going diving for a couple of hours. Laura was off to illustrators club and they parted company until the afternoon. As Ben and Hitti moved away from all the hilarity, Ben heard the wailing sound again. He could tell that Hitti heard nothing. It was he and Laura who were somehow chosen for this mystery solving and he was determined they would do just that.

The school had an unusual old indoor pool built around 1927; it was huge and surrounded by a mosaic floor. This floor had been made by the pupils of the time and looked more like a Roman villa than a modern day effort.

Mr Goving looked after the club, as he was a past swimmer of some note himself. He rarely got in the pool these days but directed and advised from the side, seated next to some rope, a life-saving ring and a large timing clock.

Boys and girls were all in the same diving club in this school. Ben and Hitti emerged from the changing room, dressed in their swimming gear to the strong smell of pool chemicals. The magnificent mosaic floor glistened in the sunshine streaming through the side windows. The high diving boards were something Ben had been getting used to lately. It was a five-metre depth and the top board was four metres high.

Whilst waiting for the remainder of the group to assemble, Ben struck up a conversation with Mr Goving.

"Did you ever know the head that was here sometime back called Mr Streeter?"

"Actually, no. He was well before my time. Did you ask because he has a similar name to yours, Ben?"

"Yes, I just noticed it on the list of heads."

"I think he had a tough time here after the end of the war and left in some peculiar circumstances," Mr Goving remarked in a matter of fact way.

Ben didn't feel a need to ask what those 'peculiar circumstances' might be and assumed they were connected to the case of Sonia. But he could not be sure could he? Up to now he only knew that the drama teacher had left after her death. He resisted the temptation to let it be known he was a relation.

Suddenly, Ben was feeling that strange feeling in his stomach he had experienced before. Usually this had been followed by strange incidents. Ben had assumed he was now in control of the powers that he had acquired. He began to worry that his conversation with Mr Goving had been the cause. Everything was connected in some way, he thought.

"Right, all get in line for forward springboard and synchronised springboard today, please. Same positions as last week."

They all made their way up the steps to use the two metre high board. Ben was third in line. Off went the other two. Ben stepped forward and jumped to spring off the board. As he flew upwards then down with his arms outstretched, his stomach felt like a powerhouse of butterflies.

He hurtled through the water curving his way to near parallel with the bottom. He was shocked! He expected to see the WISPA sign adorning the bottom of the pool. It had vanished. He could see the words 'help me' instead in a similar semicircle.

He came up panting and shaking. He knew it was another sign meant for him. No confusion about that this time. He pulled himself out by the steps and looked back at the watery sign on the bottom of the pool. He couldn't read it outside of the water too easily. It was very deep, but the sign seemed to look the same as usual. He calmed himself.

In line again for a synchronised dive, his partner was to be Hitti. On the way up the stairs he made a suggestion.

"Hitti, when we get to the bottom, meet me at the WISPA sign before you come up."

"OK my friend. No problem." A few seconds later they were bouncing off their boards to the sound of the start whistle. Down in the water they went, at almost exactly the same moment. They both arrived at the sign. Ben gulped some water in his mouth. His jaw had nearly dropped open. Hitti and he were both there for about a second, looking at the same thing he hoped. The sign had changed again! It simply said, Sonia. Up they both came with Ben panting and shaking again. Hitti saw the state of Ben.

"Are you all right?" Ben was choking up some water. "What's it all about, Ben? You knew that sign was weird didn't you?" he said as they swam to the side.

"Uhmm. You saw it then?" coughed Ben recovering. They were levering themselves out of the pool as they spoke.

"Of course I did, you crazy nutter." Hitti wondered why Ben had even asked if he saw it. "Who would change it to say Sonia?"

"Ssshh," said Ben stopping Hitti's announcement. Everyone who swam knew it said WISPA. He had placed his finger across his lips. He was now sure Hitti had seen the same thing. "It's all part of what I was telling you Hitti," he whispered as they walked. "The girl I mentioned who died was called Sonia. That's why we're going to the museum."

Hitti was plainly shocked and didn't speak for some time. He didn't know what to think. He hadn't really believed the story about it before. Now he had first-hand experience of something weird and supernatural.

They all dived a couple more times. Hitti sidled up to Ben at the end of the session speaking quietly through closed teeth.

"It's changed back to WISPA."

"I know," said Ben. Hitti had such a pained expression on his face; people began to enquire if he was feeling OK.

"Hurry up everyone," called Mr Goving through the doorway. "The canteen will shut if you don't get a move on." It was canteen day today.

Just outside, the clerk of works called Mr Burton, but known only as 'Bertie', was passing. He noticed Mr Goving leaving the pool complex.

"Ah, Headmaster Sir," he said greeting Mr Goving with his usual old-fashioned manners.

"Bertie! How are you? Haven't seen you about lately."

"Busy as always, Sir. You knows me. I just wanted ter tell yer, I've checked the floor under the staff room like you said. There's nuffink wrong there I could find," he concluded.

"Oh really? Well, thanks for checking anyway."

"I got rid of this enormous insect nest I found while I was at it," added Bertie. "All full of sticky jelly-like stuff," he added, not knowing if it was important.

Ben and Hitti had finished changing and went to the school canteen for lunch. There was a long queue that started in the open corridor outside. Ben and Hitti started their wait very near the school noticeboards. Hitti was glancing at them.

"Hey, Ben. Looks like a message for you up there." Ben strained to see it. As they got closer, it was plain to them both that the small sealed envelope was addressed to a 'Ben Streeter', and not just Ben Street.

Ben had to think quickly. He thought it quite possible it was for him, because he now knew his family's former name had been Streeter. However, who knew *that* except him and what would it say? He worried that if he took it in front of everyone, they would start asking questions.

"It's not quite my name is it?" said Ben as if not bothered at all. "I'd better take it to the office after lunch and ask if they've just spelt it wrong before I go opening it."

He took it down as he spoke and replaced the drawing pin back on the board, before putting the unopened letter straight in his pocket. He carried on waiting in the queue.

He felt a massive temptation to freeze-frame everyone in his sight so he could take a peek at the letter. He couldn't bring himself to try it. There were far too many people about and he was still outside.

Laura had been sketching and clay modelling all morning. Her charcoal sketches were becoming famous within the school. She had built up quite a collection over the term. Most were of known figures around the school, be it pupil or teacher. She was working on some that might be used for a new book about the school.

As Ben and Hitti reached the canteen doorway they could see Laura and some of her illustrator friends already eating. They exchanged waves across the hall and then joined them on the same table.

There was a most revolting beef stew being served. At least that's what it was called. It was more beef fat than meat. Ben decided his mum's cooking was quite good after canteen experiences, until he remembered the dreaded marrow. It was all eaten very quickly in a rowdy atmosphere. Sadly, plenty was thrown in the bin.

"I'm just going to the school office," Ben said to Laura.

"Have we got time? It's nearly two o'clock and our team pick session starts in ten minutes," Laura pointed out.

The canteen was already emptying. Ben leant towards Laura and whispered something in her ear. They stayed together and slipped away in the crowd and into the library lobby nearby and sat on one of the sofas. No one was there, not even a teacher. Ben removed the letter he had stuffed in his pocket and started to open the envelope.

"It's got the name Streeter, Laura, but that was my family name until about forty years ago or something. I don't underst—" Ben stopped in his tracks. They both saw the three words that were etched in a spindly scrawl on the paper: Scarigus is watching. Ben went very pale and Laura was feeling frightened by this whole episode.

"You remember that name don't you Laura?" Ben asked almost trembling.

"How could I forget it?" Neither of them had dared go back to the local history club since the first time many weeks ago.

"I keep on getting signs," said Ben. "We've got to do something about it now. This is getting serious." Neither had taken their eyes off the letter. To their amazement, it then folded itself up and flew off out of the door and disappeared.

They both made their way to the Peter Phelps Theatre calming each other as they went. They could not wait to go back to that museum and start trying to find answers.

*

Ben and Laura arrived just in time to hear the announcements about the afternoon's event. Mr McKinley had risen to his feet and was standing at the microphone on the stage. They quickly sat down at the edge of the theatre.

"A bit of listening is what I want from you all now. That way we won't have people asking silly questions all afternoon about the order of events. Quiet!" He shouted, pointing at a group of four boys chattering at the back. "If you don't want to listen, then you'll be quarantined. Do you understand?"

Being quarantined was just about the worst fate that could befall anyone at WISPA. It meant exclusion from all teams and the Comp at the end of the year. For most pupils and parents, it was the single most important event on the school calendar. There was immediate and absolute silence after that announcement.

"Good. Now there are three pupil judges and myself. That's Fiona, Tom and Gordon over there. I have the final say on any decision. I am here to make sure the teams are picked fairly. You'll all have a good chance to show us what you can do individually and most of you in your dance or singing or mimicking groups or whatever it may be.

"A fair mix of each of the disciplines will be in each of the three teams. I will place anyone still not picked at the end of the session. Remember, you could get picked for any one of your skills during this session. You will do all that you've put in for, whether you are already picked for a team or not.

"The idea is that you all enjoy yourselves. You can't perform if you are too uptight. Just relax and it will all fall into place. Only clap at the end of performances please. Any questions, come and see me quickly in a minute. Any of you who need to change for dance had better go and do so now. We'll be starting with the ventriloquists group in about two minutes and then dance groups."

He studied a small list. "There's five of you down for that." The theatre silence was broken and quiet chattering resumed.

Ben had already left to put on his dance gear returning within minutes.

"Right. First on, please welcome Liam Bidwell." Liam made his way to centre stage. He was about sixteen and looked as if he had only just got out of bed. He had his own dummy this year, dressed like a football player. He did his bit and was followed by the other four who trotted out their sketches. And so the afternoon proceeded with the teams gradually taking shape.

Then it came time for Ben's dance group to appear. Hitti was among them. They had prepared a choreographed dance and song routine like you would see in a musical. The song was actually written by Smudge and choreography done by Ropy and Smudge together.

Smudge was there to play the piano part. It involved a mixture of tap and jazz movement merged with hip hop. Ben and Hitti were smiling as they warmed to the music and began the singing and dancing parts. It was all going great until there was a loud thump coming through the bright lighting. The music stopped.

"Ben, you must be out of place," Mr McKinley insisted, pointing to his group. Without hesitation, Ben looked— clicked and freeze-framed the entire theatre full of people. They were all in his vision easily, being in the centre of the auditorium or otherwise on stage with him. He stepped over to the correct position a few steps away. Again he looked— clicked and unfroze them all.

"It is correct isn't it?" Ben questioned, looking toward Smudge for confirmation. Smudge looked up from the piano for the first time and nodded. Mr McKinley was no longer sure of himself.

"Oh, sorry. I thought you were—well, we'd better let you start again."

There was muffled chattering around the theatre and a sense of confusion over what had been seen. The music started up again and Ben caught Laura's eye. She glanced across with a look on her face that said she knew just what Ben had been up to. This time the entire routine was completed to rapturous applause.

Then the team picking took place on the basis of this performance. It was Fiona's turn to pick next. She chose Kirsty Robinson, an athletic wee girl of just thirteen with beautiful flowing blond hair, tied back for the performance.

Next, Gordon had his pick. Ben crossed his fingers and hoped it would be him. He had seen Gordon at a seniors dance class recently and thought him quite magnificent. He kindly said it was a tough choice and then went for Amelia Montague. She had an older sister at the school called

Millie Montague. Amelia was new and still only twelve. She had come on a scholarship just like Ben and impressed many with her nifty footwork and developing voice.

Ben felt very disappointed and his mind started to drift. There was a droning in the background as the team picking continued.

He came to and realised Tom Cortazzi was speaking. Ben just didn't want to be picked by Tom Cortazzi. He didn't like his attitude and had confused his feelings. His little speech was agonising. Ben couldn't believe he'd want him any way after the way he went on in the corridors whenever they happened to meet. Tom had already secured the major part in the end of term play and Ben was not even in it.

"And that's why I chose him for the Cortazzi team." Tom stopped speaking and a few claps were heard. Ben turned to Hitti in confusion.

"Who did he choose then?" asked Ben.

"You, of course! Didn't you hear it?" Hitti half smiled and shook his head slightly in vague disapproval.

Ben's heart sank. He had no desire to be in the Cortazzi team. There must be a way out somehow. But how? Poor Hitti had not been chosen yet and Ben had not noticed this either.

The afternoon continued to its conclusion. Laura was picked for Fiona's team and Hitti, for his excerpt from *Macbeth*, was picked for Cortazzi. Ben decided he wouldn't worry about being in Cortazzi after all, now that Hitti had joined him.

In between their performances, Ben, Hitti and Laura had firmly agreed that tomorrow night after the school party, they would go to the museum. As soon as the team pick was over they grabbed their school bags and made their way home.

That night Ben had the same dream troubling him ever more frequently. He was imagining hearing wasps and flies buzzing accompanied by the smell of jasmine. This time his bed was floating above the school as if on the hunt for something, but what? He woke with a start hearing his mum calling.

"Come on Ben, you'll be late if yer don't get up soon."

She was right. It was seven forty-five already and the bus went in five minutes for WISPA. He rushed to get washed and dressed and left without breakfast.

He heard his mum calling after him as he ran for the bus. "You won't do no dancing wivout yer porridge." He didn't even look back. It was going to be a most important day.

That day was the last but one before the end of term. It ran as usual. The school party was an afternoon affair and held no interest for Ben, Laura and Hitti who thought of nothing but their quest.

Towards the end of the party as pupils and staff were leaving, the three of them sneaked over to the area by the indoor pool building next to the museum.

Being December in England, it was virtually dark at just after four o'clock and there was little lighting in that area since the pool was closed. The lights were still on in the museum. None of them wanted to be spotted or even seen together. Ben whispered the plan to them. After a few minutes they were ready to go in.

"OK then, Laura, when you're ready," announced Ben quietly but in military fashion.

"Yup," sighed Laura who for once worried what her parents would think if she was caught. But it wasn't exactly naughty was it? It was important work and no one else would do it. Laura was the first to make her way in. She checked across the parking area. A few cars remained, but no one could be seen. She nipped up the steps and in through the museum door. She relaxed as she made her way into the second room.

By now, Mr Bodkin the caretaker had begun his rounds. He was leaving the first toilet block and on his way towards the theatre with his large jangling bunch of keys about him.

"Go on, Hitti. Let's get it over with," instructed Ben, still in charge. Hitti walked from the dark area by the pool entrance and along towards the museum steps. He just walked quite normally. They were still allowed to go there at this time, so he didn't worry. He heard a car moving off behind him. He didn't want to turn and look. He jumped onto the steps and hurried in to meet Laura who was waiting anxiously. Ben was still outside.

Mr Bodkin had now reached the front of the grand entrance hall and was about to enter the car park. Ben couldn't see him around the corner of the building and set off. They were within about ten metres of each other and seemingly about to meet. Ben heard the footsteps and he was still a few seconds away from reaching the museum. He had almost decided to abandon the museum and just walk away, when the footsteps stopped. He could still see no one. Ben looked around and quickly scuttled up the museum steps.

"Hey, quick," he loudly whispered to the others. "Hide behind the cabinets and don't move or breathe." They knew the museum was locked about this time every afternoon and opened at about seven each morning.

Mr Bodkin had stopped and locked the large outside cupboard door that housed school sports and drama equipment. He resumed his nightly mission and came up the creaking museum steps, pushing the door slightly ajar.

"Lock-up time now if anyone's in." The school clock struck four fifteen. There was a loud creak from the wooden structure. Mr Bodkin peered in and extended his gaze for several seconds, checking. Laura breathed very slowly. The lights went out. The door closed with a thud and the unsettling sound of a turning key in the lock was heard inside. The sound of footsteps on wood, then gravel and tarmac, gradually faded.

"OK, we're on our own now I reckon," Ben whispered. He reached in his bag and retrieved a torch that he switched on keeping the beam low to avoid the windows.

"How will we get out? He's locked us in," Hitti said forgetting about whispering already.

"Check the windows," whispered Laura and Ben almost simultaneously. They all tried the nearest window to where they stood. All were locked! A mild panic set in as they tried the rest. Ben had assumed that from the inside he could just open a window and they could leave when ready.

"Ben!" complained Hitti. Laura just stood speechless.

"Look, let's do what we came to do and then I'll find some way out of here," Ben explained confidently. But he was anything but sure. With some relief, Ben pulled back the sliding glass doors of the cabinets containing school records and magazines. At least they were still unlocked!

Ben directed their efforts. "Right, we're looking for something about a Sonia Bird who died; anything about anyone called Sonia who would have been a past pupil here."

"Isn't it the mid 1940s onwards?" piped up Laura.

"Yes, about then. That headmaster's letter was from around then wasn't it?" replied Ben. Hitti was filled in on the details. As Ben spoke a low level hum of insects buzzing began. They hardly noticed at first, but as the seconds ticked away, the noise became quite pronounced. All three stopped and looked at each other.

Ben asked, "Can you hear that buzzing sound guys?" The others nodded. "It's the same noise that keeps on following me. It must be a sign."

"Oh, I just wanna get out of here," said Hitti as he made to move away. Ben grabbed his shoulder.

"Don't you see? Whatever it is wants you to go away. It means we are on the right track." There was a long pause while both Ben and Hitti looked at each other, motionless in thought. "Stay," urged Ben.

"OK, but I'd better not get into trouble over this."

After an hour or so, Hitti noticed a list of pupils in one of the volumes of records. "What about this? It's got a Sonia

Bird on this list as being here from 1946 to 1949." They all took a look. Ben was suddenly enthusiastic.

"Yep, that's gonna be her! The name Sonia Bird sounds right." The others wondered how he was so sure. Pointing at the page, Ben said, "See here, after her name. Those letters decd." The other two were none the wiser and just frowned at Ben. "That means deceased or dead, you dumbos," whispered Ben flatly.

"Wicked!" enthused Hitti, rather pleased with himself.

"We'll need to find anything about Sonia Bird dying then," Laura announced rifling through school magazines. She started thumbing through them quickly. Ben grabbed a few and did the same.

Suddenly, Laura saw an article in a 1949 edition entitled, 'Service held for our lost soul Sonia'. She leant over to show Ben and Hitti, when the most enormous thunder crack erupted, shaking the whole museum. It was followed by the largest loudest streaks of lightening any of them had ever experienced. The whole museum temporarily lit up from the light as if someone had forced the moon in through an open window! The storm had begun with a vengeance as huge hailstones and heavy rain battered the thinly tiled roof. Ben looked at Laura.

"I'm not going out in that," he said.

Laura showed Ben and Hitti the article. It seemed poor Sonia had fallen to her death from above the scenery at the Peter Phelps Theatre, whilst working backstage. The drama teacher of the time, Tim Dreante, had not been found responsible. They turned the page to find the second half of the article was ripped out. Searching all round there was no sign of it or any other information.

"So what are we supposed to do about that?" asked Hitti. "Isn't it on the internet or somewhere?" he suggested. Ben sat pensively, sighing to himself.

"I've tried the net. Not a thing. It's probably too long ago and no one has bothered to put it on there." Laura tapped four fingers across her lips, whilst she thought it through.

Ben suddenly called out, "Sonia, is that you?" He could see something. Hitti was not impressed.

"Come on, stop playing around," he said.

"I can't hear you properly!" Ben cried out. He had now gone very pale and was trembling. You couldn't fake it. He was lying on the floor perched up on his elbows. Laura and Hitti moved away from him and huddled together, frightened. They could see and hear nothing except Ben's reactions until without warning, Ben's body rose about ten centimetres clear of the floor. The look of terror on Ben's face told the story.

"You're crying Sonia. It was an accident. What can I do about it? Speak to me!" Ben was almost shouting.

It was about six o'clock by now. Hitti and Laura were desperate for this to end. They began to wonder if Ben was possessed by some evil spirit!

"You've really gotta tell me. I can't take much more."

The wind and rain were beating hard against the side of the museum. Laura and Hitti could both hear a faint wailing sound, but saw nothing. Ben's fixed gaze towards the other room displayed that he was definitely seeing something. It was Sonia's ghost standing right in front of Ben and this time only he could see it. Sonia cried out but it was hard to make out what she was saying.

"I was terminated and it was his fault. He was in charge, but he was not a man," she wailed. "My father did not mean the creature any harm. He was just a scientist doing his work."

"Whose fault? What creature? and what are you on about, terminated?" Ben shouted. "Not a man? What do you mean?" The wailing voice and apparition grew faint. Ben couldn't really make any sense of her words any more. All he could hear once again was the sound of an insect buzz around them. The ghost of Sonia Bird had disappeared. Ben dropped back to the floor. He sat still recovering for a minute.

"It's over. Gone." He paused. "I think she was murdered," he said in a quite serious voice. "It was no accident. This is the murder case of Sonia Bird!" There was silence. Laura and Hitti gulped.

"We've gotta go to the police then," said Hitti, relieved at the thought of a solution. Ben sighed.

"Just how would you explain what happened here? Sonia died in 1949. We've seen her ghost!"

"I didn't see a ghost!" interrupted Hitti.

"Nor me," added Laura.

"No, we only heard it."

"Ooh," Ben sighed as he took it all in. "Well you saw me lifted off the floor. They won't believe it and even if they did, what'll they do about it now?" he ranted. Hitti and Laura had to agree that the police were no answer. "Sonia said she was terminated. That means murder to me. Then she said something weird, like 'he' was in charge but it was not a man!"

"Let's go home now," said Laura, interrupting Ben's hypothesis. Ben took no notice as he continued to think aloud.

"Well, according to the article, Tim Dreante was in charge. That's a man's name!"

"Yes, probably a monster," Hitti added flippantly. "I'm out of here." He walked to the doorway.

"Brilliant," remarked Ben. "It was a creature, not a man. And her father?"

"Let's talk about the information on our way home. I don't want to stay here anymore," Hitti replied. Laura and Hitti made to leave with Ben still deep in thought, following and mumbling various possible answers to himself.

In the Munday household, Laura's mother was now very concerned. It was well after six. Laura's bus usually came in about half past four or quarter to five.

"Rupert dear, shall we ring the school?" They were sat in their very posh living room watching the evening news. Mr Munday had his feet up relaxing.

"Haven't they had a school party today Patricia? She's probably a bit late and just enjoying herself." By the look on his wife's face he could see this would not satisfy her. "I'll try ringing the school then, but I doubt I'll get an answer." He stayed seated and used his mobile.

"It's just an answering machine I'm afraid," he said. They decided to wait for another fifteen minutes and then they were going to call the police.

Meanwhile, the Street household were beginning to have similar worries.

"What time does Ben's bus normally come in then, Kate?" Ben's father queried.

"Oh, anything between four and five I'd say. Never known him later than half past five, Jim." Ben's mum sounded quite jittery.

"I could drive up there, I suppose," offered Jim.

"Nah, he's either on that bus or he ain't and we'll be calling the coppers in," Kate replied. They both agreed that by seven they would call the police.

The home of the Singh's was not so quiet. As he had three brothers and two sisters, his absence wasn't even noticed yet. He sometimes went to other friends and came home at eight o'clock. His parents were easy going.

Ben, Laura and Hitti agreed to find the rest of the article that had been ripped from the magazine. After all, there must be some reason why someone managed to take that exact page and no other from one school magazine printed in 1949. Someone was hiding something and Ben was going to find out who and why.

As they wandered over to the door chatting, they had forgotten all about the fact that they were locked in the museum. The school clock chimed seven o'clock reminding them they had been hours! None of them had a mobile phone with them. Ben and Hitti didn't own one and Laura

CHAPTER 1

The darkest day

Wiltshire, England – 1946

The sound of excited laughter could be heard coming from the children of the William Ingram School of Performing Arts on their annual school trip. They poured from the bus without hesitation, and then stood marvelling at the stone structure before them. An ancient civilisation had placed these great, tall stones, called Stonehenge, in a circle.

The day had started out bright and sunny. As eleven o'clock approached, the kids were all grouped in the centre of the monument, listening to the gentle rise and fall of their teacher's voice, as Mr Streeter held forth on the history of Stonehenge. Suddenly, a shadow began to gather right over them, and then gradually spread out and moved sideways over a nearby field. It was not a cloud. It formed a perfect square of absolute darkness. The children gasped and stood motionless, their eyes transfixed skywards.

The black mass grew by the second. Suddenly, Mr Streeter called out in panic, "Run for the bus! It's a meteorite!"

The galloping herd of terrified kids and teachers were all back in the bus and driving away in seconds. Within minutes, the bus was several miles away. The meteorite struck earth, causing an enormous tremor and a terrifying bang, which reverberated around them. The bus wobbled and kids collided with each other. Shaken up, they looked

1

out of the windows to see a massive mushroom cloud of dust rising into the sky.

The following morning, Dr Edward Bird was working diligently in his laboratory at the Department of Entomology. A slimly built man, his frame bore out his name. With his tufted hair going grey where he wasn't losing it, his bushy eyebrows, and his wide eyes behind round spectacles, he looked very much like some rare bird as he perched over his laboratory desk, pecking away at his latest theories. Suddenly, the telephone rang, jarring his concentration. Despite being the foremost living expert on insects, calls to his lab were very rare.

"Edward Bird speaking," he said into the phone.

"Dr Bird, this is Tony Chatterton, the Minister of Defence," said the voice on the line. "Please listen carefully."

The doctor went pale as he listened over the next several minutes and then replaced the receiver with a shaking hand. As he turned, he spoke sharply to his assistant, who had been watching the scene with growing interest. "Jeffrey, gather up a set of sample bottles, the largest cage we've got, and all the antidotes," he ordered. He began racing about the lab, placing surgical instruments into his case. "Don't stand there gawking, man. Move!"

"Yes, Doctor," said Jeffrey. "But what's it all about?"

The doctor paused, looking deep into Jeffrey's eyes.

"That thing that landed in Wiltshire. You must have heard it on the news. The Minister of Defence, by order of the Prime Minister, has asked us to go and urgently investigate—" The doctor hesitated to finish the sentence. He started to whisper. "Look, this is top secret. Not a word. Our lives may depend on it. That square meteorite which landed yesterday split into four perfectly shaped pieces. It's been seen crawling with unknown giant insects. The army has cordoned off the area."

The doctor's lips quivered with nervous tension. He snapped closed his briefcase and picked up the phone ready to call his wife. "You'll have to come too, Jeffrey. Don't know if I can manage it on my own. Go and pack up the things I need, and then call your wife." Shocked and worried, Jeffrey went away to comply with the doctor's orders.

Dr Bird rang his wife, doing his best to sound calm. "Heather, my love," he said, lightly into the phone. "I'm so sorry, dearest, but I've been called away on urgent government business. I don't expect to be back tonight, unfortunately."

"Oh, Edward," exclaimed his wife. "Of all the days! You know how Sonia has been looking forward to this evening!"

"Why? What's Sonia doing today?"

"Today is the Ingram School's song and dance competition. You know she's entered, and she's been practising for weeks, in class and out," chided his wife. "She'll be crushed if her own father isn't there."

"I am so sorry, darling," said Dr Bird. "I am afraid it can't be helped. Do tell Sonia I'll make it up to her. I promise."

He said his goodbyes and dropped the phone down. As alarmed as his wife had been the day before when Sonia had returned from the school trip with tales of being nearly crushed by the meteorite, he could only imagine how Heather would react if she knew he was going to return to that very site today. Particularly if she knew what he suspected was awaiting him there.

It was several hours of slow driving in a small black Austin van before Dr Bird and Jeffrey arrived at the site of the meteorite landing. As they passed the army checkpoint, the soldiers looked perplexed, and plainly relieved to see them. Dr Bird smiled at them confidently as if he'd seen it all before. But nothing could be further from the truth. The soldiers, obviously agitated, escorted the two scientists from their vehicle to the site, brandishing machine guns.

"You're not to shoot anything unless I say so. Is that clear?" insisted Dr Bird. The soldiers nodded, but nervously fingered their weapons, nonetheless. Dr Bird strode quickly with his instrument case toward the meteorite's resting place, his leather coat flapping against his legs, as Jeffrey followed behind, clumsily struggling to carry a large glass and wire cage.

As the group slowly descended into the crater made by the fallen rock, a large black insect the size of a full-grown cat suddenly sprang from behind an oblong stone. The insect looked around wildly, then peered at the men with a menacing turquoise glare. It waved its huge, wiry legs around, bounced momentarily in front of them, and then flew off like a small rocket. In less than a second, it was completely out of sight. All four men stood rooted in shock.

"Has anyone logged how many of these things have flown off like that?" Dr Bird said sharply.

"That's the third one, sir," replied a sergeant. "The other two came down somewhere nearby."

"I want all of you to stay here," Dr Bird commanded.

"But we were ordered by General—"

"I don't care what you were ordered," snapped the irritated doctor. "This is a job for me and me alone. Jeffrey, I'll have the cage. You carry my bag and follow ten paces behind." He set off without waiting and walked out of sight in between the oblong rocks. Jeffrey picked up the bag, and meekly followed his mentor as instructed.

After a few minutes, there was sudden clamour, and Jeffrey heard Dr Bird shouting for him. "The antidote, Jeffrey! The antidote, over here, quick!" Jeffrey ran in the direction of the voice, and found Dr Bird lying on the ground, clutching his left forearm, which was dribbling blood. Next to him was the cage, now containing one of the giant insects, which clawed and scratched viciously at the walls of its prison.

Jeffrey withdrew an antidote kit from the doctor's case and the doctor nodded to indicate one of the substances. "Inject it in my left arm above the elbow," ordered Dr Bird. Jeffrey hesitated for moment, the needle poised above the couldn't find hers in her bag. Everywhere was locked. Ben tried the door with all his might but it would not budge.

"I'll try my kinetic power," he said to Laura.

"Your what?" crowed Hitti in disbelief. Ben had forgotten Hitti had never seen him use it and even if he had, wouldn't have known how it happened. Laura and Hitti stood back. Ben looked and clicked his eyes thinking of the door moving. It creaked and moved a millimetre or so in its place. But it was locked and Ben could not unlock it whatever he thought about.

"I can see the door move a bit, but that's the wind or something. Come on!" said Hitti in disbelief. Ben did it again and Hitti's mouth dropped open as he saw the door move up and down on its hinges. But Ben couldn't open it. They knew they were in trouble. The last bus went at six or just before.

Laura's father was calling out up their stairway. "I've phoned them, Patricia. They've sent a patrol to drive the route between here and the school and they're radioing around." Laura's mother was emerging from their bedroom as he finished.

"No need to shout, Rupert. I can hear you!" Their phone started to ring. "I'll get that," she said disappearing back into the bedroom. "Hello?"

"This is Hently police, Madam. Are you Mrs Munday?"

"Yes."

"PC Shaw here. I was talking to your husband a few minutes ago. Don't want to worry you Madam, but since then we've had a report of another missing person from the same school, called Ben Street." Laura's mother's head began to spin. Was it good or bad she thought, two of them missing together? "Do you know anything about him, Madam?" asked PC Shaw.

"I know he's friends with Laura. We've only seen him at school a couple of times, that's all."

"That's about the same as the Streets seem to think. If you hear anything about him, then call us please. They may well be together."

"Yes, all right. We'll do that. Phone us whatever the time won't you?" said Mrs Munday.

"Of course, Madam," said the officer. Mr Munday had joined his wife in the bedroom.

"What's happening?" he said.

"I'll tell you downstairs, Rupert. I've found Laura's mobile in her bedroom sitting on her homework. She must have forgotten it, so no wonder there's no phone call."

By now the Singhs had decided their son was on the missing list and called the police. After another round of calls from the police to each missing pupil's home, all of their parents were now aware there were three of them out there somewhere, missing!

Ben, Laura and Hitti had resigned themselves to sleeping on the floor of the museum. It wasn't very late but they were all drained by their weird experience. It was going to mean big trouble in the morning. They put their school bags down to act as pillows and decided to get some rest.

Ben was lying with his head facing towards the door. The light of the moon flickered in from time to time between the clouds that were now clearing.

He squinted and looked again towards a shape he had spotted to the left of the door. There was a little box about a metre from the doorway hanging on the wall, at eye level. Ben looked at it several times when the light shone in. He had a suspicion and just had to get up and look.

"What's up now?" asked Hitti who was already dozing. Ben said nothing and marched straight up to the small box. Laura turned round to see Ben pulling at the wall.

"What are you doing?" she called.

"This might help," Ben laughed as he turned about smiling. He held up a key, which he had just prized from the little box. That little box had scribbled upon it the words 'spare' in very small old writing.

Ben tried to put the key in the door. But it didn't go in! He pushed harder. He was exasperated at his effort leading nowhere. Suddenly, as he pushed hard, there was a click and it fell into place. Ben slowly turned the key. The door was unlocked. The three of them grabbed their bags, made for the door and Ben replaced the key in the box.

They stepped out sheepishly, closing the door behind them. Down the creaky steps they went with little but the moonlight and one car park light to guide them. Luckily the rain had stopped for now.

"How are we going to get home? What'll we say?" Laura said with a slight panic in her voice.

"OK. We've got a problem," agreed Ben. "The truth's no good is it?"

"Hey, guys," added Hitti, "I reckon we should just keep it simple. We were together after the party sorting out some school history and the time just passed."

"Brilliant!" said Laura. Little did they know the police were out looking for them. They walked across the school car park and passed the front of the entrance. They had no phone and there were no public call boxes around.

"I'm sure there's one of those emergency roadside call boxes on the main road, not far," remarked Ben. In hope, they all set off on foot.

By now all their parents were getting very worried. They had only walked about two hundred metres from the school entrance, when a police car pulled up. Now they felt under pressure.

"Are you Laura, Ben and Hitti?" asked the uniformed officer, PC Welch.

"Yes," they replied together. It was a relief of sorts. At least they were going to be whisked home to their parents. Pointing to the police car he issued the expected order.

"Get in here please. Your parents have reported you three as missing persons. In view of your age, I'm going to take you home and the questions will come tomorrow I expect." None of them were worried about that just now.

115

"Alpha Foxtrot forty-two to base," said the officer, speaking into his car radio device. "I've picked up the three missing youngsters. Yes, that's them, Sarge, you can call the parents," he said. "Home, yes. Will do," he continued.

He said nothing else and simply delivered all three of them straight home, one after the other. Hitti was first. His anxious parents simply hugged him, thanked the officer and took him inside. Ben was next. Once inside his mum wanted answers. She slapped his face, not hard but enough to show her upset.

"Now what's this all about? We was worried sick."

"I'm sorry, Mum. We just got a bit carried away doing our school history and didn't notice the time," Ben tried explaining.

"I'll give you school history, my lad. What's wrong with the phone then, eh? Are you dumb as well as stupid?" she screeched.

"Hey, hey, hey. Stop this, both of you!" intervened his father. There was a short pause for calm. "Just don't do anything so daft again. You phone, or you're for the high jump. Got it?"

"Yes, Dad," agreed Ben somewhat relieved it seemed to be over. Somehow, in a way, parents were more annoying than ghosts weren't they?

"Now, I saved you a bit of me cheesy marrow dish," said his mum. He knew he couldn't disappoint his mother again, when it came to the question of supper. He bit his lip.

"Lovely, Mum. I'm really hungry."

At about this time, Laura was just being delivered to her mansion house behind the iron gates. Her parents had calmed down since they heard the police were on their way with their daughter.

"Thank you so much, officer," smiled Mrs Munday rather falsely. Laura was taken straight in and the huge double doors bolted up. Both her parents hugged her and then looking hurt, her mother spoke first very firmly.

"Your father and I need your explanation and now." Laura's face was red with emotion.

"I'm really sorry. We were doing some school history stuff and forgot about the time and it—"

"A likely story," she raved.

"Let her finish, Patricia," insisted her father.

"It all went a bit pear-shaped," Laura concluded slowly, sounding less convincing as she went.

"Who were you with?" said her father rather directly. Laura gulped.

"Ben and Hitti." Her mum and dad seemed relieved even though they didn't know much about Hitti.

"Listen carefully, Laura. I've spoken to the headmaster this evening. He will see you and those others tomorrow morning in his office, before school at eight-thirty and he'll deal with you all together. The police are leaving it to the school and parents fortunately." Mr Munday looked very grave. "Really, Laura, I thought better of you, not even phoning." He walked off to his study. Her mum just glared at her.

Laura didn't want to make it worse. She just bowed her head, took herself to the kitchen for a snack and made her way to bed. It was an early bus tomorrow and the last day of her first term at WISPA. She could only ask herself over and over again, what would become of her school career now?

The following day was a Friday and a cool clear day with a little ground frost. Laura was first on the early bus. Ben and Hitti got on at their stop as well and it was obvious by the looks on their faces they had all been told the same thing. They were headed for a rocket from Mr Goving.

The headmaster's office was an enormous room with wood panelled walls, a large meeting desk and an open area for polite parties or receptions. It felt like a small courtroom and very formal. It had floor to ceiling bookcases as well, containing leather bound volumes on everything and anything about the school. No doubt they formed the definitive set.

The three of them stood outside the door nervously waiting the five minutes until the allotted time.

Mr Bodkin had opened most of the school's buildings and was making his way up the steps of the museum. He placed his key in the lock and went to turn it. The door was already unlocked.

"That's odd," he muttered. "Must've done it wrong I suppose." He tried the door, shut it again and walked back down the steps.

Outside the head's office the time had come.

"You knock the door, Hitti," said Ben.

"Not me, it's all your fault we're here anyway," he replied without hesitation.

"Let's get it over with," said Laura softly and knocked on the door herself. There was silence. They looked at each other for a few seconds when they suddenly heard the voice of authority.

"Enter," said Mr Goving. Ben turned the handle and pushed the door open. "You three can stand in front of my desk." They walked into the office and stood there like soldiers on parade. "Ben, you tell me just what went on here last night please." Mr Goving was galloping his fingers on the desk menacingly. Ben breathed in heavily.

"Can I just say—" Mr Goving immediately stopped him.

"Answer the question and nothing else please." Ben felt cornered but determined.

"After the school party, Sir, we decided to look into some school history. We found out about someone who was here in the past and it was really interesting." Ben paused.

"You did not arrange it with your parents or put yourselves on the after five-thirty list of persons in the building. You caused the police to be called and a great deal of worry to your parents."

"Yes, Sir. It won't happen again," said Ben in a formal manner.

"Hittendra? Same question."

"Well, it was like Ben said and I'm very sorry for the trouble." Hitti couldn't bear it! Mr Goving spoke in a sarcastic tone of voice and fixed his gaze on Hitti.

"Hmmm. You like school history too, do you?"

"Yes, Sir," replied Hitti nervously.

"Laura, what was the school history about?" Mr Goving asked screwing up his eyes slightly.

"We just wanted to find out about someone who came here and something happened. It was in a very old article. They died in the theatre." Mr Goving glossed over it so quickly it was strange. Had he never heard of it? Or did he have something to hide? He brushed it aside.

"Look, you need to grow up. Consider the safety issue, the disrespect to your parents and having to involve me. You are banned for the rest of today from associating with each other. Do not ever do it again. Ben, I'm afraid this is going in your scholarship report. Now please leave."

Ben tried to speak but wasn't allowed. "You've said enough, Ben. Leave while I'm still feeling lenient."

Outside the relief could be seen on their faces. They just had to avoid each other for the rest of the day. Too easy! Next term was just a few weeks away.

CHAPTER 8

Unexpected information

The holidays and Christmas passed peacefully. Ben had been careful not to use any of his powers or upset any of his neighbours. He would just take himself to his own room occasionally to check he still had his kinetic power and he only freeze-framed his mum when his dad was at work. She never knew, but had formed the opinion that he was mighty quick at chores in the house and was well impressed.

On the day before term started, Ben was sorting out his school gear in his room. He heard the familiar voice of his mother flowing up the stairs.

"I bet you never cleaned that bathroom like I asked you?" his mum enquired very nicely. Ben came out and looked down the stairs and immediately went, look—click—freeze-frame. Mrs Street was rooted to the bottom step, with her apron moving in the wind of the fan heater across the hallway.

Ben slipped past her, and into the kitchen. He returned with a bucket and cleaning agents. He scrubbed up the bathroom for five minutes or so. It wasn't like a proper mum would do it but a lot better than before. He ran downstairs, put the bucket and cleaners away. Then he ran past his mum to the top of the stairway. Look—click—move.

"I did clean it. Have a look," said Ben smiling. His mum was already on the way. She looked in to see a relatively clean bathroom. Her eyes twinkled as she thought how

120

much Ben had changed since he went to WISPA. Like most parents, she didn't really know very much did she?

"Ben, you're a lovely boy," she said as if she hadn't noticed Ben was nearly thirteen and actually a young man.

"If you say so, Mum," Ben replied.

The next morning Ben could hardly wait to get back to school. It had never left his thoughts that it was *he* who was going to uncover the mystery of Sonia's death. It was murder and he was going to find out who or what did it.

As soon as he left Macey Avenue, he was virtually street dancing his way along the road to his bus stop. He met up with the usual WISPA crowd on the bus, except Laura was missing. As soon as he walked through the school entrance, he saw a parked Bentley. Laura would surely be there already.

The whole school were putting their bags in lockers and things on pegs before going to assembly in the Peter Phelps Theatre. They were jostling their way to their seats when the familiar sound of thumping began. The enormous spoon was out battering the poor side table again!

"Quiet please for the headmaster," shouted one of the prefects. The theatre gradually came to a silent halt. Mr Goving stood right beside the little table and put down some of his notes.

"Welcome back! We had a good start to the year last term. Before I get on to events, I just wanted to make sure you are all aware of the five-thirty list."

Ben was drifting already. I'll bet he says nothing worth knowing Ben chuckled to himself. He felt a little flutter of excitement in his stomach. He must resist the temptation this term, he thought. His powers were for unravelling an important truth and not just for laughs, weren't they?

Ben's resistance was waning fast. He found himself focussing on the rolled up scenery just above the headmaster. Mr Goving's little habit of rising onto his toes and down again as he spoke was just too convenient. It made a slight squeak on the theatre floor.

Look—click—move, down, down and down. The painted scenery of some country farm, edged down on its roll a few centimetres and down again, all in time with the headmaster's feet. Any sound of moving scenery was muffled. Gradually it was noticed by everyone except Mr Goving. He bowled on regardless.

The scenery had now moved down so far it was moving just in front of the table but just behind Mr Goving. No one dared interrupt, not even the other teachers present. They all looked on with disbelief and anticipation. What would happen next?

As Mr Goving put out his hand to reach the next set of notes from the table, the whole school descended into laughter. The table had disappeared behind the scenery! His hand collided with a painted bucket on the scenery instead and he nearly jumped out of his skin.

Look—click—up. The scenery rolled itself straight up as if the headmaster's touch had caused it. A confused head was left looking up into the theatre backstage and listening to the loudest laughter he had ever heard. He raised his hand for quiet and seemed pleased at the hilarity he had unwittingly created. The theatre slowly calmed.

"Well, glad you liked the show," chortled Mr Goving. He reached for his notes. "Just the notices then. Please check the board for your Comp teams and rehearsal times. Missing them won't do. Put them in your school diary today."

Filing out had already begun. Ben went past the noticeboard in the crowd, smiling. Then he saw his name on the Cortazzi team. Not so good he thought. Ben's first period was a piano lesson in the music school. He saw Ned Elliot going towards the science labs and he waved. That was in the next block along. Ned waved back.

Laura and Hitti came trotting by and Ben stopped to speak with them. After a brief chat about their Christmas breaks Ben had something important to say.

"Remember when we had to go to Mr Goving's office?" Laura and Hitti nodded. How could they forget?

"There was loads of school mags there. I want to get the rest of that stuff on Sonia that was ripped out of the one in the museum. I bet it's in his office. Yeah?" Ben was looking for approval of his plan.

"Well, let's just go and ask for it," Laura said.

"Oh no, not after that dressing down on school history. No way. He didn't believe us anyway," Hitti said. "He'll think we're taking the mick and we'll get detention or something."

Ben was nodding in agreement. "Yup. He was weird about it, Laura. Something just didn't add up the way he went on."

"I thought that too," Hitti piped up.

"There's no way out of it, Laura. We'll just have to borrow it somehow. We can put it back can't we?" Ben was going to have his way. The three of them agreed that as Mr Goving would be away next week for a conference, it would be the perfect moment. They went their separate ways.

Ned had walked into the science labs and joined his group of friends. Dr Metanite was already there as they wandered in. He was taking little notice of any of his pupils and seemed to have constructed a miniature steel bridge with all sorts of tension struts attached. Suddenly Dr Metanite came to life.

"Right, class. Can I have your attention please," he yelled in his unusual voice. "We're going to study the metal composition of this bridge structure and also something on how engineers might go about designing them. Gather round," he instructed. The bridge was on his very large fixed desk at the front of class. Dr Metanite was moving around from side to side adding parts and getting more and more excited. His long spindly fingers appeared adept at attaching the tiniest of nuts and bolts, and so quickly too.

"If we change the central zone this way," he demonstrated, "Do you think our bridge will be stronger or weaker?" Nobody really knew, but there was a fifty percent chance of being right, Ned thought.

"Weaker," he answered, hoping for the best.

"Correct!" came the teacher's reply. Dr Metanite threw up his hands in a victory wave and knocked his own briefcase onto the floor next to Ned, on the other side of the desk. The case had come open and papers were spewing out of it. Dr Metanite rushed around the table and was already there as Ned bent down to start picking them up.

It all seemed to be old science books, pupils' homework and parts of old school magazines mixed up. Ned was just thinking, what a messy case it was when Dr Metanite's spindly fingers grabbed the outside of it and banged it shut. Some of the papers were sticking out of the edge.

"I'll sort it out, Ned," he said looking rather unsettled. "I think you can go back to your places now and, erm, erm—" Dr Metanite had clearly lost the thread of his lesson as he put his briefcase in order.

"In your workbooks, I want you to draw three types of possible bridge construction. Tell me what they would be made of and which one would be best for putting over the River Thames in London." Luckily, Ned liked drawing and cheerfully began his task, but couldn't help thinking Dr Metanite was a bit weird. "I'll come and talk with anyone who needs help," said Dr Metanite. At least half the class put up a hand straight away.

Later on that day, Ned saw Ben and Laura on the bus home. He walked part way down the aisle looking for a seat. He only needed to get to the first village and quite often walked the fifteen minutes it took, but today he treated himself to transport. A voice from behind piped up in a snide way.

"Ned fancies Becky." Ned turned to the front.

"Leave it out!" he snapped. He wasn't sure who said it and didn't really care. He noticed a seat next to Ben in the back row and sat down. The bus moved off.

"Hi, Ned," beamed Laura, sitting beside Ben. Ned got out his science homework sheet so he could do it on the bus quickly before he even arrived home. It was multiple choice, tick the answers you agree with, type of homework. Ben saw it.

"Oh, not that; we did it last week. There's some weird questions on it," said Ben. Ned responded without a moment's hesitation.

"Well, no surprise if it's to do with Dr Metanite. You have him for science don't you?" Ben and Laura nodded. "Well, I think that man's nuts," said Ned, still confused by his lesson earlier on that day.

"Have you seen his crazy fingers?" said Ben.

"Not that! It's coz today he went on and on about bridges and stuff we hadn't even done. Then he only went and knocked his own case on the floor and all these old magazines were in it. Then he went kind of crazy," Ned said.

"Magazines?" queried Ben.

"Well bits of them," Ned added.

"What sort of magazines?" asked Laura.

"You know, science stuff and old school photos and rubbish," Ned explained. Ben and Laura looked at each other as if they knew something.

*

The rest of the week came and went. The following Monday it was lessons and drama classes as usual. Ben, Laura and Hitti were coming out of the theatre heading for their lockers. The end of school bell had just rung out. They had all agreed it was going to be tonight.

"You did tell your folks you'd be late today didn't you?" Ben checked with Hitti.

"Yeah. Extra history," he replied.

"Same here," said Laura. Ben looked satisfied.

"Good. Let's just go and do our homework in the library and wait for about five. Hardly anyone around by then."

Sure enough, by five o'clock the school took on a deathly quiet. Mr Bodkin would likely appear to lock up before long. Being a British winter it was pitch black outside at this time of year. WISPA was too far away from a road for street lamps to reach it. There were only a few security lights here and there.

"OK, let's go," whispered Ben. They walked along the school corridors and on their way put their bags back in their lockers. Ben had it worked out, or so he believed. He marched his crew of two to the bushes outside the head's office. There were no lights except in the very large porch on the side of the building. Ben knew they would never get in by that entrance. It would be via the kitchens.

Somehow they had to get around to the back without anyone noticing. The yard at the school kitchen area is not somewhere you could just walk in to. No one ever said it was not allowed, but it was for staff only.

The three of them crept past the building entrance in the very wide flowerbed backed by huge old bushes. There was a shed in there although you'd never notice it. As they reached the side, a torch came over the flowerbed from an upper window. Laura nearly let out a scream, but managed to swallow it.

"Crikey," Ben said quietly. "That came from Bertie's flat, I swear it. You know Mr Burton, clerk of works."

They all crept around the other side of the shed and scuttled over behind the wooden gate in the fence that led to the kitchens. At that moment the giant old front door in the side porch creaked open and out came the searching torchlight, moving from side to side. They ducked behind the fence. They watched through a crack in the slats as Bertie, dressed in an old overcoat and boots wandered across to the flowerbeds. He trudged about pointing his torch in all directions.

"Come on out. I heard yer," he was muttering several times. Then he kept mumbling, "I'll wait here all night if that's what it takes. Bloody tomfoolery, that's what it is."

They couldn't wait there all night, Ben thought. He knew he must return home for dinner! He went look—click—freeze-frame. All three could see Bertie standing there like a statue, lit up only partially by his own torchlight. Hitti yelped at the sheer power Ben had displayed. The problem was he was standing in the middle of the flowerbed. His light was pointing straight outwards, over the low fence along a small service road upon which there were several cottages lived in by younger staff like Mr McKinley. Someone would soon notice.

"We can't leave him like that!" objected Laura. She hadn't yet considered the torchlight and was worried about where he was standing.

"OK," said Ben. Again he used his kinetic touch. He looked—clicked—and moved. The small shed, barely visible in the bushes lifted up and Ben used his eye click to direct it right in front of Bertie. The torchlight was now barely visible. He was standing facing the shed, well into the flowerbed and bushes. The torch was up against the side of it. You would never have noticed him from the pathway.

Suddenly Hitti got up. He had seen all this and not been asked for an opinion once. He ran from behind the fence with Ben and Laura whispering loudly.

"Come back!"

Hitti sprinted to the bushes and reached Bertie in seconds. Ben and Laura didn't know what he was going to do. Hitti reached out towards Bertie and put his hand on the torch. He felt around the edge until he could put his thumb on a button. Off went the torch. He ran back to the others and they all laughed that Ben had moved the shed for nothing!

"Easy really," said Hitti, rather pleased with himself.

"Right. We need to move it," urged Ben.

"Not again," crowed Hitti.

"No not that. I mean get a move on! Let's go." He started to walk off behind the kitchens and realised after a few steps Hitti and Laura hadn't followed. He turned to see Hitti's index finger beckoning him back.

"You're not thinking, Ben. Bertie came out of there." Hitti pointed at the large old entranceway and front door. Ben closed his eyes now blinded by the obvious.

"I knew you'd be useful," said Ben shaking his head at himself. "Hope it's actually open then," he added.

"Hey, this doesn't count as burglary does it?" asked Hitti nervously.

"We're investigating a murder. Not trying to steal stuff," hissed Ben. They walked the few steps over to the door in the dim light. Laura slowly approached it first. It looked closed.

"I'll do this," whispered Laura. She grabbed the handle and started to turn it hoping the door would open. With a slight push it opened ajar. They all breathed heavily for a few seconds. Then realising they were in the light of the porch the three of them rapidly walked through into the hallway.

A feeling of guilt was rising up in Ben's thoughts. It didn't seem like something any of them should be doing. Ben would not normally have dreamt of doing anything of the sort, until that is, the mystery of Sonia came to light.

The hallway was not lit, but the light of the porch way shone through the large glass pane at the top of the door. There was enough light to see the doorways in the passage ahead. None of them had ever entered the building from this direction.

"Which door is it? Any ideas?" whispered Ben. The others pointed down the passage. It had to be one of the three doors on the right that led to the headmaster's office.

Ben, Laura and Hitti walked a few steps as if on eggshells. Ben noticed there were framed photos on the wall of past heads of the school. He could just make out a photo of a Mr Gareth Streeter. It was dated 1950. A little feeling of pride entered him, as he already knew this was his great grandfather.

The floorboards creaked slightly and they stopped in fright. Just at that moment a small amount of extra light entered the passageway. A wave of fear entered their bodies. Laura looked up. There was a pane of glass above each of the three large Victorian doors and the middle one now had light coming through it. Ben whispered very quietly indeed.

"It's the deputy head's room. I forgot that's next to Mr Goving's." The fact was, the door on the other side of the building was normally used for entering these offices and not the doors from the posh passage they were now in. Someone was now in the middle office. They had no choice but to press on.

"It's the last door; I'm sure," Ben whispered ever more quietly. He moved very slowly step by step, followed by Laura and Hitti. Ben put his hand out and turned the handle. It was locked! He knew his kinetic power did not work on locks. They remembered what happened in the school museum. They all grimaced at this setback.

"I bet the kitchen passage is through there and the other door to the office," Hitti suggested in a whisper, pointing onwards to another door at the end of the passage.

There were creaks from the deputy's room. They all started to move much more quickly. Suddenly none of them wanted to be there at all. Mercifully, the door at the end of the passage was open and they exited to a corridor they knew well – the other end was the canteen entrance now locked up and this end was the usual door to go into Mr Goving's office. Ben led them straight to the correct office door.

He put his hand out to turn the door handle, but before he could do so, the sound of a light-switch being pressed permeated through the door. A thin beam of light immediately shone out around the doorframe. Someone must have gone in there!

"I want to get out of here," hissed Laura, now very nervous. It was clear they would not be able to complete their plan. But how would they get out? Ben looked about behind him.

"We'll get out through the kitchen. Follow me," Ben indicated by mouthing the words in the dim light. As Ben moved, his jacket caught on the door handle and pulled at it. The handle flicked up and down making quite a racket.

They stood deathly still for a moment waiting to see if there was any reaction. Phew – nothing! They delicately tiptoed away. The door from the corridor to the kitchen was open and they went right to the other side. Ben opened the exit door to the outside using the key sitting in the lock which was inside. Once out, they ran around to the fenced area where they had begun and prepared to bolt away from the scene.

"Let's get right out of sight and then I'll unfreeze Bertie," said Ben.

They all ran as quietly as they could to the other side of the quadrangle so they could barely see Bertie anymore. A voice called out in the darkness.

"Come back here. This is out of bounds at this time of day. I'll call the police." It was only about five thirty but pitch black. None of them could see the owner of the voice, but it was probably the deputy; someone you never really saw called Nathan Gale.

They stopped to catch their breath. Smudge suddenly came into view. She was walking very quickly on the other side of the quadrangle. She looked very preoccupied and didn't appear to notice Ben or the others. She went through an ornamental archway underneath the bursar's office near to the headmaster's porch. This eventually led out to the main road. There were few lights on. It was all very strange. She had what looked like a couple of jam jars with her.

"What's Smudge doing?" said Ben observing her unexpected activities. He had a suspicion the jars contained something green.

"I hope she doesn't ask us the same thing!" commented Hitti sarcastically.

"True. Look guys, we need to plan things better next time," said Ben still panting a little.

"Next time!" yelped Hitti. "Are you mad? We were so close to being caught, I can't believe we weren't."

"I'm sorry. I'll think it through. Let's just get out of here," he replied.

"Don't forget Bertie," said Laura. Look—click—move, went Ben. Bertie could be heard mumbling in the bushes as the three of them carried on walking away to get their bus home. Just as they went to turn the corner out of sight, the light of his torch came on again.

"At least I know he's all right," commented Ben somewhat relieved.

"But what about the shed?" exclaimed Hitti. "You've left it in the wrong place." Ben tried to stay calm. They all waited a few seconds until they could see Bertie go back indoors. Then Ben kinetically moved the shed back to its original position. As soon as it landed they all bolted like horses out of a stable.

That night Ben had a lucid dream. This was nothing like he had experienced before. He knew he was dreaming, but at the same time he felt involved. He could remember this dream in detail when he woke up the next day. It must be important he thought.

It had all started at the school at the time his great grandfather was the head. He saw a beautiful girl dancing and singing gracefully and receiving a prize to great applause from the audience. A piece of rope and a pulley kept on appearing over and over again with the sound of wailing and buzzing insects accompanying it.

WHEN BEN AWOKE HE WAS IN A SLIGHTLY
SWEATY, TENSE STATE. THE FIRST THING HE
THOUGHT OF WAS LAURA'S WONDERFUL
SKETCH SHE HAD DRAWN THAT FIRST TERM AT
THE CLUB FESTIVAL DAY. IT WAS THE *SAME*
GIRL IN HIS DREAM; THE ONE HE NOW KNEW
WAS SONIA BIRD, THE GHOST!

CHAPTER 9

The suspicion grows

Some days later Ben was at school as usual. It was morning break time. He was sitting alone eating an apple and thinking about his future. Laura and Hitti had both experienced similar dreams to Ben in recent days. He tried to get on with his life, but the mystery of Sonia was literally haunting him.

He realised that he must wait until the headmaster was away from school in the daytime and just walk into his office to borrow the school magazine he wanted. Mr Goving published a schedule of his diary for all to see on a weekly basis. Ben ambled along to the noticeboard in the covered corridor. There were few times Mr Goving would be away from his desk when Ben could go there himself, except one! What about next Monday lunchtime?

Mr Goving was due to be away from one o'clock in the afternoon at a local heads meeting. Laura and Hitti would probably be able to help him at that time too.

Ben quickly returned just in time to join his maths class with Mrs Rigging. As she entered the room the class were faced with Ropy's new hair do. It was rather short but no doubt easy to keep neat. However, it looked extremely severe, quite like her mood these days. Her bob was no longer. She had taken to wearing jeans with a white top and little else on a daily basis.

The lesson got underway. Pupils were moving to and from the front of class to do long division. It was one of those days when Ben could not concentrate and he looked about the class in a bit of a daze. After a while he heard his name. Mrs Rigging stood in front of her own desk before the class.

"Ben, can you do this one please?" Mrs Rigging was looking towards her maths problems displayed on the board. As she looked forward a flickball passed from behind Ben perilously close to her and landed on a shelf of books. She didn't notice. Mrs Rigging sometimes liked pupils to demonstrate their working out to the whole class on the board. Ben was awake enough to know he had to get to the front of the classroom. He got up and performed the calculation.

"Easy," he said. It was not the best thing to say to Mrs Rigging.

"Well, we'll see about that," retorted Mrs Rigging. She bounced up to her board and put two more sums up, making them progressively more difficult and returned to her place. Ben had started to walk back to his seat. Mrs Rigging pointed at him and indicated he must do the further questions now on the board. At that exact moment Ben turned very pale. Everyone was mystified. The ghost of Sonia was coming through to him. Only Ben could see her.

"Use all your powers, Ben. It happened in 1949," wailed the ghostly form.

"I don't know what to do," said Ben. Mrs Rigging was not impressed hearing him speak like that. She had no idea he was actually speaking to a ghost!

"You will do them or it'll be detention for you young man," screeched an ever more irritated Mrs Rigging.

"You can get the answer. You are the chosen one," wailed the ghost again. It was hovering right in front of Ben.

"I'll use all my powers," Ben said hastily.

"You will indeed," replied Mrs Rigging in the belief Ben was talking to *her*. The long pauses after she spoke was too much for Mrs Rigging. "Come on. What are you waiting for?" she yelled. Ben stood still.

"Pray for me," the ghostly girl wailed as she began to fade away.

"I'm praying I can do it. But I'm not sure what I'm supposed to do," said Ben.

"Enough of this insolence," Mrs Rigging ordered. "You'll do it now and quick!"

Now the ghost of Sonia had gone Ben started to listen once again. He hadn't looked at the extra sums Mrs Rigging had put on the board before he blurted out yet another cheeky remark.

"OK. I'll do them before you can even walk back to the board," said Ben in an apparent about turn of attitude. Before he finished saying it, he wished he hadn't. You could hear the whole class go very quiet and Mrs Rigging was now very confused.

"I don't know what on earth you're playing at. But you'd better get your act together and quick," Mrs Rigging said firmly. Ben and Mrs Rigging looked at each other with steely determination. Ben had walked to the front of class and he moved his head towards them all. Then he went, look—click—freeze. The power of freeze-frame to the rescue! The whole class was frozen to the spot.

One hundred and two divided by six: seventeen. Two thousand six hundred and sixty four divided by eight: three hundred and thirty-three. Nine hundred and eighteen thousand, two hundred and fifty-two divided by nine: one hundred and two thousand and twenty-eight. Ben worked them all out by exactly the correct method in about forty seconds. Look—click—move, he thought, looking at the class again.

"Done it!" Ben said grinning. Mrs Rigging and the class were stunned at the apparent speed with which the answers had appeared. They had no idea they'd missed forty seconds of consciousness. All that is, except for Laura who guessed exactly what was going on. A slow outbreak of giggling began as a few seconds passed and Mrs Rigging contemplated her options. She would not be beaten or humiliated.

"Right Ben. Three more," she announced and marched to the front with three ever-harder questions to solve and a rather grim expression on her face. Ben adopted the same tactics. Look—click—freeze. He put the answers up on the board taking about another forty seconds. As the class unfroze this time, their amazement increased, as did the laughter.

"Silence," shouted Mrs Rigging. She tried for a third and last time hardly believing it possible. Three of the hardest equations were put on the board. Again Ben freeze-framed them all, did the answers and returned everyone to normal.

The confusion in class was now enormous. Mrs Rigging was fuming. She was trying hard to control her emotions. Ben's fellow pupils did not seem to be laughing any more. The atmosphere was electric with anticipation. What would happen next?

"Just how did you do that Ben?" Mrs Rigging asked. She was frowning and believed some trick must be involved. Ben thought for a few seconds.

"Quickly?" he replied cheekily. This answer did not satisfy Mrs Rigging who was shaking her head.

"Back to your seat then," she commanded. Mrs Rigging began to walk back to her usual place. Ben looked at her white tee shirt from the back and just as she went to step up onto the raised platform where her teacher's desk sat, he lost his battle with temptation.

He went look—click—move! It was a quick movement and just raised Mrs Rigging across the step and a couple of paces forward. She felt like she had walked on air and arrived just a moment quicker than anticipated. It was so unexpected she just looked around herself to see what had transported her along. No one was behind her. To the class it looked as if she had leapt into position in front of her board. Now her pupils were all looking at *her*. She seemed to be in disarray.

"Right," she said slowly. "For next time—" The end of lesson bell drowned her voice out. The relief around the class could be felt. They all left very rapidly.

Ben, Laura and Hitti wandered off with Ned to the canteen. By the time they reached it there was a long queue. As they stood waiting to buy their lunch, Ben noticed the table of teachers sitting on the raised area allotted to them. He tried to ignore it, but somehow they all seemed to be looking his way and talking. Mrs Rigging for one was sitting next to Smudge and Splinter, engrossed in conversation.

"How do you find that boy Ben Street?" Mrs Rigging asked Smudge and Splinter.

"I wasn't sure at first, but I think he has some remarkable talents," commented Splinter.

"Yes. You need to watch him though. You're never quite sure what he's thinking," added Smudge. They all took a couple of mouthfuls of their green soup, which allegedly contained pea and ham. The flavour was less convincing than the title.

"I don't know how to deal with him," Mrs Rigging half whispered. "One minute he's in a world of his own dreaming blankly, the next he's performing like some superstar. I can't make it out."

"I've taught a few like that over the years. They're gifted kids and hard to motivate on a day-to-day basis. Lot's of them swing from boredom to excitement. I'd give him different, harder homework and just not worry," Splinter advised kindly. He was pushing some bread around his soup bowl soaking up the curiously green liquid.

"Don't think I'm crazy, but I get this feeling something's in the room with us when I teach Ben. It never happens except when he's in my class. Today it was awful. Ben did the board sums in about two seconds. They were hard ones too. Unbelievable." Mrs Rigging was looking quite perturbed by the thought of it.

"Don't worry," soothed Smudge as she put an arm around Mrs Rigging who wriggled a bit, unsure of this touchy feely approach. She stood up and went to the hot plates for her main course. It was braised beef in gravy with mashed potato. Smudge leant over to Splinter slightly.

"Do you think our Ropy's all right? She seems very upset. It's not like her is it?"

"She's right, you know. There's something about that Ben Street. Can't put my finger on it," Splinter concluded between mouthfuls of bread. "He's always with Laura Munday and Hitti Singh. Can't believe he's ended up in Cortazzi's team for the Comp."

"Hmmm," Smudge hummed. She was very suspicious of Ben and intended to keep her eye on him. There were several other teachers there; all very artistic types and dressed imaginatively. They did not look like a bunch of the usual teachers at a school, except perhaps for Mrs Rigging who dressed down by comparison.

Ben had reached the front of the queue and was choosing a sandwich. He sensed the teacher's continuing curiosity about him.

"Guys, come on. I want to talk something over with you," Ben said to Hitti and Laura. Hitti was helping himself to some noodles and Laura a wrap. They followed Ben to a table. Ben sat carefully so he could see the teachers' eating area and still talk to his friends.

"I've got it all planned this time," said Ben quietly looking up towards the teachers and back to his own table. Hitti and Laura guessed what would be coming next. They listened with some trepidation. "Mr Goving is away next Monday lunchtime. That's our chance. I want to just go to his office, borrow the 1949 stuff and get outta there. Will you come too?"

"What if we get caught? I mean do you need me?" queried Hitti. He was not sure about anything after his last experience with Ben trying to get into Mr Goving's office.

"Yeah, course I need you, Hitti!" Ben said. "We need to stick together. School history project and all that." Ben was nudging Hitti with his elbow.

"What if the office is locked?" interjected Laura.

"I don't think it will be during the middle of the day because it leads through to other offices doesn't it?" Ben replied hoping he'd be right this time. "Anyhow, we've got to try it. It won't be much hassle to go and see."

"Monday lunchtime?" Laura questioned. "There's no time then really. We've got Comp practise that day and after lunch you've got to get straight into your costumes for the afternoon." Hitti was nodding agreement.

"I'd forgotten that. Still, there's always an hour or so, at some point when you are waiting isn't there? Once we've changed and know when we'll be on, we could just go and do it quickly and come back. In fact that'd be better. Less people about."

Laura and Hitti agreed to help. How could they refuse their friend? None of them had thought about how it might look for three costumed pupils to be seen meandering past the staff room, past the kitchen passage and towards the offices. At least it was a stage school!

They'd all eaten their lunch quickly during the conversation and were about to go and change for afternoon sports. Suddenly there was a commotion in the teachers' eating area. Smudge had collapsed. Splinter was holding her by her arms and lowering her to the ground and checking her pulse.

"Call an ambulance," he shouted to an anxious Mrs Rigging. She was nearest to the telephone on the wall and immediately took action. Smudge was panting and wheezing obviously in considerable discomfort. The whole canteen had become silent and was now viewing the spectacle. The door to the corridor outside the kitchens had been opened by one of the cook's team and within seconds Smudge had become ill.

"Are you allergic to anything, Smudge? Can you tell me?" Splinter asked in a worried tone of voice. He was tending to her and she appeared to recover a little.

"I can't move my legs," she complained from the floor, ignoring Splinter's question.

"Are you taking any medicines?" he tried. Everyone was looking on in horror and surprise. She seemed such a fit person and only about thirty-five years old.

"No. I'm not allergic to anything either," she responded in her befuddled state. Now she seemed to be improving and sat up. Her beautiful ring was ever present, sparkling away even if she wasn't. "Look, I'm going to be OK. Just fainted, that's all," she announced suddenly.

"An ambulance is on the way, Smudge," said Splinter.

"Oh, call them back and tell them it's not needed." By this time Smudge had started to get up.

"Are you sure?" Mrs Rigging asked as she picked up the phone again.

"Oh yes, I don't need an ambulance," Smudge replied looking ever better. Splinter looked at her quizzically and spoke to her again.

"Has this ever happened before?"

"No, never," she said firmly.

"Go and see the doctor. Have a check up. Please."

"I'll do that," she mumbled. With that, she got up and walked out into the fresh air followed by the other teachers. Splinter found the whole incident peculiar. Ben had looked on with a feeling of unease. It just did not ring true or strike him as real. The boot was on the other foot now as Ben viewed Smudge with suspicion. It was rather like Smudge viewed Ben. Could she have acted the whole thing and what for?

Ben, Laura and Hitti made their way out into the hallway leading past the main corridor adjacent to the kitchens. As they passed by, the cook's assistant came from the opposite direction spraying something into the air.

"The way that food smells you'd need air freshener," suggested Laura.

"Stinks more like fly spray to me," said Ben. The small crowd of young people were dispersing for the afternoon's activities when Ben felt the familiar handgrip of Tom Cortazzi on his shoulder. For once he was smiling. Ben turned round.

"Hi, Ben. Loved your dance movements last time. You're going great." Ben had become used to Tom and his brash manner. "Could you come early on Monday? I want to go through a bit of the routine with you, so you can show the others out back." Was this a compliment or was Tom trying to use Ben? He wasn't sure. In any case he had other plans that afternoon hadn't he?

"Will it take long because I've got a few problems with that afternoon?"

"If you come at one fifteen it'll be ten or fifteen minutes, just you and me. Our team's not going to be on until about three fifteen or even half past," Tom replied.

You couldn't really refuse Tom. He would probably turn on you if you did. He did the nice guy, nasty guy pressure tactic on people.

"OK. I'll be there then," agreed Ben hastily. What had he let himself in for now? Only time would tell.

CHAPTER 10

The surprise on the shelf

"When is the end of year show, Laura?" asked her mum from the bathroom. It was Monday morning and Laura had already started worrying about the mission to Mr Goving's office. Her mum was in her suite helping her get ready for school and came out of the bathroom with towels in her hand.

"It's about June, Mum. The date's on the school calendar isn't it?" Laura said.

"Oh, I must check. Your dad has in mind a business trip to Rome one weekend in June and the babysitter will have to stay here for you."

"Oh," said Laura, sounding disappointed.

"Don't worry, dear. We won't miss your show. Couldn't possibly." Laura felt relieved.

"Is Ben in the show too?" she asked. She didn't have a clue and was beginning to get on Laura's nerves. Parents never stop asking pointless questions do they?

"I don't know," Laura said. She did know of course but had other things on her mind and needed to stop the barrage of parent questioning. She walked towards her bedroom door. "Got to go early today, Mum. Lessons and rehearsals. Might be a bit late." Detecting her mood, Laura's mother called down the stairs.

"Don't you go doing anything silly today will you? I've got a little supper party tonight; the Van Berkels are coming."

Laura had already unlocked and pulled open one of her large Venetian-style front doors and was heading for the bus stop.

Ben had only just got dressed and was coming down the stairs to have a very quick breakfast. His father was very chirpy that morning.

"Ben, they've come."

"What's that, Dad?" No doubt it would be car parts or a new cold frame for marrows. "The seeds. I'm going to grow courgettes this year as well." He nodded to himself in some form of pleasure. Ben just thought of more mushy dinners.

"That's good, Dad," he said, forcing a smile.

"Yes and when I've got a good crop we'll—" Ben switched off at this point and luckily heard nothing else. His mum never emerged that morning in time to say goodbye after breakfast. She had the courgette announcement to look forward to, thought Ben sarcastically.

Ben wasn't late for his bus and found Laura at the back playing a game on her Nintendo. Ben would never get one. His parents couldn't afford things like that, but he was happy enough all the same. He had a turn and soon they were outside WISPA ready for the day.

*

The afternoon couldn't come quickly enough. Ben, Laura and Hitti had all come with their own packed lunch that day. It was good planning. They went to the junior common room near the canteen to eat it because that was the rule.
As they passed the fateful corridor leading to Mr Goving's office, there was a triangular sign up saying 'out of bounds'.

As they looked up the corridor, they saw that a painter was busy roller painting the ceiling. Whatever would they do now? That was the only route to the head's office apart from the grand entrance they were not allowed to use. They had a debate over their quick lunch.

"Why don't you freeze-frame him, Ben?" suggested Laura.

"Too dangerous. Bound to be seen by someone." Ben was suddenly feeling negative about the whole thing.

"I could try and distract him somehow and you two go down and do whatever," said Hitti. Ben thought for a moment.

"It sounds all right 'til we take too long and he comes back or something." Ben got up and looked out of the window. He saw Mr McKinley talking to one of the groundsmen. He was deep in thought. "I know what to do," he said suddenly. "Let's go."

The three of them left the room and made their way around the corner to the corridor. It was already ten past one and Ben needed to meet Tom soon. He had no time to lose. Laura and Hitti just had to trust that Ben knew what he was doing this time!

"Hi," he said, smiling as sweetly as he could at the painter who was hanging off a stepladder. "Do you mind me asking how you're getting on down there?" The painter was not accustomed to being spoken to by pupils who mostly took no notice. He looked up.

"Not at all. I thought no one would ever ask! It's all good up here thanks, as it happens." He smiled back.

"It's just that we'll need to get down there a bit later on and seeing your sign."

"No bother, me lad. I'm probably finished within the hour anyhow. But if you need to get by before just ask and I'll sort it."

That was a relief and really quite easy thought Ben. He left Laura and Hitti to finish their break and rushed off to meet Tom Cortazzi at the theatre. The moment he stepped onto the stage Tom threw him a white cane. It was the kind you could use in dance routines.

"Glad you remembered," he said in a sinister sort of way. There was no waiting.

"Now watch this, coz I want you to show the others these steps and add them into our routine at the end. OK?"

"Yup," said Ben. Tom set off across the stage with a blistering pace performing tap steps Ben had not learnt before. He was a magnificent dancer for his age. He was dancing around the cane, twiddling it with his fingers and throwing it to catch whilst dancing. Ben looked on in amazement. He felt much more comfortable with the hip hop, street dance they were going to do as their first routine in the show.

"Can you remember that?" Tom asked, looking very directly at Ben. There was a feeling of dread inside Ben.

"Can we do it in stages?" Ben dried up and doubted himself. "Course, of course," Tom spouted reassuringly. "I know you can do it. That's why you're here now and that's why you're in my team. No one has ever done this as a group in the Comp as far as I know." That comment didn't inspire Ben. It just made him feel even more nervous. Tom performed the first part again. Ben had a go. He tried again. A backwards half sit-down and get up manoeuvre was new to him.

Gradually over the next fifteen minutes Ben, who was a very quick learner, mastered the steps. He hadn't quite the poise of Tom, but he *was* about three years younger.

"Ben. You're a genius. I had to find out you see."

"What do you mean?" Ben asked.

"When I was your age, I was shown the steps we've just done. I was told no one had ever done them in a show here in their first year because it's too advanced really. They didn't let me do them that year. I can see you're just like me, Ben. I want us to prove them wrong. You can show the others. All of them except one is older than you and none of them are better." Ben was bowled over by all these compliments.

"What if the others can't do it?"

"Have them do one of the three parts. Not all of it. Only *you* do all of it."

Lots of other people were coming by to get to the changing area, wondering what was going on. Ben rushed off to find his group and organise a meeting to teach them the new steps. How would he fit in his planned trip to Mr Goving's office? His pulse felt fast at the excitement of it all.

Mr McKinley and the other team leaders, Gordon and Fiona, were all milling about giving instructions. Mr McKinley used a backstage microphone.

"Order of events will be announced out front in two minutes. All please come out front of stage."

Ben, Hitti and Laura all sat near to one another. The announcement was made and the three of them worked out that none of them were needed from two o'clock until a quarter to three.

Ben organised two sessions for teaching his group around it. One was right away so he left the auditorium signalling to his team of dancers to follow. That included Hitti as the only other younger member for the Cortazzi tap team. Laura's jazz dance team was to be on at quarter to three and she watched the proceedings for the next twenty minutes or so until the two o'clock window of opportunity arrived. She just slipped off as if going to the girl's room. No one took any notice.

Ben and Hitti were already outside. All three of them were dressed in their dancing clothes, but each had been given characterisations. Ben had a white top and black dancing trousers, ready for part of the routine. He left the hat behind. Hitti had the same but with white trousers and black top. Laura was adorned in a pink, skintight dancing suit.

They made their way to the dreaded corridor leading to Mr Goving's office. The painter was just leaving and picking up his sign.

"Good timing," he pronounced and walked off.

"Right, let's go," said Ben with urgency in his tone. They all walked straight along the corridor and were outside the office in a matter of seconds. The cook had caught sight of these dressed up youngsters and stuck her head out of her kitchen door and looked at them.

"Theatre's that way love," she laughed, pointing back the other way. Ben was in charge still and sighed at this new hurdle.

"Hi. We've forgotten something. Just getting it and back to rehearsals." Cook was not concerned and went back into the kitchens. She had a visitor anyway.

"Come on. I want to be the one to try the door," Laura said under her breath. She had gone into the front position. She put her hand out almost as if she expected an electric shock. In fact Ben had a very odd feeling brewing inside him. Not another visitation he hoped! His hair was standing to attention as if all gelled up. The handle pulled down instantly and Laura pushed the door open. No one there. They all felt a sense of relief and the three of them hopped inside and closed the door.

The shelves were full of so many books and bound-up magazines. Luckily they were marked by their dates. For 1949 there were three on the shelf. They could all see them. But these were floor to ceiling bookshelves and this ceiling was tall, very tall. None of them had a hope of reaching the books without standing on something. Hitti signalled that Mr Goving's chair might do it. Ben shook his head.

He signalled for the others to stand back. He looked very carefully at the three books and went, look—click—lift. They edged their way from the high shelf and came floating gently downwards. But somehow there were four! Ben grabbed at them in the air. One unintended book that came too ended up lying on the floor behind them. Ben handed Hitti and Laura one of the school magazine bound books each.

"Find that article and then we can borrow just the one," whispered Ben. They each thumbed through at lightning pace until Laura indicated it was found. It was a complete article about Sonia Bird and just what they came for. Ben sent the two magazines not needed back to the shelf. Up they floated as he concentrated on them. They were all about to leave when Hitti noticed the extra book still lying on the floor.

"What about that one?" asked Hitti quietly. Ben picked it up without speaking. It was a special school photo album. Laura had already opened the door and didn't know whether to shut it again or just stand still. They all felt an icy cold wind come at them. The sound of insects humming was all around them. It was vile and unfriendly. It felt like a presence. Ben shut the photo book and the chill died away. He looked at the others. This could be important.

"Can we just go?" Hitti implored in his loudest whisper ever. Ben was not listening and Laura was twitching with tension. Ben opened the photo book again and the chilled wind started blowing gently at first but increasing with each second. It fell open at a group photo and the humming, buzzing sound intensified. 1948. There in the centre was one Gareth Streeter, then headmaster and Ben's own great grandfather. Ben's hair was completely standing on end.

"I'm taking this one too," said Ben as he shut the photo album. The wind began to ease. The humming insect sound ceased.

Laura was facing Hitti and Ben with her back to the door she had propped open. Suddenly a hand landed on her shoulder from behind. The large face looking in was none other than Captain Blakey.

He was a retired career soldier who ran the school army cadet training for those that wanted it. He was a huge man, towering above anyone they had ever seen. He was wearing his full army uniform and captains hat at an angle. A little of his gingery hair was visible below the edge of his hat. He had the thickest eyebrows you've ever seen and an evil grin adorned his craggy face.

"What might you three rascals be doing here?" he demanded. He was tapping one of his over-polished black boots on the floor as he spoke. All three of them began to babble at once. "Quiet!" Silence reigned for a second. "I know you. You're that Ben Street aren't you?"

"Yes, Sir," answered Ben in military fashion almost ready to salute.

"I've listened to three different explanations already. One of you is gabbling about forgetting something, another about school reports or school history or something. I want you to tell me the truth young man." Everyone knew about Ben whether he'd properly met them or not. His hair still seemed to be pointing north, but he was calm.

"It's about school history. We're doing our own project on it and needed to borrow something from here because it goes back to the late 1940s. Mr Goving wasn't here, so we just thought we'd look. We'll put them back," Ben pleaded.

Captain Blakey drew in a full lung of air whilst he tried to decide if he believed this explanation. He couldn't think why anyone would want to see these old magazines except for school history study.

"Well, all right. I'm sure the headmaster would want you to ask before you go doing it. You should've waited for another day when he was here."

"I'm sorry," said Ben.

"It's OK. There is a signing out book for these you know." They didn't know. The Captain gave them the benefit of the doubt and counter-signed the two books out just as required. He noted down everyone's names in his little notebook, rather like a policeman.

"Now be on your way. You must be rehearsing today, dressed like that?"

"Yes, Sir," chanted Ben in military style. They made their way back out. Cook stuck her head into the corridor again.

"Captain, those spicy chicken wings dear. Did you want them?"

"Oh, yes please, darling. Enough for fifty like the rest." He turned to the kids he was escorting. "It's my birthday on Sunday and Cook is doing the party food for me. Mr

Goving's coming. I'll mention I signed you out some books." Ben felt a looming fear of seeing Mr Goving after the last time he had spoken to him about their interest in 'school history'. What would he say when told they had borrowed the books? Before they all reached the end of the corridor Cook suddenly screamed out.

"Oh my God!" The Captain marched back up the passage and into the kitchen. In the kitchen on the other side of the wall from the floor to ceiling bookshelves in Mr Goving's office, there was a huge cupboard full of crockery. But Cook had just been to it and found all the crockery on the floor in neat piles, with none broken!

"How the heck?" spluttered the Captain. "We were talking over there." He pointed to the other end of the kitchen about fifteen metres away through an arch. "I didn't hear anything or anyone—"

Ben, Laura and Hitti, hearing the commotion had come back too and looked through to see the amazing sight. Ben gulped. Had some of his kinetic thoughts travelled through the wall? Either way, they decided to make quick their escape. The Captain gave up and had no explanation except some practical jokers may have been involved. He still had some suspicion over the three, but never saw a thing.

The Captain left, walking quickly across the quadrangle and out of sight. He lived in a cottage on the school grounds somewhere, but no one could see it properly. It was very well camouflaged by bushes.

Laura was due on stage any minute. There was no time to lose. All three ran back to the theatre entering via a backstage door. There was Smudge fussing over her choreography moves and speaking in her calm encouraging voice. Laura went to the edge of stage and just managed by a second to tag onto her group of dancers who were joining arms in a movement from the wings straight onto stage. Across she danced and then letting go of each other they continued in formation.

Ben remained backstage where he secreted the magazines in his clothes bag. Dr Metanite was in the changing area getting some equipment out of a cupboard. Ben looked around himself, not sure if anyone noticed him hiding the magazines. He walked around and gathered his team together taking them to a rehearsal room. He was at the door ushering them all in when he noticed Dr Metanite again. He didn't seem to be doing anything, just hovering, holding some props.

"Hullo, Ben. I've been asked to help out backstage today. Smudge can't do it when she's teaching her choreography as well." He hadn't said anything when he saw Ben the first time a minute ago.

Dr Metanite then entered a caged staircase to access the upper levels of the theatre where some scenery controls were placed. Ben was looking at him from below as he walked up a few steps. Without thinking about it, he accidentally clicked his eyes on him with a 'move thought' in his head. Dr Metanite moved upwards rapidly and gave out a little squeak of surprise. Ben, realising his mistake had no time to consider the best course of action. He just looked—clicked and freeze-framed Dr Metanite to the top step. Ben's team were asking for him to get on with it, in the rehearsal room. He was in the doorway and seemed to be waiting for nothing. So he had no choice but to leave the doctor motionless, high in the theatre's backstage. In the back of his mind Ben worried that someone would see him before he could sort it out. He had better move quickly!

He continued showing the team all the extra routine steps Tom had taught him earlier. They worked very hard at it especially because Ben and not Tom was teaching them. Perhaps that was Tom's plan. They sang one of the song's verses to warm up their voices.

They were nearly finished when suddenly they all heard the sound of shouting outside. No doubt about it; that was the voice of Smudge. Ben opened the door.

"Where the hell is my ring? Who's got it? It must be here somewhere," she raged. Smudge without her famous ring? No one could remember seeing that. As she ranted and raved moving around backstage the racket was so loud it was permeating through to the auditorium. Mr McKinley began to look perplexed at the noise.

"Can you be quiet out back," he balled, not registering it was Smudge causing the row. Others were joining in the call for calm. The good mood in the theatre evaporated to one of sheer irritation. Ned passed the screaming Smudge and shouted back at her.

"It wasn't on when you arrived!" She was stunned into silence. The show continued on stage whilst she stood still, not wanting to believe what she had just heard. After a very long pause she regained control of herself and spoke in her usual voice.

"It must be here. I saw it on my finger only a short time before this session began. Everyone start looking," she ordered.

Luckily no one was missing Dr Metanite still frozen to the spot, but out of the way. Ben knew he must undo this situation and fast before someone noticed. He went round the corner and looked upwards. Look—click—move. He could see a confused Dr Metanite just carrying on to his destination and looking at the stage pulleys. It was the longest time by far Ben had freeze-framed anyone; about fifteen minutes. What a risk of discovery that was!

By now news of the missing ring had reached Mr McKinley who temporarily stopped the show for everyone to look. Nothing was found and the show was restarted.

The Cortazzi team were called on. Ben, Hitti and the others bowled onto the stage with renewed enthusiasm. They were all dressed in a group style and hip hopped away in a street dance type routine doing their crip walks, knee drops, glides and slides in great style. They stopped to change into tap dance shoes and returned after another short act performed.

Finally, they tapped away in an amazingly complex routine as they sang together. Ben had a few lines of the song to himself, which pleased him. They were all over the stage, tapping in unison and singly or in pairs as the routine dictated. There was one stumble about half way. Even so Mr McKinley knew he had not seen the like of it before. It ended to considerable applause from the watching pupils. Tom Cortazzi beamed like a Cheshire cat.

Despite their strong performance it was still true the competition was very tough this year. Ben left the stage fairly breathless. He had been in every part of the routine. Laura had already changed and waited for Ben and Hitti in the theatre auditorium. There were one or two more performances to go. Ben gave a little wave from the side curtain and Laura joined them backstage. Just as they were about to leave they overheard Smudge speaking to Dr Metanite.

"I'll just have to go and retrace my steps. I can't be without my ring. Can you cope here and uhmm—"

"Don't worry, not much left to do here. It'll be somewhere," he said with feeling. That was unusual for him. His spindly fingers ushered Smudge away in a surprisingly kindly manner. He was fond of Smudge and in a peculiar way she was fond of him. He saw Ben.

"I don't think I'll go up there again. Something seemed to come over me," he said pointing up the steps. Ben didn't know what to say and wondered by the tone of it whether Dr Metanite had some suspicion of him.

"Are you OK now?" asked Ben, trying to give nothing away.

"Yes thanks, just a bit dizzy." By now Smudge had left the back entrance. Laura and Hitti were waving vigorously at the doorway for Ben to hurry up. He trotted off and out they went.

"Come on, I want to follow Smudge," said Hitti excitedly.

"What's up?" asked Ben.

"Didn't you see the way she went on about that ring? She went loopy," Hitti exclaimed.

"She was upset. So what?"

"Her face said there's something weird about it all. No one's ever heard her screaming like that. I wanna know where she goes on the hunt for that ring." Ben was walking quickly to keep up with Hitti and Laura. Smudge was right on the other side of the quadrangle now.

"She just lost a ring and threw a wobbly. That's it," offered Ben confidently.

"No. Hitti's right," began Laura. "There's something not right with that woman. We saw her a couple of weeks ago being pretty odd when Bertie was frozen by the shed. Remember?"

Ben decided to go along with it. All he actually wanted to do was go home and look at the school photo book he had borrowed earlier.

Smudge was seen entering the school chapel. She never went to services there so far as anyone knew. Ben, Laura and Hitti peered through the glass canopy into the front of the chapel. Smudge was on her hands and knees looking under the pews. She kept on looking about herself like some common shop thief about to steal.

After a few minutes, she left the chapel and virtually tiptoed to the library. Keeping their distance Ben and the others positioned themselves in some bushes outside. The long windows allowed them to keep watch. She was seen in the science aisle. Not even her subject, Ben was thinking when without warning Smudge moved right up next to the window nearest them. She looked out from inside just past them and seemed to have a look of surprise on her face. Ben noticed part of Laura's bag sticking out in full view! He pulled Laura's arm to indicate a departure was required.

All three reversed out as quickly as a bat flying from a belfry. They scuffled their way into the covered corridor area. The theatre was emptying. The Comp rehearsal must have just finished. Smudge would have to re-enter the corridor area herself to exit the courtyard entrance to the library.

A moment later she appeared and found Laura, Ben and Hitti apparently reading school notices. She looked carefully at their bags as she went by saying nothing. Laura had forced her bag into Hitti's. Laura looked at Smudge's ring finger as she passed. It had a mark around it.

"She is just so suspicious of us. It isn't just about where her ring went. I reckon she's spying on us. And you know what?" asked Laura intrigued by what she saw.

"No," said Ben and Hitti together.

"That ring was on very tight. Her finger had a deep red mark on it. I can't see how it would fall off."

"Maybe she took it off and forgot what she did with it? She's probably going home now anyway," said Ben dismissively. However as they watched, her slim frame was seen to enter the science labs. She didn't teach science and so their interest increased. The three investigators kept an eye on the building. After waiting about ten minutes Hitti indicated it was enough for him.

"She might have left by some other door out back. I think we should pack it in for now." All agreed and made their way to the bus stop. Laura retrieved her bag from inside Hitti's and they waited on the pavement chatting about the school magazine and photo book they had borrowed. It was agreed they would look at it together the following day and Ben would just take both books home for safe-keeping. Just as they'd given up on Smudge she came down a pathway that sided some terraced homes opposite the school.

"Look at the smile on her face," said Ben now feeling more curious than ever.

"Must have found her ring," commented Hitti. They could only see her top half over a low garden wall that was between them and her. When she emerged to the roadside it could be seen that she was holding about three or four jam jars. They looked green enough to contain chutney or apple sauce even under street lamps.

Ben wondered about the green shade of the substances in those jars! It just did not look quite like anything he had normally seen in a jar. She crossed the road, went to the school entrance and out of view. None of them could actually see whether the ring had re-appeared on her finger.

"More jam jars!" said Laura. "See, Ben. There's something about her. You can see that now can't you?"

"Laura, I saw it by the time she was in the library," Ben replied thinking it all through. "Maybe she overheard us talking about Sonia's murder," he whispered. "I wonder if she knows something and is covering it up?"

"She's certainly weird, but I can't see how the ring incident means much," remarked Hitti. Ben was itching to get home. He already knew he would not be able to resist looking at the school photo book, whatever he said earlier.

It was not very long before Ben was walking down Macey Avenue with a little skip in his step that late afternoon. There was progress in all he had achieved that day. He used his house key and went in the front door to the Street family's tiny hallway.

"Hi, Mum," he called towards the kitchen. There was steam blowing about and the smell of cooking as usual.

"Glad your back love," she said lovingly. "Your dad's just phoned to say he'd be late, but we can have our tea anyhow."

"What's up? Something at work?" asked Ben as he put his bag on the coat peg. He unzipped a section and took out just the photo book.

"He's advising on gardening at the skittles club. Says they wanna to grow veg and seeing how he's an expert."

"He'll love that," said Ben mustering just a little enthusiasm. Ben was not sure if he should show his mum the photos after what happened in Mr Goving's office. The book was in his hand and he found himself ambling into the kitchen during his conversation. Mrs Street was well on the

156

way to finishing supper. It was butter beans in tomato sauce and with a cheese and bacon topping. Not too bad, thought Ben. He decided to go and get changed.

"What's that book then?" said his mum, before he could leave the room.

"It's old school photos. There's one with great grandad in it, so I—"

"Ooh, your dad's gonna be well interested in that." Ben started to open the book.

"Show me at supper love," added his mum as she started to empty a hot saucepan of steaming beans into a dish. A chill wind blew across them both and a distinct insect buzz entered the room. The steam went sideways.

"Blimey, what was that?" she screeched. Ben shrugged his shoulders, but he knew didn't he? Something was in that book and he was going to be the one that must get it out. He left for his bedroom and as he stomped up the stairs he heard his mum call out again.

"Ten minutes, Ben." He carefully shut his bedroom door and plopped onto his bed. Ben concentrated on the book of school photos. 1948 was printed in gold letters down the spine of this bound book. It seemed ancient to Ben, but it was only twenty years before his dad was born. It had obviously spent so long on a shelf that it appeared almost new. How and why did this book hold some chilling power? Two cold eerie winds had already come out of it today. Ben could not know what would happen if he held it open, but there was no alternative.

He opened it slowly, right in the middle. The book creaked liked an old wooden door as it gently released itself with a rising humming noise. The wind gathered pace, blowing from the centre until it felt like a small gale blowing in his tiny bedroom. It was as cold as ice. Ben had a job to hold on to the book. It was trying to blow out of his hands with a tremendous force and his hands were white with the freezing wind. Ben looked at his curtains and they were still as a duck pond. Nothing was affected except him.

157

He heard a wailing noise and a male, evil laughing sound above the hum of a buzzing insect nest. He was fearful, but somehow felt he had been chosen to beat this thing.

He fought with the wind trying to look downwards. It was forcing his chin up as he pushed in an effort to look down at the photograph. He was determined and pushed down with all his might. He caught sight of his great grandfather. But what would cause this extreme power?

The photograph began to detach from the book. It was becoming three dimensional and seemed to want to leave the book altogether. It urged its way out of the book to appear like a hologram. Sitting next to great grandfather was another teacher Ben presumed. The name at the bottom of the photo could be seen. It was Mr Tim Dreante.

Ben knew he'd already heard of that name. It was the teacher in charge when Sonia Bird was killed. Ben looked at the picture with steely determination and refused to look away. The face of Tim Dreante appeared as a misty blank. His hair seemed visible as did his clothes, but all facial features were otherwise missing. That confirmed Ben's worst fears. The plight of Sonia had something to do with this past teacher. He didn't recognise any of the other teachers. The wind began to subside and the warmth started to return to his fingers. They had never been so cold and were quite pink with the experience.

"Supper's on the table," came the call from downstairs. Ben composed himself.

"Coming, Mum," he replied. He opened the book again very slightly. No wind. He opened it more. Nothing happened. He chuckled to himself, pleased that he seemed to have purged the book of some peculiar power. Would it last though? He put the book away in his bag. He couldn't show it to his mum, not with that blank face in it. There'd be another picture of his great grandfather somewhere he hoped.

The supper was surprisingly good and Ben was very hungry. He had only eaten a few mouthfuls when the phone rang.

"I'll get it," offered Ben, hoping it was for him anyway. He went quickly to the hallway and picked up the receiver.

"Hi, Ben," said Laura, "I need to talk to you urgently." Her greeting tone had changed immediately from normal to worried.

"What's up?" Ben asked, concerned already.

"I was going upstairs at home about ten minutes ago when a sudden rush of cold wind came past me with that buzzing noise. Then, I was in my bedroom just a few minutes ago, when the most violent cold wind I have ever experienced blew at me. It was freezing and I could barely move, Ben. It'll be to do with that stupid ghost of yours," Laura screeched.

Ben had never heard her speak like it before and her worried tone was turning to anger. Ben heaved in a lungful of air.

"I'm *so* sorry. I really, really am," he accentuated. "I reckon it was the photo book"

"Ben, *you* have the photo book!" she said very directly. Ben swallowed wondering what mayhem he had caused. He would have to admit it.

"It's just that I opened it and out came that cold wind, like you're on about. I wasn't going to let it beat me and held it open. Then it stopped. It must have connected to you somehow." There was a lengthy silence.

"Hullo, are you still there?" Ben asked.

"I am, Ben. But I'm furious, you frightening me like that! We agreed we'd look at this stuff together. At least I would have known what it was when this wind came out!" she choked. Laura was almost in tears over it. Ben couldn't apologise enough and promised not to touch it before they met with Hitti at school. He put the phone down and went back to the dining area to finish his supper.

"Something up?" enquired his mum. She had heard all the apologising.

"Oh, Laura didn't want me to look at the photo book."

"Well how would she know you did and why would she mind?" asked his mum quite astutely. Ben was fast going into hot water over this explanation.

"Well, I said I wouldn't coz we're going to study it together, but when she rang about something. I had to admit I had looked in it." Did this add up? His mum mulled it over for a moment.

"Anyhow, you were going to show it to me. Where is it?" she said, enquiringly between mouthfuls. Ben had to think quickly but what could he say?

"It isn't the right photo of great grandad I want you to see that's in there."

"But it is a photo of him isn't it?" she pressed.

"Erm, yes," he replied reluctantly.

"Well, we can see it and see the other one another day," she insisted. Ben knew he was stuck with it. After supper he went to his room. He quickly flicked through the photo book and no strange events happened to his relief. He noticed another photo of great grandad at the front of the book. He was with some pupils. His mum could see that one. He just hoped she'd not notice the other strange photo with the faceless Mr Dreante in it. Ben's father came in the front door as Ben arrived at the bottom of the stairs.

"Hey, Ben. I've been invited to judge the Skittles club annual gardeners show!"

"Oh—good," said Ben instinctively. His dad was so pleased and went straight to tell his wife the news, with Ben following into the living room. After the congratulations were over, the photo book had to be seen. Ben held it open and cleverly showed them both just the black and white print he wanted them to see.

"I CAN SEE THE FAMILY RESEMBLANCE. HE LOOKS QUITE LIKE GRANDAD AT ABOUT THAT AGE," REMARKED HIS DAD. WHEN THEY APPEARED SATISFIED HE WHISKED IT AWAY TO HIS SCHOOL BAG ONCE MORE.

CHAPTER 11

The 'Bickie'

Ben managed to catch an earlier bus for school than Laura and Hitti the following morning. The first he saw of them was when they approached the locker area outside their form classroom. He had already been looking at the busy schedule that faced them in the next week.

"Hi," he said to both. Hitti came straight out with it.

"Ben, I've had this freezing wind frightening me like Laura had. And the noise. I thought I'd be attacked by a nest of wasps or something." No doubt Hitti and Laura had chatted on the bus.

"I want out of this now! I've had enough. I was in the bath, when the water came up around my throat and this massive wind froze me. It made ice form on the bathwater right round my neck!"

Ben was shocked and fell off his feet onto the nearest bench in the corridor. He had put both the 'borrowed' books in his locker. When he recovered his composure he took Laura and Hitti to one side.

"Look, I'm really sorry, but we're near to finding something. I can feel it. I reckon I now know why it was me that started getting messages and weird powers. It's to do with my great grandad," Ben said thinking they would instantly understand.

"Your great grandad!" Laura and Hitti shouted together. Other people looked over at them.

"Ssshh," said Ben putting his finger across his lips. He quickly explained his family name change from Streeter to Street and therefore his connection to the former headmaster Gareth Streeter in the 1940s.

"Look, Hitti, I understand if you don't want to be part of it anymore, but I have no choice."

"I'll think about it," said Hitti.

"There's nothing we can do about it this week anyway. The schedule's so full I can't believe it." They all agreed Ben was right about that. The books were destined to stay in Ben's locker for a while yet.

*

This was the week in which the annual 'Bickie' took place. The name went back long before anyone could recall. The first three letters stood for 'Bike In Costume'. This had evolved into the word 'Bickie' as a kind of nickname for the event. It had all the letters for 'Bike' in it and seemed apt.

There was to be a bike race of about fifteen kilometres all done in costumes. All pupils and staff were invited to take part, this Friday. The very oldest costumes, no longer used by the school were saved for this event. There were prizes for the best character outfit and the first three across the finishing line. This meant the scramble to choose a costume was an important part of the day.

It was Friday morning and a very strange sight indeed greeted pupils and staff alike as they arrived that day. Smudge was riding into the school smiling. Her enormous ring had reappeared and it was on display. No doubt she was up for the Bickie. She had already dressed in her costume.

She was wearing a Victorian-style cream coloured frock with frilly bloomers showing beneath it and a small crown.

Her progress was quite rapid. She rang her bell as she went rounding the corner of the main building towards the bike sheds. She didn't seem to bother that people were moving out of the way to avoid her! Her bicycle moved along smoothly and without slowing, she rode straight into a bike slot wedging her front wheel in very firmly. The force of her instant halt made the rear of the bike fly up like a bucking horse. She held onto the handlebars tightly as the back end of the bike bounced back down with a thud onto the ground.

She was still smiling like a tipsy teen. Smudge swung off the contraption sideways in a very ladylike fashion. Picking up her period satchel, she strode off in the direction of the staff common room, looking just like a film extra. She skipped up the steps and burst through the door in a very theatrical way, screeching, "Eureka! I'm fully trained for the Bickie." There were a few grunts from the three or four teachers already in attendance. Smudge was the only one who had arrived togged up.

Mr Goving arrived by car as usual and parked in his designated spot opposite the museum. Ben, Hitti and Laura were wandering past on their way to the costume store as Mr Goving opened his car door and emerged with a large handful of papers in an elastic band.

"Ahh, the school history brigade," he announced, as if there was an audience. "The Captain told me you'd had him sign out some books," he said jovially. Goodness, thought Ben. He must have changed his mind about us after our telling off.

"Oh, yes we did Mr Goving. I hope you didn't mind," replied Ben very politely. The others kept quiet.

"Mind? Of course not. The resource is there to be used. Let me know how you get on. Maybe you could do something for next term's magazine, eh?" Was it possible he'd swallowed their excuse they gave last term for being at school so late? Either that or his memory was going. None of them had expected this positive attitude from Mr Goving. It was a considerable relief, peppered with a new problem.

"Can I think about it?" asked Ben, knowing he wasn't interested in the slightest about writing an article for the school magazine.

"Tell Stewbog. He edits it." Mr Goving went inside the building to go to his office.

A short stroll later and Ben, Laura and Hitti had joined the queue for costumes. The door hadn't been opened and there were at least one hundred eager participants in line. The building was probably an old wooden boathouse and not in great shape.

Without any notice, the double doors were flung open from the inside. The one hundred pupils pushed their way in like an endless scrum. The girls were worse than the boys. Did anyone know what he or she wanted? Ben was none too sure. He found himself carried along in the crowd. Once inside, everyone spread out and started pulling at costumes, one after another, looking for the perfect fit or style. Ben saw outfits from musicals of old, Shakespearean-type clothing, chain mail, wigs, joke costumes, devil outfits, roman togas and any other style you could mention. This ill-lit den of character outfitting was heaving with activity.

Ben looked hard and settled on a King Arthur costume, complete with chain mail and red cross on white background. The chain mail was a woollen knitted material sprayed with silver paint to look realistic. He checked it out with the attendant who put his name on a list.

Hitti meanwhile had found himself a footman's suit, rather like you'd see being worn by those outside a posh hotel.

Laura was still looking and they had to wait a few more minutes. She emerged already wearing her outfit; a blue cat suit complete with tail.

"Where did you get into that?" asked Hitti, thinking of the masses of onlookers.

"I just went in an old changing cubicle I found out the back," she chuckled.

"It looks great," enthused Ben. There was only about thirty minutes to go before the race began. A vast juggernaut truck pulled into the school grounds opposite the pool complex. It had bikes for everyone, all the same and unisex with a low crossbar. No one could have an advantage by the type of cycle they rode unless they were one of the staff with their own like Smudge. Not that hers was an advantage.

A large crowd of expectant onlookers was gathering on the school playing fields where the race would begin. They comprised locals and many parents. Laura's parents were there much to her annoyance. They stood behind a long tapeline supposed to keep them in check. The trouble for Laura was that her mother would call out so everyone heard. As the cyclists lined up at the start she began.

"Laura, darling! Go, go, go, my cat girl," she screeched in a nauseatingly posh English accent. As there were so many entrants, they formed a crowd of costumed cyclists at the starting line. Bunting had been erected so the school looked ready for an Olympic event. They lined up in eager anticipation.

Mr Goving was there with a starting pistol wearing his overcoat. Stewbog had a loudhailer and liked to do a commentary of the beginning and end of the race, more like a horse event. Even before it began the rain started to fall, lightly at first.

"Just a few drops," Mr Goving was heard to say. "At the sound of the pistol you may start!" shouted Mr Goving reaching into Stewbog's loudhailer. "On your marks, get ready, BANG." The pistol rang out drowning the word, go, which Mr Goving shouted. Stewbog was ready:

"And, they're off, with Splinter up the front in a fine musketeer get-up flanked by Josephs as Ratty and Montague in full police regalia on the chase. Look at her go! Smudge as Queen Victoria followed by Matt Fingle in a puppet suit." Stewbog did not draw breath. "Here comes Tom Cortazzi as the devil himself. No change there, with

Gina Watson as the Angel Gabriel moving up from the outside, harp at the ready. Look at Johnson the Tin Man thrusting forward into third place behind the leaders. It's Ricky Lund leading as Richard the Third by a neck to Ned Elliott, Roman Emperor Caesar. Back comes Millie Montague trying to arrest the situation. I think she has it from Caesar and the Tin Man. Pushing from the rear is King Arthur Ben Street making headway into the centre ground grouping nicely with Rear Admiral Mrs Rigging, entertaining us all this afternoon. On the inside gaining ground is Archbishop Gordon Munzer, pressing into fourth place now from Caesar but still trailing Sergeant Millie Montague firmly in second place as they reach the first kilometre."

The commentary continued unabated. But the weather was changing rapidly. The slightly grey dripping sky was darkening and hard rain began to fall. Some teachers were muttering into the headmaster's ear about calling it off because all the costumes would be ruined, but he refused.

"They've set off. I'm not disappointing them now," he fumed at the suggestion.

Mrs Munday couldn't keep her embarrassing voice down. "Can't see the Archbish anywhere," she bawled. Of course, being a parent she had no understanding of how silly she sounded and looked. At least the cyclists had deliberately dressed for amusement. Mrs Munday was wearing a cocktail dress of black and white silk and a light overcoat, with matching hat, as if she was at the races. Not only that, she was dripping with jewellery. Other parents were mostly sanely dressed in normal clothes.

The first fifty or so had safely passed the drawbridge across the canal and were chasing up the muddy towpath in pairs and threes. Ben was steadily making ground, as the race was becoming a battle of distinct groups. The cyclists had spread out across the course. One young fellow named Roger Lawson had dressed as a first world war motorcyclist and strapped a piece of cardboard to his front bicycle fork to sound like a motorbike. It was causing considerable annoyance.

As Ben went by, he locked his eyes momentarily onto the cardboard. Look—click—pull, he thought. This immediately dislodged the cardboard. Ben looked back as he overtook. Unfortunately for Roger Lawson, Ben had inadvertently also undone his front wheel nuts. Ben saw the front wheel wobble for a second or two and then come clean away from his cycle, causing his front bicycle forks to dig themselves straight into the mud. Poor Roger was flung straight over his handlebars and onto the muddy ground beneath.

As Ben looked back for a second time, he saw Roger up on his feet holding the detached front cycle wheel mystified by what had happened. Ben pulled up behind a group of four who were battling it out, probably twenty-five from the leaders who were all ahead but out of sight.

Roger's plight had given Ben a mischievous thought. It was not that he wanted to win the race by cheating, but he could have some fun couldn't he? The rain was now pelting down. No one's costume would survive this. Many were like drowned rats already.

The only problem for Ben was that he was never quite sure of the exact effect his kinetic power would have. He had tried using various command words and different things had occurred. His practising had only shown him how limitless the power was, but not how he could control its every move.

The next group ahead of Ben comprised four, led by the devil-dressed Tom Cortazzi and his followers who all seemed to be dressed as henchmen. Ben was about three metres behind when he saw a convenient and very large puddle approaching. As soon as all four were entering the puddle, Ben looked hard at their rear wheels. He went look—click—and unscrew. To Ben's surprise nothing happened. He almost fell off himself with the shock.

Ben was now only two metres behind. There was a gap of several seconds when suddenly without warning, young Longwragg, one of the henchmen, fell off into a mangled heap. His bike chain was twisting and his rear wheel edging away. Ben swerved to avoid him, but as he did, Bligh, the next henchman, fell sideways as his biked seized up, throwing him off into Ben's path. He manoeuvred again and saw Tom still peddling furiously at the front, oblivious to the disappearing followers. They had barely made a sound from the shock of their sudden unexpected dismounting.

I'll try again with these two, schemed Ben to himself. Ben pushed harder and harder at his pedals in an effort to overtake. Very slowly he gained ground and was now level with Tom. Up ahead was a stream that had to be crossed somehow. It was running at a fierce pace.

"You'll never beat me, Ben," shouted Tom, who was reluctant to allow this surge from Ben to take effect. The last henchman riding alongside was actually a girl dressed as boy, called Juliet Baring. So there was the three of them hurtling towards the water as fast as they could. Ben knew this would be his chance. He swished through the muddy path throwing up filth with all his might and cleanly overtook Tom and Juliet. He had pulled in front and had every intention of cycling right through the shallow stream.

As he looked over his shoulder he saw the Rear Admiral, Mrs Rigging, in the distance cycling fast and smiling. There was no one else in view except Tom and Juliet just behind him. He looked back and prepared for the stream ahead, pushing at least five metres ahead of them. Here comes the stream! One, two, three and through Ben flew.

During his passage through the watery crossing, Ben turned his head for a second or so and, look—click—water freeze, he thought, concentrating on the stream.

Tom and Juliet reached the water about a second later, too late to even realise what was happening. Tom slid sideways at break-neck pace skewing into an unwieldy Juliet over the few metres of frozen ice that had instantaneously formed. Both ended up in a heap on the ground. Ben was cycling away feeling a little mean, but he had his wits about him. Look—click—water unfreeze, he imagined. The water became the wet runny stuff once more; almost the same second Tom and Juliet hit it from their fall.

Tom and Juliet had fallen into water and mud not ice. By this time 'Ropy the Rear Admiral Mrs Rigging', had gained ground on them all and was within thirty metres of this mangled duo of devil and girl henchman. What on earth would she make of it? Ben felt worried, thinking he could have gone a step too far? But he couldn't change it now and raced on.

He had the leading two packs of cyclists in his sights as he pushed uphill towards Starboard Meadow, the great expanse of green near the school and a major part of the circuit. Mrs Rigging stopped to help Tom and Juliet.

"Are you all right?" she queried as she dismounted her mountain bike. "I saw you both go down," she added walking over to help untangle the humans from the bikes and bike chains. Neither spoke and were still plainly speechless at what occurred. "Well, I don't know. I've never seen so many fallen heroes in my life," she said, referring to the others she had passed on the ground or getting up. Tom managed to untie his tongue.

"It went just like an ice rink. I didn't see anything, but it was so slippery it was ridiculous," he complained. "That blo..."

"Hey," Mrs Rigging interrupted, enforcing good behaviour. "There'll be no swearing in my presence." She kindly bent down, with her boots in the shallow stream and pulled up Juliet's bike. It had caught its chain around her stripey wide bottomed pants and seized up. Mrs Rigging turned the rear wheel back and she became free. Juliet jumped up and brushed off the mud and wet from her side. Tom was still stuck underneath his bike. Mrs Rigging had to pull him up with the bicycle and found his devil tail had lodged into the rear wheel spokes. A quick yank and it was released.

"No one has caught up with us even now. You can choose to carry on or go back. Up to you," she beamed. She had no inkling of the real cause of this chaos. She pushed her own bike through the water whilst on foot and remounted, pedalling away at a good pace. Juliet couldn't believe what she thought she saw.

"That looked like an ice sheet, Tom," she exclaimed. "It felt like that when we slid over."

"I never saw any ice," replied Tom with incredulity in his voice. "It's water! Probably just the wet weather that did it," said Tom not sure what he believed. By now Tom felt some suspicion over Ben's involvement, but Ben had been ahead of them, so how could it have been his fault?

He brushed off the filth and wet as best he could. The rain had already made it very wet and heavy. However he was determined not to give up. Both of them set off again and quickly passed Mrs Rigging again, still smiling. There were others not far behind who had caught up due to their mishap.

Ahead of Ben was Hitti, in a group of five contestants, doing very well in his drenched and dirty footman's uniform. They were no more than twenty-five metres away but going over the crest of the hill down into the meadow. Ben felt a surge of power as he looked behind him to see Tom and Juliet some way off. In the extreme distance he could just make out the vague form of Rear Admiral Mrs Rigging.

Whilst all this was happening, Dr Metanite was still in the science labs. He was not a very sociable man at the best of times and devoted to his science research. The idea of him joining the fun of the Bickie would be madness. He was the only staff member not either watching or participating.

Ned was right. He was nuts in his own way. The school had regarded him highly as their mainstay of science for many years.

The cleaner, Marjorie Sims, was doing her bit around the labs and could hear Dr Metanite from the corridor outside in full swing. She heard gurgling and bubbling and boiling and croaking coming from his laboratory. She'd heard it all many times before and no doubt would hear it all again. She often wondered what it was all about, but assumed him to be a 'mad scientist' type. The sort of person so engrossed in their craft they don't even notice their own appearance or even care.

That day she felt the corridor was very warm and she noticed a large number of flies were circling around and by the doctor's doorway. He must have made something attractive to them, Marjorie thought. She carried on mopping the tiled floor and gradually made her way towards the lab. Of course she had a key. So out it came on a piece of string attached to her cleaning pinny. She unlocked the door and pushed it, wedging it open with her vacuum cleaner whilst she went to unplug it in the corridor. She had a trolley for mops and cleaning gunk that she pushed through into the lab. Instinctively she greeted the doctor.

"Hullo, Doctor," she said as she shoved the trolley and awaited the reply. Busy bending down to get her cloth for the next task, she hadn't really looked across the room. There was no reply, just a pungent smell of acid and chemicals and the sound of those pesky flies buzzing around. "Are you here, Doctor?" she called. She frowned and opened a window to relieve the stench a little.

As she turned back, the doctor emerged from behind his large desk on a raised platform at the other side of the room, clutching his stomach.

"Yes," he coughed, sounding like a person choking.

"Is something wrong, Doctor?" Marjorie questioned anxiously. He looked a bit pale and was clearly having difficulty breathing.

"A bit of asthma. I was just inhaling when you came in," he replied, speaking in his unusual voice.

"You had me worried for a minute there," she said relieved. She saw he had a variety of laboratory receptacles out on display, attached by tubes and a couple of empty ordinary jars sat at the end clearly having contained a green or brown liquid. The doctor made no comment and continued tinkering. It was bubbling away at one end and a substance was being gradually produced into a glass beaker at the other. The doctor was making notes in a book on his desk as he watched the experiment progress.

"These flies are becoming a nuisance. Shall I speak to Bertie and see if he can spray something round here for it?"

"No need Marj. Spoke to him the other day about it. These things are cyclical and the wet weather's bringing them in I fancy," he replied quite excitedly almost as if he was quite happy about the flies and just making a feeble excuse. It was the most conversation Marj had experienced with the doctor in years. What was this potion the doctor was making? It all looked much the same every time Marj saw it and that was over years and years. For once Marj decided to ask.

"I know it's none of my business, but may I ask what you are working on today, Doctor?" she said very politely.

"It's isotopes," he said coldly. "I work on isotopes and molecular structure mostly," he added without batting an eyelid. That put paid to any other conversation didn't it?

Marj didn't have the foggiest notion what Dr Metanite meant. The wind kicked up in a wild gust at that moment and forced itself into the laboratory, through the open windows with considerable ferocity. Suddenly the warmth vanished together with the flies and all returned to calm. Marj completed her minimal cleaning.

"See you, Doctor," she said bidding him goodbye. He mumbled some response. He was often there you see and Marj knew it would not be long before she saw him again. There was no need to say anything else. She left with her trolley heading towards the toilets next door.

As she went back into the corridor it felt cold, in fact very cold. Marj began to wonder if she was ill, blowing hot and cold like this. The science block had a temperature chart in the corridor and colours showed the temperature. Marj looked across at it. Strange spring, she thought. It's showing nearly freezing. But it was much warmer earlier she remembered. She shrugged her shoulders and went into the toilets with her trolley, leaving the vacuum cleaner outside.

In the Bickie, Ben had passed the hillcrest and freewheeled at a breathtaking speed into Starboard Meadow and most of the way across it. He was now only two or three metres behind Hitti and four others. There was Jenny Holt as a mad hatter, Mick Mercer as a priest, Yasmin Flaxing as a rooster and Sallyanne Niarchos as a grim reaper all accompanying Hitti as a footman.

Ben's chain mail felt very hot and he had undone it at the front. Not that you could easily tell what his costume or anybody else's was any longer. They were all so covered with mud and grime and soaking with rain that they were merging in appearance.

Ben panted along behind the pack. He looked behind him and no cyclists could be seen due to the terrain. But he suspected they were not very far behind. The entire group just in front of him veered through a chicane-like sweep, the roadway passing through a lightly forested zone on the edge of the meadow. No one else in sight.

Ben looked at the five just ahead of him. He couldn't resist it. Look—click—freeze-frame. The cyclists halted, statue-like, so instantly that Ben nearly crashed into the grim reaper at the back, narrowly averting his own catastrophe. He passed ahead and not quite out of sight before he turned and—look—click—unfreeze. Instantly he saw them continue as if they hadn't stopped and their forward inertia was uninterrupted.

Ben hurried on having in his sights the two leading packs of cyclists. In fact he could see them ahead returning to the school grounds over the bridge across the canal. They had now become one large pack of leaders, about ten of them. The sight of Richard the Third, the Tin Man, Caesar and a policewoman in hot pursuit with others, was causing huge gales of laughter amongst the passers by walking their dogs or rambling across the meadow. The rain had eased but the mud had not! The spray coming from these cycles was quite tremendous.

There was Splinter still going strong next to the Archbishop amongst the rearguard, his fake musket hanging off his back like some bit of silvery driftwood. Ben could not easily catch them up in time although still gaining ground. They were back on the school playing fields and making their way across the one hundred acres to the finishing post. Ben went over the bridge into school territory.

Suddenly he could hear cheers from the expectant crowd as the leading pack came into distant view. The muffled sound of the loudhailer had begun again. Ben was now about two hundred metres from this pack. Behind him the group containing Hitti were also gaining ground. It was the last frantic push.

Unexpectedly, Ben saw Tom had now overtaken the group behind him. He was rapidly closing the gap on Ben. He noticed Tom was smiling and holding something as he rode, but he couldn't make out what it was. He looked again and noticed it was a piece of tree branch about one metre long. As Tom grew closer still, he called out.

"Ben, I'll have you. Dunno how you got up in front, but I'll have you!" he cried menacingly. Ben did not reply but tried to stay ahead. Without warning Tom put on a huge effort with all the energy he could muster and drew alongside Ben just long enough to shove his metre long stick straight into the spokes of his rear wheel.

There was an almighty crack that was heard right as far as the waiting crowd in school. The wooden branch momentarily slowed Ben's cycle, but then split in half and

175

fell to the ground with the thrust of his forward motion. It had not pulled him off his bike! Ben carried on cycling to the sound of Tom cursing and panting behind him, obviously slowing up. Tom was a spent force.

Ben thought Millie Montague dressed as the policewoman so funny, with her enormous comedic black footwear; he wanted to give her a chance. She was flanked on either side by other eager cyclists. She was boxed in beside the Archbishop who had moved forward with Richard the Third on the other side and Caesar just in front as the current leader.

What could Ben do now they were all in view? Ben thought carefully, looked forward and concentrated intensely behind Millie's bike. Look—click—blow wind, he thought. A rush of cool air brushed past them, separating the front pack and gently opening the opportunity for Millie to have a go. I can't leave it there, Ben considered. Again he tried with kinetic power aiming to keep it subtle.

Look—click—blow wind. He concentrated just on Millie this time. She floated forward about two metres ahead of everyone. That's it, decided Ben. If she has it in her to maintain the lead, then she deserves to win.

Hitti had all but caught Ben up and had long since overtaken Tom. They were both beginning to feel the heat of the battle and their pace was gently flagging.

"How did you pass me?" panted Hitti from behind. "We never saw you overtake."

"Dunno. You just didn't notice me s'pose," said Ben.

Stewbog was in full swing at the finishing line. "It's Millie Montague policewoman arresting the race, with Ned Elliot Caesar and young Mr Lund our own Richard the Third neck and neck for second place. But wait, here comes Archbishop Gordon Munzer, into service from the inside, praying all the way now. Tin Man Gary Johnson is rattling along with him. It's still anyone's race. Millie Montague policewoman still leading by a nose as they head towards the finish. Splinter is battling it out with the mighty Caesar behind the leading pack."

At this point the rather damp crowd were treated to another spectacular. Mrs Munday, Laura's mother, was cheering like someone possessed.

"Come on Archbish. Go!" she screamed in her poshest voice ever. People turned to look. Those who knew who she was were muttering, "Lucky Laura's not here yet." Why she was so attached to this Archbishop character is only guesswork. However, the best was yet to come!

The mud and rain had mixed an evil cocktail. The moment the passing cyclists hit the crowd, they sprayed huge quantities of wet filth all over them, like a mud hose. Mrs Munday was at the crowd-edging ribbon. Her cocktail dress was speckled brown as if the mud had hit a fan pointed straight at her. She stood motionless for a second before waving her arms around and marching off in disgust.

It was rapid and continuous along the length of the crowd. So quickly did it happen that there was no time to react. The roar from the crowd was stupendous. The cyclists were going as fast as they could these last one hundred metres. The loudhailer continued come what may as they crossed the finishing line.

"And it's Millie Montague policewoman by a whisker from Tin Man Johnson with Archbishop Munzer for third. What a race ladies and gentlemen! You have the winner. Millie Montague!" Cyclists were now pouring past in ever-greater numbers increasing the mud spray.

Millie was thrilled. She had never won a race before. She was about fifteen and had taken part on the two previous occasions. She hopped off her cycle, but due to the size of her comedy shoes and the mud, slipped straight over completely covering one side of herself in the brown mess that was everywhere.

Ben and Hitti came in about twelfth after the final rush of effort.

About five minutes later as preparations were made to award the prizes a large number of the entrants appeared in one damp and disgustingly filthy pack. At the front of this was Laura. Her cat suit had been blue once, but sadly it had turned a shade of mostly brown with blue patches here and there. Her cat tail had torn off and she looked as bedraggled and soaking wet as the rest.

Still the crowd, not caring anymore about the mess, cheered them on as heroes for finishing at all. Amongst them were two more staff, Smudge and Mrs Rigging, who had stopped for a rest until Smudge turned up and they continued together. They came in one after another looking like twin pirates covered in mud. Smudge's renowned ring was there on her finger. It was displayed curiously clean and shining like a light despite the mud everywhere else. The dim overcast afternoon did not seem to make any difference. Ben saw it as she came by. He was given to wonder again about Smudge and her unusual ring.

Mrs Munday never saw the splendid sight of mud and mayhem because she left in a huff. Some parents can be so childish can't they?

The prizes were handed out to the first three. There was a cup for the winner and a new mountain bicycle. Second prize was a signed prize certificate and a voucher for two West End theatre tickets. The third place award was a prize certificate and a book voucher.

Mr Goving also had another job to do. He was to announce the winner of the 'best costume choice' prize. He stepped up onto the platform with mud spray all down his overcoat and across his face. Taking the loudhailer he made the announcement.

"This year has been marvellous. It's been quite the funniest Bickie I've ever seen and helped by our wonderful weather. I do have a winner for 'best costume choice'. The most amusing costume this year was clearly Archbishop Munzer, our own Gordon." A round of applause met with the result. He too received a book token. Ben had enjoyed it all so much, he couldn't wait until next year to do it all again.

At about the same time as prizes were being awarded, Dr Metanite was finishing up in the science labs and preparing to leave. His lonely existence didn't bother him a bit. He left the door into the corridor and saw Marj wheeling her trolley in order to exit the building, having finished her cleaning round. She looked at him. He seemed very red in the face.

"You don't look yourself today, Doctor," she commented.

"I don't feel too good today, Marj," he replied. His mouth was quite bright red when he spoke. It was most alarming.

"Perhaps you should see your doctor," she suggested in a friendly manner.

"I'll be all right soon thanks," was the curt response. He left as she did, out of the main door into the fading afternoon damp weather, locking the door behind them. Poor old Marj was only trying to be pleasant. She found herself muttering.

"There's some beyond help in this life. Call themselves fancy doctors or not."

Outside, the bikes were being returned and the costumes taken off. They were put in one enormous pile for the laundry service to salvage and sort out. Ben saw Millie Montague outside the changing rooms while he was waiting for Laura and Hitti to come out and catch their normal bus together.

"You were brilliant, Millie. You just seemed to power through the others didn't you?" said Ben with a cheeky grin on his face.

"Cheers, Ben. Did you see me at the finish then?"

"Only from about ten behind," he replied. Of course, 'powering through' is Ben's speciality isn't it?

When Ben got home that evening, he was exhausted and ravenous. He hadn't enjoyed his supper so much for ages. It was nothing unusual mind. There was rice, beans and marrow with minced meat filling. Absolutely no flavour enhancements had been applied to this dish, but it was plain and beautiful all the same.

"Goodnight," Ben announced to his mum and dad, the moment he'd eaten. He couldn't wait to get into bed for a long, deep sleep.

That night Ben had an unexpected dream. It was nothing he had ever dreamt before. He witnessed a school assembly being addressed by his great grandad, Gareth Streeter. There was no mistaking it. Mr Streeter was addressing the school over the tragic death of Sonia Bird. Ben was experiencing disturbed sleep over this. He half wanted to wake up and half wanted to see the end of the dream. He didn't hear much that was said. There were snatches.

"None of you who happened to be there should blame yourselves in any way. Mr Dreante has given the police and myself the fullest account possible," stated Mr Streeter. Ben could see other teachers on the stage with the headmaster and looking on very sadly. The man beside the headmaster seemed particularly forlorn and for some reason his face felt familiar to Ben. Could this be the face of Mr Dreante, Ben thought? Was it the face missing in that strange school photograph book? The dream continued in movie-like fashion. "The life of the school must go on, but we must pay our respects to those—"

Ben wrestled in his bed trying to get a better look at the teacher, when he noticed something terrifying in the background. There it was, hovering behind Mr Streeter and the teachers. The same ghostly form which appeared to Ben and Laura in the local history clubroom and told him to stop 'meddling'. It was the same form that had been grappling with the ghost of Sonia. It had the word 'Scarigus' across the front of it. There was no mistake! As hard as Ben tried to see more, the picture faded until there was just a wisp of mist.

Ben woke up with a start, perspiring profusely and coughing. He felt unsettled at the episode. He wearily reached out to grab his wristwatch and see the time. It was ten past six in the morning. He would normally wake at quarter to seven. He lay in his bed reflecting on his lucid dream, realising that he could remember it all. Another message in the puzzling case of Sonia. Ben still thought it unlikely he could do anything about a death in 1949 to make it right so many years later. He sat up and was about to get out of bed when he heard a voice. It was a girl speaking.

"He's still there. He's still there. He's still there," the voice half whispered three times.

"Who's still there?" Ben said out loud. The voice had gone. It had to mean something. If it was Sonia why didn't she appear? After all, Ben knew he was not mad and didn't imagine things. Not that his parents would believe that. He came out of his bedroom and walked towards the bathroom. His mum called out from her bed next door.

"Why are you talking to yourself, Ben?" she laughed. What *would* he say?

"LINES IN A PLAY, MUM." BEN CARRIED ON ACROSS THE LANDING INTO THE BATHROOM AND SHUT THE DOOR. PHEW HE THOUGHT!

CHAPTER 12

'Finger power' day

It was two weeks later before Hitti finally came to terms with his experience of being frozen by wind whilst in his bath. Laura was angered by her blustery event but after a few days felt at ease with Ben again. The Bickie had somehow drawn a line under the episode.

Ben persuaded them to meet and examine the school magazine and photo album from 1948. With school life being so busy every day, there just hadn't been time to do it before. They arranged to meet backstage in the Peter Phelps Theatre after the last lesson of the day.

It was two fifteen and time for a lesson with Stewbog who taught English literature. As they filed in, Barry Trinder was just behind Annie Stapleton squeezing a soft plastic container towards her collar without her noticing, at least not at first. As soon as she reached her desk, she started to feel uncomfortable and itchy.

"I'm very sorry, Stewbog," she said wearily, "I think I need to go to the toilet for a moment." Stewbog gave her a barely concealed filthy look.

"Surely not at the beginning of the lesson? Do sort yourself out before class another time please. Quick as you can then." Annie rushed off to wash. She was starting to scratch her itching neck the minute she left class. She resolved to find whoever did it and deal with them in her own way. She had no wish to tell Stewbog about it and he saw nothing. That was often the way it worked.

Stewbog's classes frequently read plays with everyone having a turn at the various parts. He was such a marvellous mimic and character actor and they had enormous fun being taught new ways to speak their lines.

"Laura, you can read the part of Cicely Parjeter. Simon, you do Captain O'Reilly. Hitti, you do—Sir Brian Dewar. Ben, I've got a goody for you," Stewbog said teasingly. "Mary Slater." The whole class erupted into laughter as they realised Ben was to play a woman. Ben didn't care. It was all part of the learning curve of show business to him. After a few minutes about ten of the class had parts and the others waited for their turns later.

"OK, quiet please," Stewbog insisted calmly. "We were at the top of page thirty-four. So it's Hitti to start please. Remember your Scots accent!" There was a shuffling of books being opened.

Sir Brian: "Och, weel, the wee boy'll run oat o' money as fast as I can drink ye dry."

Cicely Parjeter: "Sir, your manners do not please me. I bid you farewell. Mary, we're leaving the presence of this insulting man at once!"

Mary Slater: "Cicely, dear. I beg of you to think again. [Whisper] I remind you we have nowhere to go."

And so the play continued. Ben read his first line with aplomb, but afterwards his mind began to drift. He saw Annie Stapleton re-enter class, but then lost track. When it came time for him to read a further line a little while later, he had completely switched off. Stewbog had to intervene.

"Speak up, Ben, it's Mary's line now! Wake up will you!" This was becoming all too familiar to teachers at WISPA – Ben Street seemingly half asleep during lessons.

Ben returned to consciousness with a start. His only defence was to turn prankster. He had been feeling particularly mischievous that day. It was the moment he would begin. In an instant he went, look—click, click, click—freeze-frame. The whole class froze in three almost immediate bites, as he looked around at them from his seat and held them in his thoughts. He couldn't quite get them all in sight at the same time from his chair. No time to put Laura to one side today.

Ben hadn't finished yet. He jumped out of his seat, making it easier to ensure control. Looking from the front he went, look—click—levitate, and—stop. The class drifted up from their seats until their knees caught them under the desk, about fifteen centimetres up. Ben had to leap forward to rescue Stewbog and suspend him before he drifted up to the ceiling! Ben had no intention of leaving it there. There was more!

He borrowed a red lipstick from Jess Brough's bag and went to Stewbog. Pulling him down a little from his floating position, Ben put round red circles on his cheeks and around his lips, until clown-like; he let him float back up to his original position.

He wasn't thinking sensibly any more. Next, he remembered that Barry Trinder had brought some itching powder to school and that's probably what he had inflicted on Annie Stapleton. Ben searched Barry's pockets one by one until he found the tube of troublesome substance. It was called 'Firkins Itching Powder – Guaranteed to have them scratching from the first puff'.

Back he went to Stewbog. He was about to apply the naughty mixture. Then he stopped. He changed his mind. It would have to be someone in class otherwise there would be real trouble. He looked around to decide who deserved it most. Barry had brought it in. Perhaps he'd better try it for himself. Ben walked over to poor Barry and pulling open the top of his shirt, directed a large quantity of powder down his chest. Rather more than Ben intended squirted out.

Ben didn't seem to want to stop! He was out of control. He already had yet another idea to cause mayhem and possible hilarity. He took a large tube of glue from the draw at the back of the classroom and prepared to glue some desk lids down! He carefully undid the screw cap and mulled over which desk would be first. Before he had a chance to squeeze the tube of glue, there was a warm gust of air blowing straight at Ben's face. A misty white fog developed in the centre of the room. Ben stopped in his tracks and suddenly felt very guilty. What the blazes had he been doing for the last few minutes, he thought! It was the ghost of Sonia appearing on her own. She began to speak very softly.

"Use your powers wisely. You will need all you can muster for the coming storm." Ben knew he hadn't been using his powers for anything other than practical jokes most of the time. He didn't exactly know what else he was supposed to do with them. Ben wasn't frightened of Sonia any more; it's just that he never knew when she might materialise.

"I'm sorry. I just don't know what to do. Who or what am I looking for? Just tell me." There was a silence, while she just hung in mid air, but her feet close to the floor. "Why can't you tell me?" demanded Ben more vociferously.

"It is the curse of Scarigus. I cannot tell or I will die."

"But, you're already dead!" squawked Ben. "How could it get any worse?" The ghostly form hesitated and then looked Ben between the eyes like never before.

"I will never be at rest, whilst this evil power holds me with its deceit. If you fail I will die another death of pain without end. You are my only hope. I can tell you no more," she wailed, virtually crying. "I need you to end my pain. The curse must be exposed to the living world or its power will continue forever in the dead world. You must use your powers wisely. They squeeze all my energy to give them to you. It is you who was chosen to fight for my peace in death."

Now Ben felt even more guilty, thinking about all the crazy things he'd done. The sound of several people's footsteps could be heard approaching down the tiled corridor. Ben's heart was racing with fear. With a large puff of wind the ghost of Sonia receded and waned into mist and then disappeared. The footsteps were even closer now and may be only seconds away. What if they came to his class?

Ben looked at Barry and noticed lots of the itchy powder had, perhaps fortunately, blown away from the inside of his shirt with the wind in the classroom. The stepping sound was now very loud.

Ben moved to the front of class so he could have everyone in his sights at once. He went 'look—click—move and fall back'. The whole lot of them dropped the fifteen centimetres or so back into their seats, with a thud. A cacophony of voices all called out in unison: "Ouch!" Ben swung into his seat at the same time and began his line in the play:

"I cannot promise—" He was cut off as all Ben's classmates burst into laughter at the sight of Stewbog's face with something akin to a clown's design upon it.

The laughter was interrupted by a knock at the door. It opened and there was Smudge with her ring sparkling. Next to her was a tall girl with long blond hair and blue eyes. Ben was nearly panting at the stress of the situation. He was certain to be caught this time he thought. Smudge looked at Stewbog who was quite confused by the whole episode. She said nothing at all about his appearance as she spoke.

"Stew, I've brought you Scarlet Scrimshaw for this class. She's just moved to the area and joined the school today. Mr Goving asked me to drop her off here.""Fine, come on in. We'll have to find you somewhere to sit," said the befuddled Stewbog. Smudge turned to Scarlet and spoke to her in a semi-whisper.

"Don't worry about his face. Probably all part of the lesson. Drama school and all that. Just call him Stewbog. You'll see." Stewbog didn't take any notice as he directed Scarlet to a spare chair at the back of class. Every one of the pupils in the class, including Ben, was unable to stop smiling at the ridiculous situation that had arisen.

"Scarlet we're in character reading this play." Scarlet looked with incredulity at the state of Stewbog's face.

"Ben's just reading the part of Mary, here," Stewbog said, handing her a spare copy of the play, opened for her at the right page.

"Right, back to you, Ben," said Stewbog.

Mary Slater: "I cannot promise you anything," said Ben. At that moment the bell rang out and the class all closed the play with one big 'bang' of books being shut together.

Laura went over to Scarlet and introduced herself, being the polite friendly girl she was. Ben just stood back and said, "Hi," listening to the conversation and waiting for Laura.

Out of class, they shuffled around in the corridor reaching into their lockers and organising themselves for the trip home. Barry Trinder was seen scratching himself and looking quite irritated. But for Laura, Hitti and Ben there was a meeting and a reading to be done. Ben had carefully secreted the school magazine book and photo volume into his bag, direct from his locker, without anyone seeing. Just as they set off, Laura wanted Ben to know she was not a fool. She knew what had been going on in that lesson.

"You can't trick me, you know," she laughed. "I'm well aware of what you did in that classroom. People don't get clown faces in half a second without help."

"Oh that," said Ben almost embarrassed. "Just needed to get out of a hole," he added sheepishly.

"You'll get caught out one of these days, Ben. Someone in school is gonna wonder about it and want to check it out. Lipstick all over his face!" scoffed Hitti.

The three of them scuttled off in the direction of the theatre backstage door. It was a door that could always be unlocked from inside because of fire regulations. There was no chance of being locked in this time! They tried not to be nervous and to walk normally. Hitti could barely contain his feeling of trepidation.

They entered and locked the door on the inside. It was quite dark with only tiny safety lights on, but they made their way to the side of the stage where a small lamp used

187

for 'prompters' was located. It was switched on; it's dim light being enough for the purpose. Not a sound could be heard in that theatre. It was a deathly hush as Ben removed a book from his bag.

Stewbog had walked towards the car park to leave for the day. He arrived next to his car and unlocked it by the light of the only outside lamp, when Mr Goving came around the corner from the opposite direction.

"Teaching clowning today were we?" enquired Mr Goving jovially.

"Clowning?" Stewbog questioned deeply. "What do you mean?"

"Your get-up, of course!"

"Get-up?" Stewbog asked, intrigued by the line of questions.

"Your make-up, man! Have you forgotten?" asked Mr Goving, now wondering if something bizarre had happened. Stewbog opened his car door instantly and sitting in his driver's seat, pulled down the sun visor to look in the little mirror.

"Argh!" he gasped with complete surprise. "How the hell did that get there?"

"You don't know?" Mr Goving said in a measured manner.

"Uhmm, must have been earlier. Uhmm, see you tomorrow," Stewbog said with a frown as he shut his car door, started the engine and set off. A bemused headmaster looked on.

"Each to their own," muttered Mr Goving as he put the key in his own car door.

Back in the Peter Phelps Theatre an investigation was taking place.

"This is the 1949 school mag book," said Ben opening it, to find the article on Sonia. He had never looked since the day it left Mr Goving's office. He flicked through the contents until there it was: 'Service held for our lost soul, Sonia.' Ben quickly turned the page. He sighed with relief.

The second page was there and not torn out. They sat on the floor and craned around to see it, all reading at the same time.

About five seconds later they all realised there were only five more lines of the article. These lines confirmed her death was believed an accident and that drama teacher Tim Dreante, had now left the school as a mark of respect to Sonia's family.

What a disappointment! It was nothing Ben didn't know already. There were no winds and no ghosts.

"You mean we went through all that bother to get this book and it's no good?" gasped Hitti. They all stood up. Ben breathed out heavily and said nothing. Laura looked at Ben quizzically.

"It's time to stop this nonsense," she announced, as if it were her decision alone. Hitti and Laura got up to leave.

"Wait," ordered Ben. "I've got something else to show you." He removed the photo book from his bag and flicked it open in the middle. Ben held his hand over the photograph that had its facial features missing.

"See this guy?" said Ben, pointing at the 1948 headmaster. "He was my great grandad, Gareth Streeter. Remember, I mentioned my family name was changed from Streeter to Street?" Hitti and Laura looked a little blank. "It's why I was chosen by Sonia. I'm sure of it; because of my connection to this school at that time."

"Can't see how it helps," Hitti chipped in. He was looking agitated as if he would leave any second and picked up his school bag.

"Have you ever seen a man with no face?" asked Ben teasing them. Laura's eyes opened wider.

"Obviously not," she said grumpily.

"Have you lost it?" mocked Hitti with a witty remark. Ben took his hand away from the photo book revealing the male next to his great grandad. Hitti and Laura both jumped when they saw it! No facial features. It was blank, but not cut out of the photo. Hitti dropped his bag.

"Someone wants to hide his face. But this is 1948. A year before Sonia died," Laura queried.

"Seen his name?" said Ben pointing to the printed list. "Tim Dreante, the drama teacher in those days." Ben nodded knowingly as if there was something he knew. Hitti piped up again.

"He's probably dead. I mean he'd have to be about eighty or ninety something at least, if he was still around. What good is it anyway? It was all put down to an accident at the time."

"Perhaps he is still around and that's the point," said Ben revealing his thoughts. "I'm not going to be given weird powers for nothing am I?"

Laura was still examining the photo. She had taken hold of the book and put it close to her eyes. She held it there for a few seconds, thinking.

"Can't see the face," she confirmed. "But, he has long fingers. Could have been a good pianist. His clothes are definitely old-fashioned teachers' clothes," she continued as if it was under a microscope. "The jacket looks like something I've seen before, maybe in the costumes store. Slightly unusual, with maybe velvet round the collar."

A blast of icy air blew at the backstage and that familiar humming, buzzing sound began again. The side curtains were held up pointing backwards towards the rear with the force. Hitti grabbed their three bags as they started to move on the floor. The three peered out of the side to see a multi-coloured ball of spinning air growing in size.

"I'm going," shouted Hitti. He tried to move but the wind force blew against them holding them all trapped in every direction. The coloured ball was forming into a flesh-like substance. They all watched in horror as it developed.

It was a monster of a ghostly form that had taken on flesh-like qualities. It was barely possible to see through it now as the huge ball about three metres high became a mass of human feet, mouths, arms, eyes and ears. There were no other features! It wobbled and wriggled around the stage moving closer to Ben, Laura and Hitti, pressing its vile flesh onto the ground. As it went, it left a trail of gooey wet mess. It smelt vile, like burning hair.

Ben concentrated on this mass of flesh and went, look—click—freeze-frame. Nothing! His powers were useless. Ben suddenly felt fear, real fear.

"Yooou," shouted the ghastly form as it paused. It wheeled slowly around to reveal the largest mouth on its revolting mass and continued speaking with it. "You cannot control me."

The mouth was disgusting; hairy round the edge of its lips, with dark green dribble and spikes sticking up inside like shining, sharpened forks. It had a furry tongue you could see and there were puffs of acid-smelling fumes emanating from it as it spoke. The smell seemed to permeate the wind, which had no effect on it as it floated past the three of them. The sound of excessive breathing was heard from the beast.

It started to edge closer to Ben who was rooted to the spot with the gusting, icy wind. Before it said anything else Ben knew it would be down to him.

"What are you?" Ben demanded. After a few seconds of nothing but wind and breathing noises it responded.

"I am your death," it replied with chilling clarity, in a gravel voice. Ben reached towards Laura still holding the photograph book. He took it from her. The form growled at Ben with a ferocious noise. The book had closed up, but Ben was determined to open it again. He looked at it and clicked his eyes onto it.

"Open—open—open, he screamed." The book began to bend and curl. "Does this book hold a secret?" asked Ben bravely.

"You cannot interfere or you will join me in an unending death," moaned the vile monster.

"Who are you?" Ben and Laura shouted together. The moving mound of flesh wobbled and cajoled itself even closer. Ben was worried it would go over them and suffocate them all as it edged slowly in their direction. The large ugly mouth coughed a mist of acidic, foul-smelling breath at them but the sound was of insect buzzing. They recoiled in disgust.

"I am Echo Spiritus, guard of the Scarigus. Stay away or you will face the consequences," boomed the low gravel voice. By now Ben had nearly opened the book. He carried on commanding it to open using all the kinetic power he had. After a few moments and with one sudden surge of power, Ben pulled its covers apart.

"It's all about this isn't it?" he blasted, showing the photo of the blank face to the ugly monster. The fleshy beast was now showing signs of tiring. Its breathing was quickening. "Well, answer me," demanded Ben like the best teacher.

An enormous cough of foul acid smell came across them all and they sheltered their faces as best they could. Ben looked back at the book to see the tips of his fingers were beginning to glow red and warming up. The warmth felt good. The red heat gradually made its way up his fingers to meet his palms. By this time Laura had taken the book back.

Ben was hearing the voice of Sonia in his ear over and over saying, "Now you have the power". Ben's fingers were not only heating up; they began to glow bright red like red-hot fired iron in a furnace. Ben could not touch anything or anyone without causing burning.

"I'm going for it Laura," Ben told her, as she looked aghast at his fingers lighting up their space. With that Ben pushed forward at the wind, fingers first. There was a crackling noise and a woody burning smell. He pushed harder. As he pushed, the vile mass of wobbling flesh howled from all it's mouths, dribbling green goo, mostly from the large ugly mouth that had spoken. He hadn't been able to reach this revolting monster.

Ben would not give in and he pushed harder against the wind force. However, the wobbling mass had reached him and was moving onto his right foot. The weight of it seemed to start pushing Ben down as it slowly crawled forward, until he finally fell down with almost half his right leg now under the fleshy beast.

Laura and Hitti could do nothing except look on in terror. Ben pushed at the wind and they all smelt more burning. Ben turned and stared at the enormous ugly mouth now approaching him, its hairy lips quivering and munching, accompanied by the sound of grinding metal spikes. The mouth neared Ben as the disgusting mound rolled up just below the knee of his right leg. One of its arms had hold of his left shoulder and was squeezing it very tightly.

Without warning Ben took his hands away from the wind he was pushing at. He stabbed his glowing red-hot hands straight into the fleshy lump crawling onto him. It fizzed and crackled and burnt with the heat. Its arm withdrew its grip. Ten holes were poked into the flesh. Ben withdrew and plumped his fingers in again at an adjacent point.

The frying monster was beginning to react. Its mouth and eyes were showing the pain. It receded slightly for a moment and then tried to move rapidly forward with a gargantuan wobbling and wriggling fit. Ben speared the flesh with his new weapon as hard and fast as he could. This ghostly monster wasn't giving up. Its mouth roared at Ben and turned at him opening its spiky jaws.

It reached forward and the metal spikes were ready to close on Ben when he saw his fingers had become so hot they were virtually white with heat. He had to take the risk. He had nothing to lose. Ben waited, poised for a second or so and then ran his fingers around the rim of the ugly mouth, immediately melting every toothy spike from its place, before it had time to think or bite.

The Echo Spiritus flesh monster backed off his leg and chewed on its own molten metal. Ben began to feel he could beat it. The wind was fading slightly. It was enough for him to get to his feet.

The goo rolled down his trouser leg and slopped onto the floor. Laura and Hitti were beside themselves and urging Ben on. The monster was flailing its peculiar arms in all directions. Ben pushed at the wind that was subsiding and yielded to his force and he stepped forward for the first time toward the creature on the stage.

Outside the theatre's foyer there was a key turning in the lock. It was Mr Bodkin, the caretaker on his rounds entering to check up, clean up and lock up. He could hear some howling noise as he entered. Nothing new, he thought. It's a theatre and there must be something on the schedule he'd forgotten. So he just carried on as usual dealing with the foyer first.

Ben pushed his white-hot fingers into the wailing mass again and it melted the flesh to liquid all around it producing holes the size of small saucepans. Now he felt in control. He swiped at this monster all over its side as it rolled around shrinking from about three meters to half that size.

Strangely the eyes and mouths moved out of the way as he speared. The form began to become misty again. Mr Bodkin had entered the back of the theatre and stood with his mouth open at the spectacle. There was Ben standing with glowing hands and apparently dealing with a vast ghostly mound of wobbling flesh. Ben pushed at the thing once more and its pathetic wail was clearly the sound of defeat. The multi-coloured mist then shrank and wisped away into thin air. Ben's hands began to calm instantly to red and then within about ten seconds to normal. The wind dropped.

The sound of clapping rang out across the auditorium. Ben and the others breathed in with relief as they turned to see Mr Bodkin by the rear exit doors.

"I loved that! It was amazing. Them special effects were a stunner," he enthused, still clapping. "Can't wait to bring me missus to the show this term." Mr Bodkin just assumed a teacher was present somewhere, but he never actually saw one.

Ben had not sufficiently recovered to reply. He breathed slowly and deliberately and then managed to speak.

"Thanks. Might not look quite the same next time. We're just going now."

"Be as long as you like. Remind your teacher to go out the back coz it's self-locking." Mr Bodkin then went about his business.

Laura and Hitti came out of the side and as they looked around, the goo that had deposited everywhere just seemed to disintegrate into powder. Ben brushed it off his trousers. Laura gave him a hug. He had beaten the beast. But still there was no answer to the mystery of Sonia's death.

Why was there a blank photograph and who wanted it hidden? Who exactly was this mound of ghostly flesh trying to protect? They stood there on the stage discussing it in the dim light of the prompter's lamp, which was now all there was.

There was a tiny thud in the wings. Hitti looked around the black side curtain and turning on the exit passage lights, saw a small piece of cut rope on the floor. It was a clean-cut, as if done with a knife. The others strolled over. As they did so a coil of rope from the upper workings of the theatre dropped down by their feet. It too had a cleanly cut end. They all looked up. There was nobody there, just silence together with a strong smell of jasmine floating by. Ben picked up the piece of rope and held on to it.

"It's another sign," said Ben philosophically. "I reckon that'll be a clue to how Sonia died. What do you think?"

"Yeah, but who's just cut that?" asked Hitti. None of them knew. They picked up their bags and Ben put the two books away. They headed towards the rear door. Hitti reached it first and put his hand on the self-locking bar ready to push.

"Wait a second," said Laura. "What's this?" she said lunging to the side and putting out her hand to catch something whirling down towards them in the air. It looked like a piece of card covered in black and white markings. Laura turned it over. It was a photograph. Ben and Hitti came back a few steps and looked at it too.

The male figure was standing. He had the same clothes and distinctive hands as the person whose facial features were missing in the group photograph.

"It can't be!" said Ben in a state of surprise. "It just can't!"

"What do you mean?" asked Laura.

"I'll think about it," said Ben suddenly not too sure what he really thought. He put the photograph and small piece of cut rope inside his bag. They all exited the rear door and headed off home. There was five minutes until the last school bus of the day was due, so they ran!

CHAPTER 13

The reflection

A few weeks passed. Ben told Laura and Hitti that as so much had happened, he needed to seek advice.

"I don't know who you could tell. Who's going to believe it? We've all talked about that loads of times," said Laura as she put her books down on the desk.

"They don't need to believe it. I just have to sort out a plan to end this thing," replied Ben. He was a bit down over it all after his success at the theatre. It would only be a few weeks until the Easter break and he couldn't let it go into another term he thought. Ben decided to seek out the advice of someone unconnected to the school.

On the other side of Macey Avenue there was a walk-in advice centre. Ben just wanted a sounding board to get it off his chest. He just wouldn't tell them names or places and it would all be all right, he told himself.

As he got off the early bus that afternoon, he walked straight there. It was not far from home. He went into a temporary building up a few steps to find a row of chairs. One of the world's lonely homeless who probably lived rough, was occupying a seat.

There was a small bell at a desk with a sign inviting you to press it. When he'd done so, Ben sat down. It was just moments before a door opened and someone came out to see him. Ben motioned towards the homeless man.

"It's OK, he's been seen and waiting for something else," said a kindly-faced lady with a soft voice. She was well-spoken, had grey wiry hair and was dressed all in yellow. She could have been anyone's grandma and was very calm.

"Come in here, young man," she beckoned pointing to a room. They both walked in and sat down in a couple of relaxing easy chairs. Ben was invited to call her Judith. She had a small form and took down Ben's name and details. She actually misheard him and wrote his family name as 'Fleet'. He didn't bother to correct her.

"Now, Ben, what seems to be the trouble?" she asked in a very friendly way. Ben wasn't sure how to begin and although he went to say something, nothing came out.

"Is it a girl?" suggested Judith.

"Yes, well no, not Laura," Ben said. "But—"

"It's OK, Ben, you can tell me anything. There's nothing I haven't heard before. It's all kept confidential here." Ben didn't think she would have heard his problem before.

"The thing is she's dead. Sonia, that is. And she's contacted me to help her," Ben spouted in an embarrassed fashion. To Ben's surprise, Judith did not bat an eyelid. She just listened as Ben gradually laid out the whole story. She never interrupted, except to say, 'uh hum' a few times at intervals. Of course, Ben didn't mention any real person's name, just nicknames. Ben wanted answers.

"Do you think a head teacher would blank out a face in school photos to hide something?" Ben asked.

"I think there must be some other answer, Ben," Judith replied.

"Well, there's this teacher with a ring who acts really weird even following me and my mates around sometimes."

"You probably need to think if she could just be going where you were anyway." Ben was not listening to her common sense and just carried on.

Could a science teacher with funny clothes be shielding the truth? How could his great grandad be involved? What about the fleshy monster? What about a mimic teacher? Was he an impostor?

"Goodness me, Ben. You are asking a lot. Now, you're quite sure Laura isn't playing tricks on you?" Judith offered innocently.

Once she had said this Ben knew he was wasting his time expecting an answer. She obviously didn't believe a word of it just as Laura warned. His powers happened without any need for Laura! Whilst Judith spoke, Ben noticed for the first time there was a full-length mirror behind and to the side of Judith's chair. As he looked down it towards his lower half, he screamed out.

"It's gone!" Ben didn't have the luxury of anything other than a tiny wall-mounted mirror at home and had never noticed what he now saw. He stood up and peered over the top of Judith.

"What's the matter, Ben?" she insisted, quite put out. "You're on a dare aren't you?" asked Judith. She was sure Ben was there for a prank.

"My leg. I told you my leg was sat on by a giant fleshy thing."

"Yes, Ben. You did," she said rising from her seat and suddenly finding it all very irritating.

"Look in the mirror," Ben cried out, almost frantic. He had seen the gap between his trousers and his sock when sitting down. He pulled up his trouser leg as Judith turned about. She leapt backwards in shock and closed her eyes.

The lower half of Ben's right leg did not show as a reflection in the mirror, the part that had been sat on by the fleshy beast at the theatre! Judith was absolutely speechless and breathless with fright. She suddenly realised this was no prank. It was for real.

She bent down and rolled up the trouser, seeing the leg in front of her. Again she gazed into the mirror to see it had no reflection up to the knee. She recovered her composure and stood up again.

"I can't advise you, Ben. Only one person I know can deal with this." Judith scribbled a name and contact number of someone onto a piece of paper and thrust it into Ben's hand. "Go, Ben. I can't see you again. Just promise me you won't come back."

Ben was shell-shocked and just nodded politely, making his way out. When he was outside, he breathed in the fresh air for a moment before opening his hand. A gust of wind took the piece of paper into the air. It was blowing Ben hard in the face. Not again, he thought! He now knew that there was still a malicious power about and it was affecting him.

The wind blew the small note straight against the side of the building and Ben reached up and grabbed it down. The wind ceased instantly. He read the name on the piece of paper with disbelief. It said 'Dr Michael Goving'. It surely couldn't be the same person as Mr Michael Keith Goving, the headmaster of WISPA?

He wasn't a 'Dr' as far as Ben knew. It must be a coincidence. The telephone number was not the number for the school as far as he could recall.

Ben wandered off across the road and around the corner into Macey Avenue. As he clutched the piece of paper, he saw Robbie McAllister further up the avenue, playing on a skateboard in the road. Robbie saw Ben, but looked away. It had been months since their paths had crossed. Clearly, by the look on his face, he had not forgotten his experience in the park!

The group of youths were all muttering, it's him, it's him, and pointing in Ben's direction. Ben put the piece of paper in his pocket and carried on walking with his bag on his back. When he reached the point of being about fifty metres away, the chance arose.

Robbie McAllister was skating over a mound of earth dug up for road repairs. Just as he swished up the mound, Ben went look—click—pull. Irresistible! Robbie's skateboard came straight out from under his feet and left him unceremoniously dumped on top of the muddy heap, on his behind.

The other lads all cheered, having no reason to know how it had happened. Ben walked up his garden path, past the car and went into his house, unable to conceal his cheeky grin.

"Hi, Mum. Hi, Dad," he called. There was a muffled acknowledgement from the back of the house. His dad must be in the garden. Marrows and courgettes sprang to mind. Ben put down his bag and went out the back to see his dad watering away in the greenhouse. Cold or not, the heater was on to keep the produce growing!

"Ben! How was school?" asked his dad.

"All right," he replied without a single detail.

"What did you do today?"

"It's just school, Dad. Nothing really," Ben responded. Not much point in starting, thought Ben. He wouldn't understand would he? His dad cut off a couple of courgettes and handed them to Ben.

"Take these beauties into Mum for supper will you?" He would have liked to throw them straight in the bin, but didn't want to hurt his father's feelings.

"Yeah, OK. Is Mum in then?"

"She was in just a few minutes ago." Ben went upstairs and met his mum on the way down.

"Hi, Ben," she smiled.

"Hi, Mum. I just put the courgettes on the side for you."

Ben carried on to the top of the stairs. He had a job to do before supper. He had to know. Ben took the portable phone from his parents' bedside table and went into his own bedroom. He looked in his pocket for the piece of paper with a Dr Goving's telephone number on it. He tried his other pocket and looked on the floor of his room. It was not there! He rushed to his school bag in the hallway downstairs and looked on the hall carpet. There was nothing! He began to feel a small panic. He pelted into the kitchen.

"You didn't pick up a piece paper on the stairs or anywhere just now, did you Mum?" He asked anxiously.

"I put something in the bin, yeah. It was by the front door when I walked by." Ben dived for the household rubbish basket under the sink. There it was, sitting upon some other rubbish, but now a much darker colour. Ben opened it up and ran away upstairs.

The numbers were fading before his eyes. He memorised them and wrote them onto his notepad. The original note was almost black and becoming quite powdery. He had not seriously suspected Mr Goving before, if indeed it was his number.

Ben punched it into the phone. It started to ring and Ben's heart began to thump in anticipation. It rang for quite some time. Then it answered. It was a recorded voice message. The unmistakable voice of Mr Goving began speaking. He was now confirmed as also being known as 'Dr' Goving! How did Judith know him and why should she suggest he could help? Ben had a terrible thought. Had she known all along that he was telling her about events at WISPA?

"Supper in ten minutes, Ben," called his mum from the kitchen.

"All right," he answered.

*

By the following morning, Ben had been thinking a great deal about what he should do. He would have to do something about his right leg and maybe that would lead him to be able to help Sonia. It felt fine, but if it couldn't be seen in a mirror that was a matter which really worried him.

He had a tiny mirror screwed to the back of his bedroom door at head height. Ben got out of his bed and stood on it in his pyjamas and socks. He slightly pulled up his pyjama trouser and lifted his right leg up quite high so he could try and see it in the tiny mirror. He could see no leg reflected in the mirror and started to gently lower his leg carefully as any dancer would. His moment of hope that this problem would have just gone away faded.

Before he had a chance to lower his leg very much at all, Ben's dad walked straight in and stopped with surprise at the sight of his son.

"What in heavens name are you doing?" his father asked. He was still standing there with one leg vertical and one of his pyjama legs rolled up!" This called for some quick thinking.

"I limber up for some dance routines like this, Dad," Ben said confidently as he slowly lowered his leg avoiding tearing any muscle. Luckily that was true as well.

"Rather you than me. Now where's that phone?" grumbled his dad as he scooped it up from the floor. "Put it back next time. I'm fed up of finding it's gone," he added. He left Ben's room in a hurry.

Time to get to school!

CHAPTER 14

There's a hole in that shirt!

It was not long until the end of the second term and the Agent's Parade or Comp preparations were taken very seriously at this stage.

Next term would be the summer term at the end of which the Comp would be over for another year. Some pupils would be offered work in film, television or theatre if they were lucky.

There was huge excitement building about the various performances that were still being experimented with. As with every day at WISPA, there were almost always normal lessons in the mornings. Today was no exception. Ben's class would have to endure double chemistry with Dr Metanite before the afternoon fun in the theatre.

Today the class was asked to dissolve various substances into sulphuric acid and note the properties of each and the substance created. It involved heating some of them gently in test tubes using a Bunsen burner and so forth. They were to work in pairs and Ben and Laura elected to be together.

Dr Metanite's voice was even stranger than usual today as if something was affecting it. He didn't have a cold or anything like that. It just sounded alarmingly different and old.

"That's all your instructions for this one. Any questions?" Dr Metanite asked. Not a soul wanted to hear him speak another word, as he sounded so croaky and peculiar. "OK, then you may start," he continued. He plodded around the class for about five minutes checking pupils had set up their equipment correctly before returning to his desk on the raised platform at the front of class.

"Can you attach these tubes here, Ben? The clamps won't go," asked Laura. Ben dutifully put it together. They both began warming the pungent liquid wearing their eye visors and aprons just in case. Ben and Laura were nearest the front of class and had the largest working space.

"Let's do the first one then." Ben was speaking as he put a spatula into a jar of white powder. He stopped and noted down the experiment in his workbook. He continued and spooned out an amount he intended to use. Laura weighed it and noted it. Meanwhile the acidic fluid was warming and Ben pushed it slightly away from the heat.

Laura took over and added some of the powder to the fluid. She turned away to note down all that was happening. It was bubbling as it consumed the added substance. Ben was looking towards the Bunsen burner, but not taking much notice anymore. He was wondering what he could do to cure his right leg. He hadn't told Laura about it yet either. He drifted a little in his thoughts. The sound of his name suddenly rang out in class.

"Street. Pay attention at once!" came the croaky scream from the front. Dr Metanite looked ready to explode, like the boiling test tube he had spotted in front of Ben. He stood up and rushed around to Ben's work area. Ben woke from his daydream in time to see the moment a large quantity of boiling fluid began throwing itself out of the test tube he was supposed to be watching.

A slow motion feeling entered the event. Ben could not think or move quickly enough. He could see the blob of fluid flying through the air in one expanding ball and making its way in an arc across his desk. He saw Dr Metanite arrive as this arc of liquid plummeted onto his desk and splashed upwards and over the work area. It went onto Ben's apron. The slow motion stopped.

"What did I tell you right at the start?" scolded Dr Metanite. Ben stood with a sorry expression on his face. "Never, ever allow your test tube to boil! It's dangerous."

"I'm very sorry, Doctor," apologised Ben. Unfortunately the mayhem did not stop there. Laura was standing back and had been unaffected by the disaster. Ben reached out to pick up the rubber gloves to start the clean up, but he knocked over the container of sulphuric acid onto the worktop.

Dr Metanite was still standing beside him as it dribbled everywhere. Even so, the doctor stayed calm as Ben was made to clear up the entire mess. Laura looked on waiting for Ben to finish. Dr Metanite returned to his desk and surveyed the scene.

As Laura looked at the teacher, she noticed there was a small round mark on one side of his white shirt, which seemed to be a curious sparkling black colour like a really small shiny button.

"Hey, Ben. Look at Meti's shirt," whispered Laura, trying not to draw attention to herself. Ben was still wiping the work surface as he looked across at Dr Metanite.

"What am I looking for?" Ben asked quietly.

"That black round thing on the front. It wasn't there just now," Laura informed him. Ben looked again. There was a mark on the left side about where his stomach would be. It seemed to be dark brown now and still sparkling. Ben returned to his wiping up. As they looked again it changed. Ben could see light in it! Laura and he looked at each other in astonishment. Ben whispered to Laura again. "I have an idea. If you go over there and open the cupboard door, you'll be out of my sight for just a few seconds."

"I know what you're going to do," Laura cut in. She made her way to the store cupboard and opened the full-length door. Laura went slightly behind it and could not see Ben. She counted to five.

Ben had moved to the side of the classroom. He went look—click—freeze-frame. It worked first time!

"You can come out now Laura," called Ben. Laura was already on the way as he spoke. There were the whole class, stiff as statues. "Oh no. We'll have to do something," Ben suddenly thought out loud.

"What's the matter?" said Laura. Ben had already marched away and was turning off all the Bunsen burners as rapidly as he could.

"Don't want any more trouble with these," he said. Now they turned their attentions to the strange Dr Metanite. They skipped around the desk to see him standing and facing the board, with his right arm holding a pen. He must have turned at the last moment. Ben bent down slightly to examine his shirt. The mark had become a hole.

"I reckon it could have been splashed by acid just now," commented Ben.

"The mark is still changing. It's weird," said Laura, who was on the other side of Dr Metanite. Ben stood up.

"What have I done?" said Ben. "I might've killed him!" Laura was still looking at the mark intensely.

"Don't think so," she replied calmly. "Just come and look at this Ben, you won't believe it." Ben came to the other side of the doctor and peered at the mark. As he bent down again he could see right in and the colour black. It was not an ordinary black. It was the black of a leather case Ben realised with a start!

"Oh my God, you can see right through him." Ben was looking through a tube that had developed in the side of Dr Metanite to the other side. He could actually see the doctor's black leather case through the hole! But it was still changing. The mark on the shirt was tiny but what you could see inside was growing. Ben decided they would examine the doctor more closely still.

"Laura, we need more light. Just stand back and I'll try something." Ben concentrated and then went, look—click—levitate and turn. Dr Metanite was gently raised in his statue-like state. His body turned towards the light of day. Now the hole was roughly at their eye level. Ben commanded the body remain still and in place for examination using his powers. Ben and Laura moved right up to the small hole and peered in. Laura jumped back in shock.

"Can you see what's inside now, Ben!" she screeched. Ben continued looking in.

"It's metal! I can see metal shiny objects!" said Ben with a stunned expression. "There's no blood in here. What is he Laura? He can't be human!"

"He must be. I bet he's had an operation or something and they've put some metal part in," she said trying to be convinced. Ben was still looking all around the doctor. He noticed something else.

"Look at this, Laura," said Ben, with a little excitement in his voice. Ben directed Laura to look inside the shirt collar and peek at Dr Metanite's neck. As he was levitated, his collar was hanging down slightly and you could see part of the side of his neck normally covered by material. There they both saw a small purple mark about the size of two pinheads that looked like a mole at first sight. On closer inspection it appeared to take the form of a small insect. You could make out the shape of a body and some legs.

"It's just a birthmark, Ben. Now you're making it up as you go; imagining things," Laura announced, quite sure about it.

"Maybe you're right," conceded Ben. As they stood there, the hole through Dr Metanite's body seemed to be closing up slowly. Ben peered inside to see what was happening. Laura looked from the other side. They could no longer see right through. The metal shininess was going and the tube way suddenly disappeared. On the outside, the flesh pressed itself closely together leaving only a tiny pinprick of a mark on his front and back.

"Weird," Ben said. They both stood there, wondering what to do next. They agreed to light the Bunsen burners together and return the class to normal. The doctor was moved back into a standing position.

"Hang on, Ben," asked Laura. "Just one more thing to do." Laura grabbed a piece of string and tied it into the belt holder at the back of Dr Metanite's trousers.

"Laura, you're becoming as bad as me!" gasped Ben. He knew she was up to mischief. She had attached the string to a small table near the doctor's desk but behind him. "Laura, quick. The test tubes are warming through. I can't wait much longer."

There was talking in the corridor and the sound of several sets of footsteps. Laura was still struggling with the knot around the table leg.

"Laura!" called Ben, in a quiet but firm command. She had finished. Ben looked at the class. Look—click—unfreeze. They all resumed as if nothing had happened. The classroom door opened.

"Ah, Doctor, I met Smudge outside and we both just wanted a word about your school magazine article," Mr Goving gushed with excitement. Smudge was carrying a small book.

"I was going to see you on that very matter today Mr Gov—" As Dr Metanite had walked towards the headmaster, the string tied to his trousers had taken the small table with him. The class looked to see the clattering noise and burst into hysterics. The table had been pulled over. A worried silence came over the class.

"Turn off your burners everyone," barked Dr Metanite.

"Who did this?" demanded Mr Goving. No one answered. Mr Goving gazed around the room and tried again.

"We have a decent tradition in this school. Those that did wrong own up. The alternative is for the whole lot of you to be in detention on Friday afternoon." Still nothing. After a few moments reflection Laura realised she would have to come forward.

"I'm afraid it was me, Mr Goving."

"Laura!" he said with a little surprise. "Be at my office, eight forty-five tomorrow morning." Dr Metanite had meanwhile untied the knot of string.

"Are you sure you're all right? You look rather pale, Doctor," suggested Mr Goving.

"I'm all right thanks. Been a bit tired after my operation at Christmas," he replied.

"Your voice sounds like it needs a good rest today." Dr Metanite shook his head.

"Nothing a good night's sleep won't cure." Ben and Laura, being at the front of class, had overheard all this and gave each other a knowing glance. Ben had not finished with his mischief today. He cast his gaze across the class and went, look—click—freeze-frame. Now all the class, Mr Goving and Smudge were frozen as statues.

This time Laura was amongst them. Ben had a hilarious plan, but he was not entirely sure it would work. He quickly levitated everyone to a standing position in front of his or her work zones. Some looked a bit crooked having been seated and then frozen. Then he concentrated his thoughts on all his fellow pupils legs and went, look—click—Irish dance. The entire room came to life again and all classmates' legs were dancing up and down in Irish jig fashion, in perfect time together. Before they had time to complain or to think about it, within ten seconds Ben had joined in but then put a stop to it.

Mr Goving interrupted the look of astonishment on their faces. Everyone turned to laughter when it stopped, not knowing how else to react.

"That was absolutely astonishing! I have never seen the like of it, have you?" he exclaimed turning to Smudge.

"I don't think I have. I haven't taught Irish this term," she added.

"Well, I do hope I'll be treated to some dancing of that calibre in the Comp. This school is going up. I can feel it!" said Mr Goving with a little dance in his step. Then he continued with his intention for attending the classroom.

"Now, your article?"

"I do have some information for the article. It's all gathered up in my briefcase. Something old, something new. You know," said Dr Metanite reaching for his case.

"No need to get anything out now. Smudge and I wanted you to have this in case it helped. Smudge handed an old book to Mr Goving who passed it on.

"Past heads!" said Dr Metanite. "That might do it."

"Good," said Mr Goving. Smudge gave a little wave of goodbye and they both left. Dr Metanite issued some more instructions on noting results and putting away their gear. Ben wasn't listening to much of it. He was ecstatic. He could use his powers for the Comp. That was definitely a wise use of his power he persuaded himself.

Outside, Mr Goving and Smudge were walking back through the quadrangle chatting.

"Have you had much contact with that Ben Street," asked Smudge.

"Why do you ask? Is there a problem?" asked Mr Goving detecting a certain tone.

"Very odd boy. Things don't seem to turn out as expected when he's around. I'm just not sure about him." Mr Goving turned to look straight at Smudge. She didn't stop speaking. "There's something unusual. You can't put your finger on it. I'm not sure he's good to have here because he affects others."

"That's some statement, Smudge. You're forgetting where he came from. His last school probably hadn't heard of manners. We had a girl like that a few years ago, but she did well once she settled down."

"I think we should watch him, that's all."

"Look, I've heard some very good things about him. I know he's a bit of a tearaway; sent to detention on his first day and all that. But I have him for diving. He's pretty well behaved with me," insisted Mr Goving.

Ben, Laura and Hitti had all met at the theatre for the afternoon practise. They had all changed and were waiting in the auditorium. Along came Mr McKinley with his three panellists, Tom Cortazzi, Fiona Payne and Gordon Munzer. Tom saw Ben and made his way over to him. Ben was never relaxed about an approach from Tom.

"Ben. Just wanted a quick word. You know this is the last rehearsal this term. We need to do well, because Mr McKinley chooses the order of appearances based on today," said Tom.

"What does that mean?" asked Ben.

"The Comp, the Agent's Parade! He literally decides what order the various routines will appear in front of all those agents," Tom enthused.

"You mean the people who could ask you to be in a film or telly part?" asked Ben rather innocently. Tom's jaw dropped slightly seeing how little Ben understood of the process.

"Precisely," Tom replied forcefully. "The later you are put on the better it is." Ben had no idea why that should be. He would do his best anyway.

The first act called on was for Fiona's team. They were singing in a group of six with harmonies. He remembered them from last time and they just sang without a movement amongst them. Ben had a moment's mischief in his mind. He could change all that couldn't he?

They started well and their harmonious sound was awesome for such young performers. Fiona had trained them well. After the first verse, thought Ben. He waited for the right point, whilst positioning himself carefully in the auditorium so as to see the singers and no one else.

Smudge popped her head out of the side curtain and eyed Ben carefully. Then came the moment, look—click— jazz steps. Ben was imagining a group dance in time to the music. Their legs began to go. They all continued singing barely noticing their own movement. It didn't seem to cause a feeling of effort, according to Laura who had explained it to Ben after their science lesson Irish jig.

The auditorium burst into applause as their unexpected dance proceeded. Fiona sat in her place with a look of astonishment on her face. She knew she had not taught her group this dance! The singers were smiling and wondering how they knew the routine. Ben kept it going for the whole of the two remaining verses of the song. Then again he went, look—click—stop. They finished in perfect time to more rapturous applause from all the waiting contestants!

Ben was so pleased with himself; he'd quite forgotten what Tom had said about his team doing well to get a good position in the Comp. Then he saw the look on Tom's face. It was a face like thunder and complete displeasure. Whoops! Ben realised he had better spread his powers about in equal measure and give some to his own team. Ben saw Mr McKinley furiously scribbling notes onto a pad.

Next up were Gordon Munzer's ventriloquist team. There were five, all with their own dummies, which were dressed in luminous clothing and their faces painted with 'glow paint'. The ventriloquists were all dressed in black except for their heads. With special lighting, all you could see were the heads of the ventriloquists and the dummies themselves.

They started to perform their sketch and it was hilarious. They did it like a playlet involving the dummies taking the parts. The ventriloquists had to run about the stage. Ben had thought of a little way to help them along. You could only just make out their legs dressed in black if you sat in the front where Ben now was.

Ben concentrated on them one by one. He caught sight of Liam Bidwell. As he started to walk, Ben went look—click—lift. Liam glided along into position with his legs going like bicycle wheels. The audience just saw the amazing smooth movement and its sheer pace. They laughed thinking it part of the act.

Then came Roger Lawson, speaking his part beautifully. He found himself gliding across the stage. But he carried on as if nothing had happened. The performers couldn't see how it was happening. Gordon's team enjoyed a great deal of applause.

When Ben saw what came next, a lump came up in his throat. He couldn't carry on could he? It was robotic puppetry, run by Tom Cortazzi. This meant team members would dress entirely as life-sized puppets with thick make-up, which looked like face masks and they would dance and sing.

First on was Matt Fingle, that strange boy who was part of the local history club. He was dressed like a hospital doctor in white. His face was made up in white with black facial lines that looked very painted as if on a toy puppet. Ben could have him moving like a puppet in no time.

Matt started the song, and as he sang, another 'robotic puppet' entered to join in. It was Josie Josephs, dressed as an astronaut. Three more entered one by one and joined in the harmony. They were a butler, a fireman and a ballet dancer. Once they were all on parade singing, Ben waited for the right moment. Their legs would be dancing in no time. He was concentrating and as usual went, look—click—but at that very moment Splinter had leant over from behind.

"Could you help with the balloons?" he asked pleasantly, meaning he wanted to put up balloons. All Ben could think of was balloons. He looked at the stage in horror as he saw all five puppets blowing up, fatter and fatter just like balloons. They were turning into floating balls of air before his eyes. There was a loud, 'Ooooh,' from those watching. They were moving across the stage, marooned in their new airborne skins and quite helpless. Ben had to act now or there would be a disaster.

He looked again and went, look—click—release air. Immediately, all five puppets began to deflate just like blown-up balloons that had been let go. They whizzed in circles and round and round in all directions finally running out of 'puff' and landing on the floor in a heap.

The noisy sound of laughter and glee was heard amongst the audience peppered with disbelief. It was not clear whether the puppets were meant to be behaving this way. The only clue was that their faces became somewhat glum on deflation when they landed quite hard on the stage floor. Mr McKinley leapt to his feet.

"Whoah, whoah. Stop!" he shouted towards the musicians in the pit. He waved at the puppets to come forward. "Just what are you doing? This is not scheduled at all." They were all speechless. None of them knew how they had inflated, let alone deflated afterwards.

"Last time we rehearsed, well, I mean, how did that happen? It wasn't meant to was it?" Mr McKinley spouted, not really sure what to ask. He jumped up on the stage and looked down the front of Matt Fingle's puppet suit, somehow expecting to find an answer. There was nothing there; no inflation equipment.

"House meeting, house meeting," he called. This meant everyone in the theatre must come out to the auditorium and hear him out. The echo-like sound of the message being passed around could be heard for several seconds. The entire cast and helpers emerged from all directions following this.

"Listen carefully. I don't know who wants to play tricks here, but this work is deadly serious. It's all about your future careers. Someone here has sabotaged the puppet act. I don't think it was funny. Someone could have been seriously hurt. Any more idiocy like that and I will cancel the Comp." A loud intake of breath could be heard all around the auditorium. "Oh yes I will," Mr McKinley insisted. Few doubted his sincerity. Ben was almost shaking. He knew he had gone too far this time.

Out of the corner of his eye he noticed Smudge. She again had her head around a black curtain at the side of the stage. She gazed at him in a peculiar way that made him feel uncomfortable. Ben began to worry that she had seen him doing something. She was pressing her fingers over her ring like some nervous twitch. He looked away making out he hadn't noticed.

After a short break the rehearsal was restarted. Ben watched the acts come and go without interference. Laura had missed out on Ben's enhancing powers for now. Then came Ben's turn. The Cortazzi team, of which Ben now felt happy to be a part, was the hip hop and tap dance highlight of the show and surely the best dance routine in this year's Comp. Hitti joined him on stage as Ben took the lead. Tom had taught him well.

However, he still couldn't resist one last little push from his powers. He went look—click—synchronisation, at the whole team. The effect was electric. Their feet danced and later tapped along in such perfect time; it was as good as any professional Broadway stage show. Although the dance steps had been seen as difficult last time, the execution on this occasion was magnificent. At the end the whole auditorium rose to their feet and cheered, including the panellists and even Mr McKinley found himself on his feet clapping. What a day!

It was now a little later than usual as pupils changed and made their way home. Mr Bodkin was on his way, expecting to lock up. The weather was very overcast and gloomy. As he passed down the dimly lit corridor he met a petite young lady he had never seen before passing the other way and wearing an old fashioned white dress. She spoke softly.

"Are you going into the theatre, Sir," she enquired. Not many people ever addressed him as Sir, which he found quite refreshing. Smiling he responded.

"Yes, I am. Doing the lock-up in a minute."

"Would you do me the honour of passing this letter to Mr Benjamin Street? I believe he's in the theatre this afternoon."

"I'm sure I can, if he's there as you say." Mr Bodkin put out his hand to accept the letter, but when he looked down it seemed to be in his hand already. He looked back up to bid the girl good afternoon, but she had gone. Very strange, he thought. He continued the few paces to the theatre foyer, locked up the entrance hall and made his way to the backstage area.

"Anyone seen Benjamin Street?" he asked the crowd of pupils leaving. He was pointed outside the exit door. Ben was waiting for Laura to get the last bus together.

"Are you Benjamin Street," asked Mr Bodkin, recognising him as a face he knew.

"Yes," replied Ben in anticipation.

"I've been asked to give you this. Lovely young lass handed it to me just now, then scarpered." Mr Bodkin turned round and went back inside. Ben looked at the envelope. He smelt a pleasing whiff of jasmine go up his nose. There was no writing on the outside. Moments later Laura and Hitti emerged from the exit door and they all left together. Ben hurriedly put the letter in his school bag and then forgot all about it.

As Ben retired to bed that night, he mulled over the amazing events of the day. He still had to pinch himself to make sure it really was real. And it was. He worried that his new powers would disappear if he solved the mystery of who murdered Sonia and what was covering it up. A part of him wanted it to go on forever, despite all the fear and danger he'd experienced.

*

The next morning Laura had to attend her unfortunate appointment with Mr Goving. She knocked on his overbearing door and entered.

"Good morning, young lady," said Mr Goving from behind his desk without even looking up properly. He was already hard at work. "Now, tying Dr Metanite to a table. What have you got to say for yourself, hmmm?" he asked spikily.

217

"I really do apologise for my behaviour, Mr Goving." There was a short silence.

"I loved your joke. Very funny," he said unexpectedly. "Just not allowed, that's all." He leant forward a little and looked over his expansive desk right into her eyes. "Detention next time, Laura. Now on your way."

It was not until lunchtime that same day that Ben was getting out his lunchbox from his school bag, when he came across the letter he'd been given by Mr Bodkin the afternoon before. He'd brought a packed lunch today, which he'd taken in his school bag to sit quietly on a bench in the school grounds next to the quadrangle.

He was munching a tuna and sweetcorn sandwich as he opened the envelope. Out came a small note. As it unfolded he realised there was no writing on it! Ben thought it a silly joke. He was about to screw it up ready for the bin, when to his surprise he heard a voice. It seemed to be coming from the piece of paper but was rather faint. Ben swallowed his mouthful and hurriedly put the note to his ear. The message was speaking.

"—and it's the twelfth book from the left. You can listen to this information again anytime if you need a reminder. That's why I have given you this voice letter. Good luck."

Ben didn't know what it was talking about. But he automatically recognised the sweet voice as that of Sonia the ghost. Ben shook the piece of paper expecting it to start the message again. He heard nothing. He turned it over, folded it and unfolded it. Nothing happened and yet he'd only heard a few meaningless words. In the end he put the note back in its envelope, put it down beside him and finished his lunch.

Ben couldn't take his eyes off the envelope. With the last mouthful of sandwich in his mouth, he picked it up again and took out the note in case he'd missed something. The moment he unfolded it, the sweet voice began speaking. This time he held it straight to his ear.

"—very important message for you, Ben. You must go to the corridor outside Dr Goving's office. The book of instruction you need will be found on the eighth bookcase, on the fourth shelf down and it's the twelfth book from the left. You can listen to this information—"

This voice letter had called the headmaster 'Dr' Goving, not Mr! What did this mean? Ben put the note straight back in the envelope and then took it out again. He unfolded it and held it to his ear once more.

"Yes!" he squawked. Ben had found the way to start the voice letter. It had to be folded and put back in the envelope first, then removed again before it would begin. He tucked it into his pocket ready to show Laura and Hitti later that day. They will be amazed by this he thought!

*

It was the following afternoon and the bell went signalling the end of the school day. By now it was the last Wednesday of the spring term. Easter was upon them. As they filed out of class and picked up their bags from the lockers, Ben spoke to Laura and Hitti anxiously.

"So will you guys come with me then?" Hitti and Laura had both heard the voice letter the day before and nodded.

"How is some old book going to help solve a murder, Ben?" asked Hitti incisively. "It's hardly going to tell you who did it is it?

"I'm not sure what it'll do, but I do know that letter means I must get that book and perhaps it's hiding the secret somehow."

"I'll come on one condition," added Laura. "If there's any sign of weird things happening, then I'm leaving."

"Same here," said Hitti persuasively. Ben, Laura and Hitti made their way to the famous corridor outside Mr Goving's office. The three of them walked along together chatting on the way.

"All I'm going to do is to get the book down from the right place like the voice letter said. Then we'll sign it out and run," said Ben.

"Is there a sign-out book in the corridor then?" asked Hitti.

"Yup. One inside and one outside his office. I've already looked. Only problem is the fourth shelf is very high up," said Ben authoritatively. They walked in the door past the canteen and then past the staff room. A couple of teachers waved as they went by. Then the three of them turned the corner into the corridor.

There were at least twelve bookcases along the wall one after another. Each had floor to ceiling books on about twenty shelves. The top shelf was about three and a half metres high from the floor. Laura was admiring the enormous bookcases when she had a thought.

"Which end shall we count from?" she asked.

"I hadn't thought of that," replied Ben as he walked back and forth surveying the situation. He started counting the bookcases and when he reached fifteen he burst out laughing.

"What's so funny?" asked Hitti and Laura in unison. Ben controlled himself.

"Hitti, you count eight along from the far end and Laura you count eight from this end," suggested Ben, smiling. Laura and Hitti set off on their task.

A few seconds later they were all laughing. Laura and Hitti had met in the middle. It didn't matter which end you started. When you counted eight bookcases along it was the same one from either end, right in the middle. They looked up at the height and knew the book could not be reached. Hitti looked along the bookcases he'd just counted.

"Hey, Ben. There's a sliding stepladder down the end. Why don't we use it?"

"Good thinking," Ben said as they walked over to the slim ladder. It was stuck on rails that ran along the top and bottom of the bookcases, so the boys began pushing it along towards the centre. As it reached the seventh bookcase it shuddered to a halt and would not budge. They shoved it and cajoled it but it was stuck on its rails.

"Look, I'll go up the ladder and see if I can reach the book anyhow," offered Hitti. Up the steps he went and leant right across as far as he could.

"The fourth shelf down and twelfth book from the left," Ben directed. Hitti could count all right. His hand was tantalisingly close, but not close enough to pull out the book.

Suddenly there was the sound of a creaky opening door. All three looked along the corridor expecting someone in authority to emerge at any moment. No one came! Then the door banged shut with a puff of wind from the window.

"Can I have a go?" asked Ben. Hitti dutifully came down the ladder and Ben went up in his place. It was no different. He couldn't reach. There was nothing else for it was there? Just a little kinetic energy, he thought.

Ben had locked his eyes on the correct book as he held onto the ladder with one hand and had the other outstretched trying to reach. His fingers were only a few centimetres away from touching it. He went look—click—pull. The book stayed put. He tried again. Look—click—pull. There was a scraping noise and a little dust fell from the shelf in front of the book. Ben looked at the others. Before he could look back, the book began to slide slowly outwards, making a noise like a train on dodgy tracks screeching into a station. Ben held out his hand as the book slid towards the edge.

"Catch it," shouted Ben. Laura was below as the book fell off the shelf. Ben never quite reached it. However, the book didn't exactly fall. It floated down gently like something on a parachute, landing softly into Laura's eager hands.

With it came a rush of light mist from the gap in the shelf. Ben hopped down the ladder to join the others. It was a strong aroma of jasmine. The same smell Ben had from the voice letter when he first opened it. They all stood there astonished as its gush slowed and faded away. Laura looked down at the book for the first time. She read the title out loud.

"*The William Ingram School Constitution.*"

"You got us here for that!" complained Hitti. "No clues or notes or anything?" Laura flicked past all the pages. There was nothing but an ordinary untouched book. Ben sighed.

"I'll just have to take it with me and think about it." Ben signed the book out on the pad attached to the bookcase. Then the three friends left for home, at least content they had not faced some ghostly nightmare or even a teacher!

The end of term came a couple of days later and Ben said goodbye to everyone. He never usually saw anyone from school in the holidays. But he did have the book to study. It *will* reveal the answer. He was sure of that.

*

During the Easter break Ben spent a lot of his time in his bedroom poring over that book. In fact, he read almost every page. On the last Sunday before school resumed he was in his bedroom studying hard.

"Come on down here," called his mum. "Hardly seen you all week."

"I'm busy, Mum," Ben called back.

"Don't you wanna come shopping? I was gonna get you some new clothes and that."

"You go ahead. I'm fine here thanks," Ben shouted out.

"You have it your own way then. If you don't like them, that's tough," his mum said, miffed at Ben's attitude. "Your dad's in the garden." Ben heard the front door slam shut followed by the car door banging hard and a roaring engine leaving the front of his house. Parents, he thought. Who'd have them?

He looked back at the book. He sat forward and read a paragraph over twice. This was it! It was called a 'Pupil's

Censure Motion'. Ben phoned Laura's mobile straight away.

"I've got the answer, Laura!" announced Ben.

"What are you talking about now, Ben? I'm out shopping."

"That book we got down tells me exactly how I can have a teacher, or another person at school up before the headmaster and the governors."

"For what, Ben? I don't know what you mean?"

"Being an impostor of course!" said Ben.

"Impostor? Now you've gone crazy."

"No I haven't! I reckon there's a person at WISPA pretending to be someone and they are covering it all up, that's what," replied Ben. "I'm going to have it out in front of Mr Goving. I just need to prove Sonia was murdered and it wasn't just some accident." Ben was upset at Laura's attitude.

"Well who is it then?"

"I'll explain when I see you. It's a bit complicated."

"Oh, so you don't really know do you?" replied Laura quite miffed.

"I sort of do, but—" As Ben spoke Laura cut him off.

Ben felt all alone about his problems for the first time. He looked at the open page of the book. The governors could hear him out and then decide what to do, it explained. This could even mean punishment, expulsion or sacking from their job if it was a teacher. There was even an application form in the book you could copy, fill in and give to the headmaster requesting the process to begin!

BUT THERE WAS JUST ONE SMALL PROBLEM. BEN'S SUSPICIONS OF WHO COULD BE TRYING TO HIDE THE TRUTH ABOUT SONIA WERE COMING TO A HEAD. BUT THERE WAS MORE

**THAN ONE PERSON BEN SUSPECTED AS
INVOLVED. IN FACT THERE WERE SEVERAL.**

CHAPTER 15

Smudge up

It was the beginning of the summer term. The annual Comp would take place in June straight after the usual, boring end of year exams.

Ben was very excited about the Comp and had high hopes. But he also had a worry. He'd made the decision. He had thought about absolutely everything that had happened since he came to WISPA. There was an answer and he was going to have it out in front of the headmaster. Ben was still on the morning bus with Laura when he told her exactly what he planned to do.

"Don't tell anyone about it. Only you and Hitti must know who it is," said Ben.

"Are you sure, Ben? How do you know you're right? It just sounds so crazy. If you're wrong you'll cause real trouble. You do know that don't you?" Laura pleaded.

"I can't go on if nothing's ever done about it. Look at all the grief we've had over it?" Ben replied. Somehow, his point was unanswerable. The bus pulled in and Ben went straight to Mr Goving's office. He had a delivery to make before lessons began. It was going to happen come what may. Ben marched up the dreaded corridor and found the door was already open. Mr Goving was standing there ready to leave.

"Good morning, Ben. Welcome back!" he beamed.

"Good morning, Mr Goving. I need to give you this," said Ben as he thrust an envelope into the headmaster's hand leaving Mr Goving looking confused.

"Is it important? Do I need to read it now?" he asked as he turned to put it on his desk.

"As soon as you can, please," suggested Ben as he walked away. He didn't want to be present when it was read. Ben walked quickly to the end of the corridor and ran all the way to his classroom as if he'd done wrong and needed to escape. Mr Goving went back into his office and picked the letter up again and sat at his desk opening it.

"Oh my God," he muttered and carried on reading. "No! How silly. Smudge was right about that boy." He put it down and gazed out of the window as if he'd just heard of a relative's death. Then, composing himself he picked up the phone and scrolled down his stored telephone numbers to the name Mr George Sayers, chair of the school governors, and punched the call button.

"George? Good morning to you too," he began. "Got a bit of a problem I need to run past you. Our scholarship pupil Ben Street has just delivered a Pupil's Censure Motion."

"No! That's a first. What's it all about?" asked George.

"Well, you'll have to see it yourself. Of course it's absolutely ludicrous, claiming a teacher here's an impostor! It's nonsense. What do you think I should do?"

"I'll check it out for you. But if it's a properly presented complaint, then we have to convene a meeting to hear it," reasoned George.

"But it's madness—"

"Doesn't matter how mad it is. We are bound to listen to it under the rules if the form is filled in correctly," replied George quite clearly.

"I've never heard such poppycock."

"Send it through and I'll be in touch. Got to go Michael," insisted George.

"We can't have this boy controlling us. It's preposterous," roared Mr Goving. With that the phone went dead and Mr Goving had no choice but to put his own phone down.

*

Later that day Ben was at home watching television with his parents after supper. It was a lifestyle programme on home renovation. Ben was regularly forced to endure such programmes. His parents always raved about what they could do to their own home. Once it ended they forgot all about it and did nothing. In fact Ben did not recall any change at their home since he was about five. Even then it was only a quick coat of magnolia paint over some old wallpaper in the hall.

"I'd love one of them canopy things round our bed, Jim. Looks gorgeous," his mum murmured.

"I like the extension they've built on" replied his dad. Ben wanted to watch something interesting like a movie, but he was stuck with boring parents. When the phone rang, Ben sprang to his feet like a gazelle and couldn't wait to leave the room. He rushed to the hallway and picked up the phone.

"Hullo," said Ben expectantly.

"Ah, Ben. Just the fellow," boomed the caller. It was the unmistakable voice of Mr Goving! "I just wanted to inform you of a few things about your complaint young man, before it's processed." Ben was off guard and felt uncomfortable.

"Yes, Mr Goving."

"You probably realise I've had to inform the chair of the school governors. You should know that the scholarship committee will be informed. It could affect future payment of your fees at the school. Did you think about that?"

"I didn't, but I'm going ahead with it anyway," replied Ben nervously.

"Do you really think accusing a teacher of being an impostor is a good idea? I think we all know this is something you've imagined."

"I did not!" said Ben rather forcefully. There was a loud sigh from Mr Goving.

"Well, then I'm sorry for you. I'll have to give you a confirmation in writing within a week with a date for the meeting before the governors," Mr Goving said very calmly.

"I know," said Ben. He had read all the rules on this over Easter.

"For the last time, Ben, I must warn you; proceeding with this could even result in you being asked to leave WISPA. I really don't want that for you. You have a great talent," implored Mr Goving in a persuasive manner.

"Thanks Mr Goving, but I have to do it," Ben replied in a very adult way. Mr Goving sighed again even more deeply.

"I've done my best to try and change your mind, Ben. Think it over. You can stop it at any time, but sooner is best." Mr Goving was about to end the conversation when Ben thought of a question.

"Mr Goving. Can I just ask you one thing?"

"Of course," replied Mr Goving hoping Ben would suddenly see sense.

"Are you actually Dr Goving?" There was a silence that made Ben wonder if the line had gone dead. "Hullo, hullo, are you there?" he asked frantically.

"Yes, I'm here," came the weary sounding response. "How did you know about it?"

"Someone I met just happened to mention it, that's all," said Ben.

"I don't use the title of Doctor. That's my choice. I got my doctorate in philosophy many years ago and then did drama afterwards you see," Mr Goving explained.

"Yeah, I see," said Ben, not really convinced. At this point they ended their chat and Ben went back to his living

228

room. Ben was sure Mr Goving had some other reason to hide his real title from people. But what was it?

"Who was that?" enquired Ben's dad. Ben didn't want to admit the headmaster had phoned him at home, let alone the contents of the conversation. A moment's panic hit him as he thought about it.

"The headmaster's giving me some notice about a meeting. He just wanted me to know. That's all," Ben answered hoping to put him off. His dad was watching a gardening programme now and so his attention span for anything else was about two seconds.

"Oh," he said, in a disinterested way. Ben's mum was engrossed by a packet of chocolate eclairs and said nothing. That's good, thought Ben as he left his parents and went up to bed. It was a calm night with a beautiful full moon shining through his curtains. He hopped into bed and slept like a log.

*

Another week passed without incident. Ben had kept a low profile since the delivery of his letter to Mr Goving, just going about his school life as if nothing had happened. Today there was an English literature lesson and he walked to the classroom with Laura expecting to find Stewbog.

Ben entered the room to find Smudge was there instead. Stewbog was off sick and she had stepped in. Ben sat down at his desk and started arranging his exercise books and got out the play they were reading. Smudge came over with a huge scowl on her face and gave him an envelope. Ben knew what that would be. He turned it over to open it and saw the little printed sign, 'From the office of the headmaster'. He couldn't resist it for a second and tore it open.

In response to the complaint made by pupil, Benjamin Street, under Section 41(b) of the school constitutional rules,

**the governors have convened a meeting
to be held in the office of the headmaster,
on Thursday 29th May.**

**At this meeting, Benjamin Street is
invited to present his complaint before
the governors and in front of any party
concerned, who may respond to him. The
governors may make such decision as is
appropriate thereafter. Benjamin Street
may bring one supporter to the meeting.**

This sounded very formal and grand! Ben was quietly
feeling very calm and confident. The letter had instantly
cheered him. It meant he was going to be taken seriously
after all. He was now sure he knew who was involved with
the murder of the lost soul, Sonia Bird, all those years ago.

"Right, I'm taking you today as you can see because
Stewbog is feeling poorly," said Smudge smiling.

"Good morning, Smudge," announced the class on cue.

"I thought we'd have a bit of fun today. So I've got a
little quiz lined up." She marched up to her desk at the front
and pressed a button on her laptop to bring up a series of
questions on the board. She turned to look at them and
check them through. After a few moments there was
muttering in the class. This didn't look much fun at all! It
was more like an English literature test.

Ben just peered out of the window imagining what he'd
say at his meeting of the governors. The quiz began.
Smudge stood in front of the class pointing to each question
and waving her enormous ring about as if she were
conducting an orchestra with it. She picked pupils in
rotation to answer the questions. You'd lose one of three
'lives' if you got it wrong. There was to be a 'play off' of
the final two pupils to find a winner. Smudge eventually
reached Laura.

"Number twenty-nine, Laura," announced Smudge.

Laura looked at the question. Who wrote *The Canterbury Tales*? But she couldn't think of the answer.

"Anyone? —No? It was Chaucer, of course." Ben was still daydreaming on another planet, which he did all too often. About ten minutes later Smudge said it was his turn. She was pointing to question thirty-seven. True to form, Ben wasn't listening.

"Ben. Your turn," she said quietly, knowing Ben was half asleep. She wanted to catch him out if she possibly could. This was the moment she was waiting for. Smudge stood patiently with a wry smile on her face.

Ned prodded Ben from behind and he regained consciousness. He took one look at the question Smudge was pointing at and knew he would have to take action. He went look—click—freeze-frame, quickly fanning his head around the room to include everyone. They all became like statues, motionless and still. Ben sighed with relief.

Ben didn't know the answer to the question, 'In which of Shakespeare's plays would you find a character called Malvolio?' However, he had a cheeky plan. He walked over to Smudge's laptop and deleted the name 'Malvolio' replacing it with the name 'Horatio'. Ben had been introduced to *Hamlet*; one of Shakespeare's most famous plays and knew Horatio was definitely one of the characters. He hopped back to his desk and sat down. Then he went, look—click—unfreeze-frame.

"It's *Hamlet*," answered Ben smiling at Smudge. Smudge smiled back.

"No, it certainly isn't *Hamlet*," she said believing Ben was wrong.

"I'm sure it is!" said Ben teasingly as he turned to the class for support. Others were nodding in agreement at Ben. There was some confusion because they hadn't seen the question suddenly change but could see the name 'Horatio' on the board.

"Rubbish! Malvolio was in *Twelfth Night* not *Hamlet*!" shouted Smudge. There was a loud muttering and whispering of the name Horatio amongst the class. Ben hyped the situation up again and called out.

"It's definitely *Hamlet*." Smudge frowned as she turned to her question on the board.

As it dawned on her that the character name of Malvolio was not there and it was now Horatio, her face turned to anger. She knew she'd been tricked and it was Ben Street in the thick of it.

Smudge rushed forward to stand beside Ben's desk with eyes as thin as slits and teeth gritted like a ferocious dog. A cloak of silence fell over the classroom as they waited with bated breath for the next move. She had obviously wanted some opportunity to deal with her suspicions about Ben her way.

The distant buzzing of a wasp's nest could be heard through the quiet. A stream of sunlight shone across Ben's face. Smudge looked at Ben. He knew she had it in for him. They had both been curious about each other for some time and that was the truth of it.

"There's something about you, Mr Street, which needs dealing with," she said ominously. No one ever called Ben 'Mr' and it sounded threatening. "You can be sure I'm going to be on your case twenty-four seven from now on." The end of lesson bell interrupted this tirade of teacher fury.

Ben began to wonder if she already knew about his meeting with the governors. Chatter broke out in the class. Just as usual, no one waited to be dismissed. The bell was all they needed and they rose from their desks to leave immediately. Ben did the same.

"Come right back here," insisted Smudge. "I haven't finished with you yet." She was still right next to him. "I've marked your card, Mr Street. I know what you're trying to do, but let me make this crystal clear; I will catch you out. No one makes a fool out of me!" she spouted menacingly as she waved her pointed finger at him. She turned and picked up her workbag, leaving without looking at anyone, head held high.

Ben's feeling of complete unease about Smudge had gone up a further notch with this episode. He found Laura outside the classroom looking rather anxious.

"I knew you'd get noticed messing around with teachers like that. What did I tell you?" said Laura, almost like a parent. She knew Ben had changed the question and made Smudge look very silly.

"I just couldn't help it."

"But now she knows for sure something wasn't right," she said.

"Something's not right with her. That's for sure," replied Ben. He had to agree with Laura that Smudge had a considerable suspicion of him. They carried on chatting on their way to the canteen.

"Laura, I've been given the date for the meeting. You know in front of the governors and Mr Goving."

"You're really going ahead with it, aren't you?" Laura frowned putting her hand up to her mouth at the thought of it.

"I can't give up now. I just can't. Anyway the date's the 29th May at midday. Let me show you the letter." Ben removed the envelope from his pocket and handed it to Laura. By now they were in the lunch queue.

"Did you notice anything?" asked Ben expectantly.

"Looks like a lot of gobbledegook to me," she replied wide eyed and fumbling for her purse. "I fancy unhealthy chips today," she added.

"Well, look at this bit," asked Ben pointing at the word 'supporter' on Mr Goving's letter. Laura vaguely looked at it.

"Chips and a pasty, please," she said to the kitchen hand.

"I'll have the wrap, cheers," Ben said to the staff. "Look, I can have one supporter in the meeting with me. It says so. I want that to be you, Laura. You're the only one who knows everything I know. Even Hitti doesn't know it all." They took their food and sat at an empty table.

"If I did come, I wouldn't have to say anything would I?" Laura queried in a concerned manner. She munched her way through the pasty while Ben cast his gaze at her and considered his reply.

"I'll do the talking, but I might want you to say you agree with me. That's all." That didn't sound too difficult, thought Laura. She wouldn't let her good friend down. Over the year, she, Ben and Hitti had become the best of mates.

"OK, I SUPPOSE SO," SHE SAID SLIGHTLY RELUCTANTLY. BEN BREATHED A SIGH OF RELIEF.

CHAPTER 16

The showdown

Some weeks later, the date for the meeting before the school governors finally arrived. Ben and Laura were as ready as they'd ever be. Ben had carefully prepared what he wanted to say and had a little folder and bag of items with him. He had dressed smartly in a suit.

He and Laura made their way to the grand entrance in the office block. Once up the hallway they found a small padded bench seat where they waited nervously. Time ticked very slowly when waiting outside a headmaster's office. There was muffled speech coming from within which must have been the governors chatting. There were some extra cars in the staff car park today.

The entrance door creaked open and there was Mr Goving, solemn-faced, ushering them in. They both got up and Ben walked in through the doorway. Laura was following.

"Wait a minute, Laura," said Mr Goving. He turned to the chair of the governors, George Sayers.

"Ben's not allowed spectators is he?"

"No, just one supporter," Mr Sayers replied firmly. Mr Goving wheeled around.

"Sorry, Laura. You'd better go back to lessons."

"But I'm coming as a supporter," she insisted confidently. Mr Goving was taken aback. He was almost angry in addressing her.

"Are you sure you know what you're doing, young lady?"

"Yes, I'm supporting Ben," Laura replied.

"Right, well, come in and we'll sort it out." She walked in to stand next to Ben in the middle of the floor. There were three governors in all, including George Sayers. The other two were Mrs Indira Patel and Mr Tony Holland. "We also have my secretary Miss Danni Dorritt who will note down everything that's said," Mr Goving explained. She had already begun and didn't look up. The governors were seated together behind a large desk with a panelled front. Mr Goving joined them.

"Mr Sayers will conduct the procedure. You two can sit opposite us," announced Mr Goving, pointing Ben and Laura to chairs nearby. "The gentleman on your right is the school's solicitor, Mr Roy Challenor. He'll ask questions of you or anyone else on behalf of the governors." By now Ben could see it was a very formal affair. He wondered whether he would cope. "Lastly, you can see Dr Metanite sitting over to our left and you know him, of course," said Mr Goving. Dr Metanite had his arms folded and he was smirking to himself. "Now I'm handing matters over to Mr Sayers."

"Good afternoon everyone. I have to state the complaint brought by Ben Street. It is that Dr Metanite, a teacher at this school, is in fact an impostor. This is a serious suggestion which if found true would likely cause his dismissal from his job. Now I have to warn you, Ben, if we find this a frivolous complaint, we are bound to report it to the scholarship committee who presently pay your fees here. Do you understand?" The sense of foreboding was growing inside Ben. He began to wish he'd never come to WISPA at all.

"I do," Ben replied automatically, not knowing what else to say.

"Good," continued Mr Sayers. "Ben, listen carefully. Having heard the possible consequences of this meeting,

236

you may still withdraw today, here and now. Nothing will happen if you do that. We will simply leave and say no more about it. Are you quite sure you wish to proceed?"

Ben's confidence was ebbing away. The pressure of it all was weighing on him heavily. Ben began speaking slowly.

"OK, perhaps I'll stop."

"No!" shrieked Laura, "You can't!"

"Just take your time, Ben. It's your decision," added Mr Sayers holding a hand up to Laura, signalling quiet. Ben just wanted it all to halt. In fact, within a second of feeling this desire, he cast his eyes around the room carefully and went look—click—freeze-frame. Apart from Laura, all of them became as still as stone statues.

"I don't know what to do, Laura?" panted Ben nervously. He stood up and twiddled his fingers about. It was quite unlike Ben.

"You're not giving up now. It doesn't matter what they say. If you give up now they'll never forget it even if Mr Sayers says nothing would happen. You can only win by having it out."

"I suppose you're right."

"I will speak up for you, Ben. Just you wait!" said Laura very impressively. Suddenly it seemed as though Laura had taken on the mantle and was exuding confidence. She smiled at him. "Just go for it!" she said enthusiastically. Ben sat down again next to Laura. He went, look—click—unfreeze-frame. Ben looked at Mr Sayers.

"I want to go ahead, Sir," he announced in a formal fashion.

"So be it," replied Mr Sayers, rather disappointed. "You must explain your complaint and any matters which suggest it's true. From time to time Mr Challenor may ask questions. After that Dr Metanite can tell us his side of it and you can ask questions of him. OK?"

"Yes, Sir," said Ben. Mr Sayers indicated for Ben to start. This was it! Ben drew in a large lungful of breath and looked at his notes.

"It all started when I found out about the death of a girl at this school who was in the theatre, backstage. It was in 1949 and she was called Sonia Bird. I read in an old school magazine that it was supposed to have been an accident. The teacher was cleared but left."

"Has this anything to do with Dr Metanite supposedly being an impostor?" Mr Challenor the solicitor called out. He was ready to end it all there and then.

"Yes," said Ben. "The teacher then was Tim Dreante. Now I looked for some photos of him. I'll come to another one later, but this one came down and landed next to me and Laura when we were backstage last term." Guffaws of laughter broke out at the thought of a photo miraculously appearing from nowhere. This was replaced by concerned frowns on the part of the governors, trying hard to look as if they were taking it seriously.

Nevertheless, Ben produced the photograph showing a face and top half. Mr Goving's mouth began to open. Ben continued. "If you look at this photo, the man's name is actually printed at the bottom as Mr Dreante. He seems to be very like a younger Dr Metanite."

The room filled with unbridled laughter and Dr Metanite seemed to be enjoying every minute of it. Ben waited until they stopped and then fired up again.

"Take a look at the clothes. This man in the photo is wearing a jacket just like Dr Metanite always wears," continued Ben. Mr Challenor leapt to his feet and challenged Ben directly.

"Are you suggesting Dr Metanite, a teacher here for about the last twenty years, *is* the person in the photograph, just because he has a similar jacket?"

There was more muffled laughter. Mrs Patel couldn't keep a straight face to save her life. Mr Sayers was trying very hard, but not quite managing it.

"Yes, I certainly am," said Ben. He wasn't giving in now!

"I have to say that clothing alone is no form of identification whatsoever. It's simply preposterous to suggest it!" With that Mr Challenor sat down and gave one big nod of his head, as if he knew it all. But then, he was a grown-up and some of them do think they know it all don't they? Ben was still not put off.

"I have with me the school magazine article about Sonia Bird. The police were involved but they got it wrong. The fact is, Sonia Bird was murdered," announced Ben.

"Now look," interrupted Mr Sayers forcefully. An unholy quiet had entered the room. All smiles had vanished at the mention of the word 'murder'. "What exactly are you suggesting, Ben? This sort of talk is beginning to be worrisome, to say the least. And it sounds very silly indeed."

"Well, I'm trying to explain that the teacher, this Mr Dreante, murdered Sonia Bird." Rather pained laughter broke out. Mr Goving's eyes were popping out of his head. Dr Metanite was looking particularly smug at this point. Again Mr Challenor stood up and looked straight at Ben.

"May I remind you, a few minutes ago you were trying to tell this meeting that Dr Metanite is in fact Mr Dreante from all those years ago?"

"That's right," Ben answered swiftly.

"Now you are saying Mr Dreante was involved in nothing less than a pupil's murder?" Mr Challenor challenged in a most sarcastic tone of voice. He was already twiddling his thumbs around the lapels of his jacket and looked ready to go in for the kill.

"Exactly," replied Ben quite unprepared for what was coming.

"Then, in fact, you are standing before us, accusing Dr Metanite of nothing less than the murder of Sonia Bird in 1949, aren't you?" There was a pause and everyone peered at Ben. He felt transparent with the strength of the gazes landing upon him.

"I suppose you could put it that way," Ben murmured.

"In that case, I will have to say, you've changed your complaint. We attended here believing you were going to tell us merely that Dr Metanite was an impostor. Now you want to say he murdered someone. That's entirely different!" Mr Challenor concluded with another knowing nod directed towards Dr Metanite as he sat down. Mr Sayers intervened.

"You know, Ben, Mr Challenor is right. We can't have you come here and just make *any* accusation you like, as you go. Now you said on the written application, Dr Metanite was an impostor. Ridiculous, of course, but we decided to hear you out. Nowhere does it say you wanted to complain he was a murderer."

Dr Metanite burst into a fit of giggles and guffaws. Mr Sayers had to ask him to stop. When calm resumed, Danni Dorritt piped up. She was taking it all down on her laptop.

"Excuse me, Mr Sayers, but I don't know if I can write down all this laughing. It's not really—"

"No need to worry about that," snapped Mr Sayers turning to Ben for an answer.

"It's kind of connected. I've got some cut rope," he said pulling it out of his pocket and dangling the small curled knot of rope in front of him. "You see the person who's an impostor is the same person that was there when Sonia Bird was killed," Ben explained carefully.

"I see. Well, we can only hear about the impostor part I'm afraid. That's what we came to hear. So please confine your remarks to that point."

"But it's all got to do—"

"No, my decision is final on that, Ben. It's the rules of these meetings," Mr Sayers confirmed firmly.

Ben looked down at his notes feeling a little puzzled. He looked at Laura, who gesticulated for him to get on with it.

"Well, I just think the police got it wrong."

"No!" shouted Mr Sayers pointing a finger directly at Ben. "One more word like that and I'll stop this meeting. Is that clear?" Ben nodded rather sheepishly. He began to worry he'd blown it now. Everyone was either laughing at what he said, or otherwise angry with him. He sighed and breathed in slowly.

"I would like to show you all a photograph from this 1948 book of school photos. I got it from the shelf right here in Mr Goving's office." Ben opened the book, marked with a piece of paper. He caught a whiff of jasmine as he did so. He arranged to pass the book around and handed it to Mr Challenor first while he carried on speaking. "When you get to look at this, you'll see the person in the centre is the headmaster of the time, Gareth Streeter."

"Similar to your name, Ben," interjected Mr Goving.

"Yes. He was actually my great grandad, but my family name was changed slightly for some reason by Grandad Street." The looks on the governor's faces and Mr Goving's confirmed that none of them believed a word of it.

Mr Challenor passed the photo book to Dr Metanite whose head curiously bowed backwards and he barely looked before passing it straight on to Mr Goving. Ben carried on regardless. "The man next to the headmaster is listed as Tim Dreante. The thing is, his face is missing. It's blank. It's not been cut out of the book. Someone must have done it deliberately. In fact I can't find any photo of Mr Dreante's face anywhere, except for the one I showed you first, that turned up backstage." Ben paused for breath. Laura put up her thumbs to encourage him.

"How do you suppose the photo of a blank face can help us identify Dr Metanite as some impostor?" asked Mr Sayers.

"I couldn't do it either." Ben was interrupted by more chuckling from Dr Metanite. He just waited and waited until Dr Metanite ground to a halt. "Until I looked at the bottom half of the photo. I don't want to be personal, but Dr Metanite has amazingly long fingers. Everyone thinks so."

"Yes, all right," snapped Mr Goving looking puzzled. He was scribbling on a pad in front of him and didn't like the personal references to Dr Metanite's fingers. Mr Sayers was looking at the photo carefully.

"The fingers of this Tim Dreante on the photo look very long too, just like Dr Metanite's," concluded Ben.

"Did you see this, Mr Goving?" asked Mr Sayers, showing him the photo again. They both peered at the unusually long fingers and shared a frowned expression. Dr Metanite had now folded his arms quite tightly and his smirk had all but gone. Mr Challenor was passed the photo book again. All of them were now staring at Dr Metanite instead of Ben. His fingers were clearly on display around his folded arms. Mr Challenor jumped up again.

"May I just say this; long fingers or not, you are being asked to believe that Dr Metanite here, is one and the same person as a Tim Dreante in these photos taken in 1948. He is only umhm—"

"Fifty-nine," said Dr Metanite precisely.

"If he was the same person he'd have to be at least eighty-five years old or more by now! It's absurd." Mr Sayers turned to Ben.

"It's rather a good point, Ben, isn't it?" Ben didn't have an answer ready and swallowed hard.

"We'll kind of come to it if you let me just—"

"Fine, but please make sure you find the answer before you finish," Mr Sayers grunted. He was fiddling with his pen and beginning to look irritated again. Ben had hoped the photos would do the trick, but now he knew he'd have to go the whole hog. Ben cleared his throat and all eyes in the room were back on him. He looked to Laura again. She beamed encouragement as he drew breath.

"There's even more on that photo. I know the face is missing, but the neck isn't," announced Ben. The governor's eyes generally drifted ceiling-wards in disbelief there could be anything else to say about the photo with no face. Dr Metanite looked as if he was squirming at the suggestion. He unfolded his arms and began to look quite glum.

242

Ben opened his bag and took out a large magnifying glass about the size of a side plate. "With this I examined the photo very carefully and found a mark on the side of Mr Dreante's neck, on his right side." Mr Sayers interjected again.

"This had better be good, Ben. Frankly you're not amusing me anymore." Ben just bowled on, taking no notice.

"And I realised a while ago that Dr Metanite had the same mark on his neck, in the same place."

"The birthmark. Brilliant!" shrieked Laura.

"Be quiet, Laura," shouted Mr Goving. "You may only speak if asked to do so," he ranted. Ben was signalled to continue.

"It's only a speck on the photo until you look with this," he said, waving the magnifying glass about. "I'm asking you all to look at the speck on this man's neck with this thing and you'll see what it really looks like."

Ben passed the photo book and magnifying glass straight to Mr Sayers who pored over it eagerly. The other Governors leant over to see, as did Mr Goving. Dr Metanite seemed to be going slightly red and now wore a pained expression. His smile had gone. His shirt collar seemed to have risen to the top of his neck as he wriggled in his seat.

The photo book and magnifying glass were both passed to Mr Challenor who also looked carefully. Mr Challenor's face now looked rather less confident and quite concerned.

"It looks like a sort of insect-shaped birthmark," said Ben. He had everyone's attention now.

"I'm beginning to work it out!" screeched an excited Danni Dorritt.

"Just do the typing please, Danni," instructed Mr Sayers, holding up his hand in a motion to stop. Dr Metanite's face seemed to be glowing an even darker red by the minute.

"I would like you to look at Dr Metanite's birthmark. It's in the same place on his neck." The atmosphere was suddenly thick with excitement.

"Hasn't this gone far enough?" complained Dr Metanite. "Surely you can see it's utter nonsense?" he added in a trembling voice. There was a long pregnant pause.

"I think we'll see it through now, thank you, Doctor," said Mr Sayers. "In all fairness we need to have a quick look at your neck please." Dr Metanite pulled his collar down in disgust and looked at the ceiling. Mr Challenor was the first to amble over to him and was seen whispering in his ear.

"Do you want to discuss anything with me outside?"

"No," responded Dr Metanite in a very grumpy voice that all the room overheard. By now the doctor was perspiring profusely and dabbing his brow with a handkerchief. Mr Challenor returned to his seat next to Ben. Mr Goving got up and the governors followed suit, forming a little queue to examine Dr Metanite's neck. They all filed away and back to their seats. Before anything else was said Dr Metanite pleaded again.

"For goodness sake, it's a birthmark anyone could have. Just a coincidence it's on my neck like the other man's."

Ben stood up and fingered along his suit lapels putting his thumbs on the inside, like he'd seen Mr Challenor do. He was feeling more confident and ready for his next announcement.

"I hope you all noticed the same thing I did," he said, gaining in stature by the second. "Dr Metanite's birthmark is the same insect-like shape you could see on the photograph, under that magnifying glass. That means he's the same man as in the photo," Ben stated, sure it would be accepted without further question.

"Right. Thank you, Ben. Now my colleagues and I will withdraw to another room to make our decision," said Mr Sayers kindly. Ben looked puzzled. Dr Metanite perked up with hope that the complaint would all collapse any second.

"But I haven't finished yet," insisted Ben.

"You mean there's more?" growled Mr Sayers.

"A couple of things," replied Ben. Mr Sayers sighed deeply.

"Well, hurry them up will you please." He looked at his watch showing more displeasure.

"You may have wondered how I knew about asking to have a meeting like this," said Ben, diving into his bag to pull out his letter from Sonia. "I actually had a message from Sonia Bird in a sort of voice letter."

"Oh my good God! What are you leading us into now, Ben?" raved Mr Sayers, slapping his hands down on the desk in front of him. Ben shut his eyes in shock at the noise. But he was determined to persist.

"Please let me finish, Sir." He smiled as sweetly as he could muster. Mrs Patel, who hadn't said a single word, intervened, putting her hand on Mr Sayer's forearm.

"Let's hear it all, George." Mr Sayers waved at Ben to continue. He had the letter from Sonia in his hand.

"When I opened this, I heard it speaking," said Ben. Heavy sighs echoed around the room. No one believed it. Ben unwrapped the letter. They could all see it was blank. All they heard was the sound of some wasps buzzing around the window ledge.

Mr Sayers was about to interject, but Mrs Patel grabbed his arm again. The voice did not begin. Ben began to feel a little panic setting in. Dr Metanite's lips were gathering into a small but discernable grin. There seemed to be a greenish shade around the edge. Ben folded the letter up again and replaced it in the envelope before repeating the process. To everyone's amazement a muffled sound began, like a girl's voice muttering something. Ben leapt forward with the letter and indicated for Mr Sayers to hold it up to his ear.

"Good Lord! It's saying there's a book outside Mr Goving's office, to be found on the eighth bookcase, on the fourth shelf down and it's the twelfth book from the left." Ben produced the book of the school constitution and rules. He politely placed it on the desk in front of Mr Goving.

"You can all have a listen. Just fold it up and put it back first, then take it out again," instructed Ben. They all began listening to it. Dr Metanite had returned to a very red colour and really looked very ill. He was clearly agitated by this process. His eyes seemed to be wider apart than ever.

"If you want to check, just go to the corridor out there and you'll see the gap in the bookcase where this book was," added Ben.

"It's a clever trick, Ben, but I really think we need to wrap this meeting up now," said Mr Sayers sourly. Mr Challenor was now speechless. Quite something for a solicitor.

"It's not a trick. I would *never* have known what to do without that rulebook."

"I'm just popping into the corridor to look," said Mr Goving. He got up and walked out into the adjacent corridor. He counted the bookcases and looked at the fourth shelf of the eighth one. He could clearly see the gap where a book had been removed. A light puff of mist blew out accompanied by the smell of jasmine. It was the same smell he had noticed on the voice letter. He rapidly returned to the meeting.

There was some muttering amongst the governors and Mr Goving for about thirty seconds. Ben waited patiently. Mr Sayers looked up and indicated for him to continue once more. Dr Metanite was clearly seething.

"I've got one more thing to tell you and Laura's going to help me this time," said Ben triumphantly. Turning to Mr Goving, Ben asked, "Do you remember that time when you came into our science lesson with Smudge? You were asking Dr Metanite about some article for the school magazine?" Mr Goving looked blank. "You know, the whole class did an Irish jig for you and you wanted to see it in the Comp or something." He still looked blank.

"I tied Dr Metanite's trousers to a table," Laura added helpfully, "And you told me to report to your office."

"Oh yes, I remember," Mr Goving smiled, thinking about how funny it looked.

"Well, I'm going to ask Laura to explain something else we saw in that lesson," said Ben with relish. Somehow Dr Metanite seemed aware of what was coming.

"It's absolute rubbish. It's all lies," he shouted. Mr Sayer's hand was up, indicating silence.

"We haven't heard it yet! Remain quiet please," he enforced. Outside dark clouds had gathered. It was so dark Mr Goving swivelled around and switched on all the lights. A loud clap of thunder was heard and a streak of lightning cracked across the sky.

"Laura?" Mr Sayers said, indicating she should start. There was a knock at the door and in came Splinter. As usual he spoke in his wonderful Welsh accent.

"Oh, I'm very sorry to interrupt. I actually came because Laura and Ben were missing from class. But I can see—" he stopped and paused.

"That's all right, Splinter. It's all taken longer than expected," said Mr Goving. Splinter nodded and left, shutting the door carefully.

"Shall I start?" asked Laura. Mr Sayers waved her on. She suddenly looked less confident now it was her turn. She began stumbling at first. "The lesson Ben mentioned. It wasn't going very well you see, because Ben had knocked over a beaker of acid and some of it splashed on Dr Metanite's shirt I think. Then I saw his shirt had a small mark on it. When we got up close I could see—"

"Stop it now!" screamed Dr Metanite very aggressively. Sweat was pouring from him and his breathing was heavy and strange. His voice had even changed to a new low sound.

"You cannot keep having outbursts, Doctor! Control yourself. Are you feeling all right?" said Mr Sayers. There was no reply. All the room looked somewhat alarmed by Dr Metanite's appearance. His head looked larger than usual as if the pressure of the accusation was making it expand. His face had turned puce with rage. His spindly fingers were moving like writhing worms in his large palms.

"I was gonna say, I saw a hole in Dr Metanite's shirt and I told Ben coz I thought his accident with the acid probably did it. Then it got worse."

"I want to stop this now! I'm warning you. These lies are treachery," Dr Metanite seethed. His voice was even lower and his mouth was a pale shade of green and foaming at the edges.

"Shut up!" shouted Mr Sayers. "If you say one more thing I will throw you out of the meeting." Mr Sayers wasn't even looking at Dr Metanite as he issued his ultimatum. Fear and foreboding was growing in the room when suddenly Danni Dorrit pitched in.

"I've got it!" No one knew what she meant, but she was immediately slapped down.

"Quiet, I say," insisted Mr Sayers. He indicated for Laura to restart.

"We were looking at the hole in his shirt when we both saw the same thing. It had gone right through and Ben went and used his pow—"

"No Laura," Ben screeched, "Just stick to what we saw." Ben was afraid she'd ruin it all by telling them he'd freeze-framed the whole class, including Dr Metanite.

"Let her say what she wants. That's what I think," said Mr Holland, who'd been remarkably quiet throughout.

"Well, we looked a bit more and we both saw right into his insides and it was all metal. We couldn't believe it," announced Laura. There was a very confused air in the room. Dr Metanite's reaction to Laura's speech was weird. But what Laura was saying sounded even stranger and most unlikely!

"Thanks, Laura," said Ben. "I would like you to look at Dr Metanite's right side because there could still be a mark there." Dr Metanite looked mortified and explosive all at once. Mr Challenor stood up and intervened.

"Looking at a neck is one thing, but someone's torso is quite another. You really need a medical for that you know. It's inappropriate."

"Thank you, Mr Challenor," said Mr Sayers. He turned towards Dr Metanite. "Are you willing to show us your chest, Doctor?"

"No!" moaned a low voice, which barely seemed human.

"Well, I think we'll have to assume there's a mark there as suggested." At that moment Dr Metanite, red faced with a swollen head and dripping with perspiration, rose up from his chair. With a strange leap, he jumped right in front of Ben growling, his long fingers curling back and forth menacingly. The governors reeled in horror. With one swipe of his right arm he swept Ben up and dragged him backwards, so they were both facing the room, but the doctor had his back to the wall. Ben panted and wheezed as he suffered the tight grip.

Dr Metanite's head was growing at an alarming rate. He was breathing and spitting green coloured fluid into the room and it smelt vile, like burning hair and acid mixed together.

"You know nothing of my suffering," began the low wobbling voice of Dr Metanite. "How would you feel if your race had to leave their dying planet? When they get here, they are treated as experiments in a science laboratory."

"Race? Planet?" muttered Mr Goving in sheer panic. Dr Metanite's head began to split down the middle in a neat line. A black inside was forcing its way out. Danni Dorrit gave out a little high-pitched scream.

"My parents were killed when we landed on earth. I was subjected to painful experiments at the hands of Sonia Bird's meddling scientist father, in his laboratory. I am the only one left of the Scarigus."

"Scarigus!" the room repeated in unison.

"I escaped the laboratory in your year, 1946. I found a young human body to be my home. I cannot survive on this

249

planet without a host body. Now after all these years I am forced to live in the same, revolting, ageing, human body, which needs daily repair it's so decrepit. He wasn't called Tim Dreante. I made that up, just like the name Dr Metanite, you ignorant fools."

The rest of Dr Metanite's head peeled away and flopped on the floor, revealing large insect-type eyes and a black gooey skull with antennae. Laura was terrified and crying. She ran into the arms of Mr Holland who comforted her. Mr Goving was frantically phoning the police, but they didn't believe a word he was saying.

"Then I had to get revenge for the ending of my race. I couldn't find the real culprit. He was protected by the government. So I sent his daughter, Sonia Bird, up the ladder backstage to pull a scenery rope. But I fixed it so she fell and died. It was me who replaced the cut rope, to avoid your sneering human detection."

Dr Metanite was nearly strangling poor Ben. This gooey black insect they thought was their science teacher was gradually emerging from the human shell in which it lived. The human body was peeling off as if unzipped and gradually descending. It was now dribbling downwards and leg tentacles were popping out. The doctor's human arms began to split apart revealing black hairy, insect arms inside. Dr Metanite spat on the floor and a large globule of green frothing liquid squirted onto the ground and it began to burn the carpet like acid.

"Then when I had to leave, I came back twenty years later using the name Dr Metanite. By then I had to use mechanical parts, to keep this vile form you call a body, alive."

He gave out a loud roar like some wild beast being slain. He started to move backwards towards the door holding onto Ben who was trying to force his way out of the hairy arms holding him. By now the human form had stripped down to the waist and bits were strewn on the floor. The mechanical metal inside had become plain for all to see.

"Let go!" screamed Ben. No one dared help the poor boy. The creature once called Dr Metanite, turned and pushed Ben closer to the door. He couldn't be seen any longer. He was trying frantically to freeze-frame this monster, but it wasn't working.

"I'll destroy you," roared Dr Metanite in a weird low voice. Ben thought his powers had deserted him just as the most critical moment of his life had arrived. Then, he felt his fingers warming.

"Yes," he shouted, to the confusion of everyone listening as this monster frothed and roared, moaned and shoved. He waited until they felt and looked bright red and even turning white with heat like fired iron. Then with an almighty thrust he speared them into Dr Metanite's metal inner workings, causing an instant knife-like incision.

The frazzle of melting metal was joined by an enormous howl from Dr Metanite as he lifted his head in pain. But he hadn't given up. The tentacle arms firmed their grip and he opened his jaws displaying green shining cutting edges. He snapped at Ben and tried to pull him nearer his mouth. The others in the room were frozen with fear and their frustration mounted by the second at being unable to help Ben.

Splinter's brother, called Branch, was working in the office next door. He heard the commotion and couldn't help but open the adjoining door to see if everything was all right. He was so shocked he fainted at the sight of it and fell on the floor next to Mr Holland and Laura.

Ben withdrew his white-hot fingers and tried again. This time he pierced them straight into Dr Metanite's neck and up towards his head. Again he howled with pain. But this time, large quantities of green slime trickled down Ben's fingers and hands and fell on the floor. Dr Metanite's grip loosened as he went down, taking Ben with him. His eyes were craning to look out at everyone until he gave a last gasp, before coming to rest, dead.

Before Ben could withdraw his fingers from the disgusting gooey mess, he felt them return to normal. He pulled them out and got up. There was no movement in the room for a few seconds as the shock was absorbed. No one had seen his glowing fingers at all. The deceased fleshy mess of enormous insect, attached to part of a human body covering, lay there in bubbling slime and steaming as it cooled. Ben brushed off the filth from his clothes.

"Oh my, oh my," said Mr Sayers at last. "Why on earth did we ever doubt you, Ben?" he panted. "I can't thank you enough for all the courage you've shown today." The others remained spaced out. Laura got up and hugged Ben despite the goo attached to parts of him.

Suddenly Danni Dorrit sprang to life. "I knew it," she said. "As soon as I typed up those names, my mind went to work. Mr 'Tim Dreante', then 'Dr Metanite'. They sounded as though they shared letters. I love a good anagram. Look here," she enthused in her eccentric manner, behaving as if it had been some stage show before her. There was a piece of paper upon which she'd scribbled the two names, 'Tim Dreante' and 'Dr Metanite' with lines going between them showing they contained exactly the same letters. "There's something else I noticed when I did that," she said. The piece of paper was turned over to reveal the word, 'TERMINATED'. "Those letters are the same as well!" she nodded, as if she had solved the riddle.

"Thank you for that," said Mr Goving completely befuddled by it all. "I need a little pause, to gather my thoughts."

"Have you got a result for me to type into the form, Mr Sayers?" Danni asked rather naively. After a few seconds Mr Sayers replied.

"I want you to delete everything you've put so far." Danni looked rather miffed at this idea. "Just say, Ben Street's complaint was upheld and Dr Metanite resigned. That'll do for the record," Mr Sayers advised.

Branch had awoken and sat up dazed and in silence. He looked confused as if he didn't believe he'd seen the earlier events. The sound of the emergency services sirens could be heard approaching. As they waited, something weird was happening. The mess that had been Dr Metanite was disintegrating before their eyes. The whole human body that had been someone turned to a grey powder and lay there mixed with a little greenish slime which was drying rapidly. The insect creature had become completely flat and thin like cling film. You could barely see it. Ben brushed off the goo and said he needed the toilet desperately. Mr Goving took command.

"I don't think anyone outside this room would ever believe what we witnessed. There's no point in trying to explain it." Mr Sayers put his hand out to pick up the voice letter from Sonia. It immediately turned to a puff of dust and floated off across the room, leaving the sweet smell of jasmine behind it. "I would like to ask everyone's co-operation that we agree never to breathe a word of it for the rest of our lives."

"Yes, I completely agree," said Mr Sayers. "You'd only make a fool of yourself if you tried."

"What'll we say went on today then?" asked Laura, sitting on her former chair.

"We'll just say we had a hearing about a confidential complaint after which Dr Metanite left his employment at the school. I think it's essential this event is never reported to the press. It could do enormous damage to the school," said Mr Sayers. Everyone agreed and nodded and grunted approval.

At this point, Mr Challenor recovered from his shock induced comatose state, to announce that his bill would be in the post. Mr Goving gave a withering wave in his direction as Mr Challenor removed himself from the room.

"OK, I've got to go. I'm bursting," pressed Ben. He was directed to the head's personal toilet. He rushed in and shut the door. He made straight for the basin mirror. He stood on the stool in the corner and lifted up his right leg and pushed up the material of his trouser.

Whilst Ben was out of the room, the police arrived and were politely told there had been some mistake in calling them. Mr Goving was gushing in his apology. Just a school prankster. Ben ran back into the room shouting out happily.

"Yes, yes, my leg's back!"

"Thank God," said Laura. She knew what he meant!

"Well, I'm sure there's a story to that," said Mr Goving, "but I think we must clear up this office and resume our day as if all was normal." He picked up the book of school photos still open at the page with a blank face. He was about to shut it when he noticed the photo had changed. The missing face had now returned to the photograph! He showed it to Mr Sayers. They both saw the name that had been Tim Dreante in the listing had disappeared. There was a space for a name but it was blank.

"Someone with a name *was* sitting next to the headmaster in this photo," commented Mr Sayers.

"I think I'm going to have to find out exactly who that was," replied Mr Goving. He then got up and began to help Danni tidy up the room. Ben and Laura helped stack the chairs.

"Ben, just look at this." Mr Sayers was still poring over the book. Ben came over and saw the changed photograph. He looked puzzled. This mystery was not quite over was it?

That same afternoon, Mr Goving told an emergency meeting of all teachers, in the staff room, that Dr Metanite had resigned and left immediately following a full hearing before the school governors.

He would not be drawn on the reason, except to say the decision over his conduct was unanimous and that Ben Street was to receive a Bravery Award for bringing the matter to the governors' attention. It was the first time this had been given for over twenty-five years. Smudge was seen leaving the meeting, incandescent with rage.

"I can't believe they'd listen to that boy," she muttered as she stormed out of the staff room. She was seen walking straight out of the school grounds passing the science laboratories as she went.

Smudge marched up Cedarcliffe Place, an adjacent road where Dr Metanite had occupied one of the terraced homes. She went up to his front door, stood on the step and rang on the bell. Receiving no answer, she pushed open his letterbox to speak through it. As it opened, a swarm of flies flew out and disappeared. Smudge wasn't giving up. She called out.

"I know you're in there. Tell me what's happened? I have to know," she insisted. After a pause she leant down and pushed the letterbox open again. "I want my jars back please."

The front door of the adjoining house opened quietly. An elderly lady wearing a scarf over her head and a blue overcoat came out with a shopping bag. Smudge turned and spoke to her.

"Oh, hullo. You must know Dr Metanite?"

"Is that what he's called?" the lady replied somewhat off-hand.

"I'm trying to find him. Have you seen him today?" asked Smudge politely.

"I haven't love. He never speaks to anyone. I've lived here for ten years and he was already there when I moved in. Very odd bloke I'd say. A loner." With that the lady wandered off down the road.

SMUDGE LEFT EMPTY HANDED AND RETURNED TO SCHOOL MORE PUZZLED THAN BEFORE. HE CAN'T JUST VANISH, SHE THOUGHT.

CHAPTER 17

The Comp

It was the middle of June. The school seemed to have taken on a calm air. Ben had found himself more popular than ever, what with his bravery award given at assembly and knowing he had rid the school of Dr Metanite. No one knew the real reason, but Dr Metanite had not been well liked by pupils, so few questions were asked.

The only person not so pleased with Ben's new status was Tom Cortazzi. They were all going to perform in the Comp that very afternoon. The day had finally arrived! Tom approached Ben as they shuffled in through the stage door. He put his arm around Ben's shoulder in an unusually friendly manner. Ben was never sure about Tom's attitude.

"Hey, Ben. We've really got to go for it today. The agents will be watching and every little move counts."

"I know. We've got a good chance, eh?" remarked Ben.

"Just don't think it'll be the same next year," Tom said unnervingly. Ben wasn't sure what that was supposed to mean. He would have to ignore it and do his best.

As the time drew nearer for the show to start, the theatrical agents started to arrive and take their reserved seats. The first one to take her seat was Yasmin Shea. She had enormous influence within the film and theatre world, helping many unknowns into show business. She had beautiful auburn hair worn shoulder length. She wore a yellow suit that looked particularly expensive.

From another agency came Jack Pelham. He was quite different. He stood stick thin, a former dancer and actor himself, with a small goatee beard, coloured dark red. His long grey hair was deliberately messy. Jack had arrived dressed informally in his jeans and tee shirt. He often helped dancers with jobs after attending WISPA.

Stephen Hollis from a London agency arrived in a blue business suit looking like an office executive.

Lastly, there was another guest. Mr Goving was anxiously showing them to their seats. No one could put a name to the extra guest judge. There was muttering it could be a film director. He wore a stylish tailored shirt, striped trousers and had designer spectacles. He oozed the look of someone wealthy and successful. He wore plenty of gold jewellery.

Meanwhile Ben's parents were on their way in the car and his father was driving.

"Thank God I don't have to go to these shows often. I don't think I could take it, Kate," Ben's father said to his mother.

"I suppose he enjoys it and that's what counts," she replied as she tried to read her magazine.

"I bet it's absolute rubbish. Most of them never get a job after this lot. I don't know what he's thinking of."

"Leave him alone. We've been through all that." There was a pause then Ben's dad piped up again.

"Wait 'til he hears I won the best marrow competition!"

"What makes you think he'll be interested in that?" Mrs Street replied not wanting an answer. Backstage the make-up and costumes were going on. Laura was already dressed and ready to go. She came out of the changing room and came across Smudge giving Andrea Suchet a telling off.

"Don't spray that near me. Can't stand fly spray. The smell makes me ill," she fumed.

"It's only air freshener, Smudge," Andrea pleaded.

"Oh thank goodness," Smudge squawked. Andrea trotted off into the changing area with the can of spray. Smudge was polishing her famous ring. As Laura passed her from behind she looked across and saw the inside of the ring where the hallmarks usually are. There seemed to be a small black 'hallmark'. To Laura's surprise it looked very like the insect shape seen as a birthmark on Dr Metanite's neck!

She rushed on saying nothing, quite upset at the thought of it. She sat down with others at the waiting area around the back of the theatre and breathed deeply. She persuaded herself it must be a mistake and she had imagined it. Without warning there was a voice behind her.

"Yoohoo," sang out the unmistakable voice of her mum, Mrs Munday. "You look simply gorgeous."

"Mum, you shouldn't be round here," screeched Laura embarrassed by her mum's arrival. "This is for performers only," she half whispered, realising that there should be quiet.

"Sorry, darling. Just wanted to wish you the best of luck." Her nauseating voice rang out and hung in the air. Poor Laura didn't know where to put herself and ushered her mum out of the stage door, instructing her to go to her seat with Dad. Off she went, oblivious to any upset she might have caused.

There were only a few minutes before the performances would begin. The tension and excitement were building as the audience of parents and locals took their seats. The three pupil judges, Tom, Fiona and Gordon would perform their own acts which they had rehearsed with Mr McKinley.

Suddenly the auditorium lights were dimmed and the voice of Stewbog made an announcement over the theatre's sound system accompanied by a perfect drum roll.

"Ladies and gentlemen, this is the moment you've all been waiting for. I would ask you to put your hands together for our performers in this year's William Ingram School of Performing Arts Agent's Parade!" A huge round of applause broke out. "Let the show begin!" was Stewbog's cry.

The first performance was from Fiona Payne's team. A good old song and dance routine. Mr Bodkin, the caretaker, was sitting with his wife in the audience enjoying the show, when he noticed his mobile phone, set to silent alert only, went off. He pulled it from his pocket and saw a message from Danni Dorritt in the school office. "Come quick. Smoke coming from museum."

He whispered to his alarmed wife and giving his apologies, squeezed past parents and others to reach the aisle. He quickly made his way out of the building and ran around to the museum area. He had a set of school keys with him. There was indeed a slight billowing of smoke coming from the free-standing wooden building used as the museum. Mr Bodkin rang Danni from his mobile.

"Have you called the fire brigade?"

"Not yet. I was waiting for you to see it," she said quickly.

"I'm already outside. I think I can handle it, but call them anyway as a precaution. It's a wooden structure," he said thoughtfully.

Mr Bodkin ran up the steps and unlocked the door. He couldn't see any fire but there was heat and he'd seen smoke was coming out from underneath and blowing around the car park area. He entered to the smell of burning, took the fire extinguisher off its hook on the wall and made his way to the second room at the back.

As he looked at the glass cases on the wall, he saw that all the old school magazines were burning inside! It looked crazy. How could they be alight on their own inside a locked case?

Mr Bodkin couldn't get near these bookcases because the heat was too great. He frantically squirted foam from the extinguisher directly at the bookcases. The foam flew off as steam but had no effect on the fire that was burning ever brighter. Mr Bodkin knew he'd have to leave it to the fire brigade. He hurriedly took a few boxes of artefacts away for a few minutes until he felt it unsafe to continue. He left, taking the extinguisher with him.

He came down the steps to see Stewbog looking on in a trance-like state. He approached him and could hear a distant roar of applause from the theatre. The performances inside were mesmerising the audience, including the judges. Ben had been gently using his powers to help. He had been so pleased to find that despite Dr Metanite's end, his powers remained intact. He was putting them to good use helping all the teams fairly! Mr Bodkin spoke before Stewbog.

"The fire brigade are on their way. I can't stop it. Seems to be inside the cabinets for some reason."

"Oh, said Stewbog," strangely uninterested. News of the fire had reached Mr Goving who had been passed a note by Danni Dorritt, who stood at the side aisle. The headmaster very discreetly withdrew from his seat and went into the foyer with Danni.

"What do you mean the museum's on fire?" he said with upset and panic in his voice.

"I've told Mr Bodkin and the fire brigade. I just saw a bit of smoke."

"The last thing I want is to be stopping that show," he spat. Mr Goving strode off towards the museum with a very glum expression. When he reached it, there was Mr Bodkin and Stewbog standing silently looking on, as ever thicker smoke seemed to pour from the bottom of the little wooden building.

"Oh, no!" said Mr Goving.

"I tried to put it out Headmaster, but the fire was having none of it," Mr Bodkin explained. The sound of the fire engine siren was now evident in the air. They would not be long. Mr Goving looked at Stewbog who stood motionless. His thin beard, probably just trimmed, looked thinner than usual. Mr Goving saw Stewbog's little purple birthmark just above his upper lip. He had never really taken much notice before. But today something struck him. He was quite shocked at what he was thinking. In fact it bothered him rather more than the burning school museum. He said nothing. He had seen the shape of this tiny birthmark and it took his breath away. It was like a small insect! No, not possible. Pure fantasy, he told himself and brought his mind back to the matter in hand.

"Right. I'm going to have to tell the audience, so there's no panic. They'll hear the fire engine in a minute. Don't want to stop the show because I can see there's no danger for any other building. Mr Bodkin; you can deal with this can't you?" Mr Goving saw a nod. "You and I can go back," he added, looking at Stewbog.

Stewbog recovered from his trance and wandered off with Mr Goving to the theatre. By now they were in full swing. Ben's performance was not due until a little later. It would be one of the last few to go. Mr Goving swung in, quickly grabbed a microphone and leapt onto the stage like a ballet dancer. He walked to the centre and the auditorium was in silence. He looked very serious.

"Ladies and gentleman. There is no need to do anything other than enjoy the remainder of the show. I just have to inform you that there is a small fire in the museum. There's no danger to any other building. You can probably smell smoke and hear the fire brigade siren, maybe now actually. So that's what it's for. I'm sure it will be out soon. Let the show go on!" he boomed to some scattered applause.

After about forty-five minutes, it was time for the Cortazzi team's final turn. Ben's group of hip hoppers, street dancers and tappers were a delight and probably received more applause than anything else during the show.

Once all the performances were over, there was a short break while the judges agreed which team had won this year. Performers waited backstage in a state of nervous tension. Laura and Ben hadn't seen each other since the beginning of the show. Ben and Hitti were chatting when Laura joined them.

"Hi, guys," she said smiling. "You were brilliant."

"Thanks," they both said together. Ben praised Laura's performance too.

"Listen," said Laura. "I have to tell someone. Smudge was down the corridor." She began whispering so no one else heard. Laura told them what she saw on Smudge's ring. Hitti laughed and dismissed it. Ben was not so sure.

Outside, the fire had been tamed by the fire brigade. In fact, the fire had hardly crawled out of the glass cases that had now been broken by the firemen and the fire within put out.

"Never seen anything like that," Mr Bodkin kept muttering. "Missed the blinking show now I suppose." The school magazines stored there had been destroyed.

Back in the theatre the tannoy system came to life.

"All performers on stage please. Comp results to be awarded in three minutes." That sent a shiver down Ben's spine.

A short time later the whole school was assembled on the stage expectantly. The theatrical agent Yasmin Shea was ready to announce the results.

"This year was the most difficult I think we've ever had to judge since I've been coming and that's ten years now. We had to come to a conclusion though. In third place was Gordon Munzer's team, but only by a hair's breadth." A round of applause rushed about the auditorium.

"I have to say that my next announcement has never happened before." The hush was electric. "Fiona Payne's and Tom Cortazzi's groups displayed an amazing array of dance moves. We were really impressed with the combination of crip walk and variation, heel toe, knee drop, glide and slides! Both teams were of such a high standard we have had to award them joint first place."

The audience erupted into rapturous applause clearly agreeing with the result. Then as the noise subsided came the surprise.

"I have two other awards to give this year. These are personal commendations for their particular individual performances. The first is 'Mimic of the Year' which goes to Barry Trinder for his quite extraordinary talent. Two years in a row; amazing."

Barry came forward and a little medal on a ribbon was put over his head. He was given two West End theatre tickets for this. A little applause came and went.

"The second is for 'most promising dancer'. This young man showed skills way beyond his years. He is Benjamin Street." This time the audience blew into a frenzy of clapping. They too had recognised the amazing talent Ben had displayed during the routine. Ben was also given his medal and two theatre tickets.

Immediately after the applause subsided, Mr Goving walked along the aisle and saw Stewbog.

"Can you introduce me to the fourth judge over there; the rather well-dressed one? Don't think I know him."

"I've never seen him before. I saw you having him seated and thought you knew him!" replied Stewbog. As they turned to look, he had vanished. Mr Goving called out to Yasmin Shea, another judge.

"Yasmin, lovely show eh?"

"Superb this year Michael. I don't know where you find the talent," she gushed.

"We work very hard at it. Yasmin, do you know the new judge who came today?"

"None of us had met him before. Mr Scarigan was it?"

"Scarigan? Can't be. You must've misheard it, Yasmin!" Mr Goving said turning pale. He marched off to the exit frowning.

Meanwhile, Ben met up with his parents outside the theatre, as did Laura and Hitti.

"Laura, my starlet. Loved it, loved it!" Screamed Mrs Munday above the sound of the entire crowd. Hitti's parents greeted and hugged him showing their pleasure. Ben's father ran over to him and gave him a huge handshake and slapped his back. His mum threw her arms around him and hugged him.

"You were fantastic," they said together. Ben almost felt a tear come to his eye. Praise from his parents was a rare event.

"I won the best marrow competition," said his father smiling.

"Well done, Dad," said Ben chuckling. "I can't wait for next year."

"A bit of Aunt June and Blackpool first?" suggested his mum. Ben was not so sure about that.